IN THE BLACK
OF NIGHT

Noco De A Oresa

D.M. MILNE-JONES

Hoover Publishing

COPYRIGHT

Dedicated to my children, Jessica Jean and Tristen Kain.

I love you both, to the moon and stars.

Chapter 1

DARKNESS WASHED over the building like a thick fog, permeating everything it touched. She noticed that during this season of the year in Black Ridge, Arkansas, the night was unusually menacing. The crisp fall air assaulted her nostrils, almost burning them. Samantha Brae stepped out of her Tahoe and closed her eyes as the blackness caressed her like a long lost lover. She had always felt at home in the dark, taking refuge in it when she had been scared or upset, finding solace in the silvery light of the moon. Tonight however, it felt different. The inky darkness seemed to take on a presence of its own and it felt malevolent. The flashing blue lights of the police cruiser parked beside her did nothing to alleviate the feeling that something prowling through the darkness was the devil in disguise, or at the very least, a demon. Whatever it was, something evil was walking amongst them, wreaking havoc upon whatever hapless soul it would encounter.

The thick smell of death filled the air, even at twenty paces from the open front door. From the outside, the two-story apartment building looked peaceful. Three apartments on each floor, then mirrored on the opposite side. The outer domiciles were two bedrooms while the center apartment was a single bedroom. The dim porch lights did nothing to dispel the blackness closed in around her, seemingly suffocating her and choking off her very life. She hurried to the doorway where an officer greeted her.

The officer on duty smiled uneasily as she approached, "Evening Detective. I'm Sergeant Clay Johnson. Here's what we've got. One body inside, driver's license was used to identify her as Cheryl Henderson, twenty seven years old. Oh, and don't mind the puke in the bushes there. The new coroner did that. He pronounced about fifteen minutes ago, approximately two minutes before his dinner made a surprise reappearance." He paused for a moment, "It's a mess in there, looks like something straight outta the Halloween movies. You should brace yourself."

The officer shifted his weight to his right foot as he made the last comment, as if to move away from the door and keep her from sensing his uneasiness.

"Thanks Sergeant, duly noted." she said as she pulled on her gloves and stepped through the doorway. A coppery smell assaulted her nose as she crossed the threshold of the apartment. The stench of death was thick, almost tangible. The living area was extremely neat. She shot two rolls of pictures to document everything before venturing further into the apartment. The occupant must have been a very tidy housekeeper. Everything was in its proper place; the picture frames on the wall were all perfectly straight, every item perfectly placed down to the smallest detail. Even the magazines that lay on the coffee table were arranged like those in a doctor's office.

The kitchen lay just beyond, separated only by a partial bar. Again, everything was in its proper place. The camera flash mimicked a strobe light as she documented the location of every inane item. There were no dishes in the sink, the countertops were clean and the utensils seemed to be placed in their proper stations. After a brief search of the kitchen area, she determined that none of the knives or other kitchen utensils were missing or had been used in this crime. Everything seemed to be accounted for.

She turned to her left and walked into the bedroom. A small gasp escaped her lips as she saw to what the officer had referred. The coppery smell was thick and somewhat greasy as it filled her nostrils, almost choking her. The room appeared as though it had been painted in blood.

A woman's body, or at least what was left of it, lay on the bed, clad only in a pair of panties. Her clothes lay in a small pile near the foot of the bed only a few inches from her severed right arm, while the left arm lay just inside the bathroom door. Her head lay at the entrance to the room, staring into the living room beyond. If Sam had not stopped when she had, she surely would have kicked it. Once again, the flash of her camera tore at the darkness of the room, capturing the grisly scene on several more rolls of film.

She squatted down in front of the head and began her forensic investigation there. The blood pooling around the neck wound suggested that the head had been placed there purposely. The young victim's entire face was battered, suggesting heavy abuse. Her eyes were swollen shut, her mouth puffy with split lips as well and her cheeks were swollen and bruised to the point of grotesque disfigurement. Then she found what she was looking for. She spied the two puncture wounds, approximately two inches apart, with what appeared to be a bite pattern running right through the idle of the marks. She documented the gruesome discovery with several more photos before starting to process it. She gently picked up the head and examined the neck wound. The flesh around the neck did not seem to have been cut. It looked as though the head had been twisted off. There were no visible tool marks on any of the flesh or bone. As a matter of fact, the bone looked as though it had been hit with enough force to shatter cement before being wrenched from her shoulders. She searched through the victim's hair for any kind of trace evidence and found one single, bright blond hair that was much too long to belong to the victim.

She placed the head and the hair into evidence bags and moved to the bed.

As she approached the bed, she felt a hand brush through her hair. She quickly turned, scanning the room for anyone else, her hand moving to her sidearm, but only the bloodstained walls of the apartment greeted her scrutiny. She stepped to the edge of the bedroom and called to the officer on duty. "Hey, Johnson, Has Will showed up yet?" As she finished her question, she hoped that he would not hear the slight quiver in her voice.

The uniform at the door stuck his head into the apartment and spoke, "Nope. Sorry Detective, no one else yet. You want me to holler at ya when he gets his lazy ass here?"

"No, that's okay Sergeant. Thank you." A shiver crept up her spine as she turned back to the grisly scene. She returned to the bed and began to examine the body. A picture on the nightstand caught her attention. She photographed it and picked it up. As she did, she caught a glimpse of what this young woman used to look like. She was beautiful, so young and full of life.

She placed the picture back on the nightstand and looked over the bed and the injuries that the victim had sustained. She noticed arterial spray on the wall that looked as though it originated from the ceiling. She documented the pattern with several photos and moved on to the blood-soaked sheet. After finding nothing but blood on the sheet, she began to print the headboard, nightstand and any other areas that the killer might have touched. She lifted several prints, but, without a microscope or computer, they all looked alike. She assumed that they all belonged to the victim, due to her assessment with just her naked eye.

While examining the victim's corpse, she photographed and documented several injuries that looked as though chunks of flesh had been bitten off but there was no evidence that the missing pieces were in the room. The head and arms had definitely been disarticulated and judging from the redness around the wounds and spray patterns it was done pre-mortem. Upon closer inspection, she noticed bruising on the victim's ribs, indicating that her body had been beaten as brutally as her face had. But Sam was unable to determine the exact cause of death.

As she finished with the body, she heard a man's voice that she knew all too well, at the door. It was her backup, Detective William Jameson. They had worked together for the better part of eight years and had almost become romantically involved. She could hear him banter back and forth with Sergeant Johnson, but could only discern that they were trying half-heartedly to make jokes. She turned back to the task at hand, moving from the body to the dismembered arm on the floor. There were also several bites taken out of the arm, but she saw no signs that the victim had been bound.

He spoke as he entered the room, startling her. "Holy shit Sam! This makes what, the fourth murder this month? What the hell is going on here?"

She turned slowly to him, and in a reverent tone replied, "Exactly that, Will. Hell. Hell has come to Black Ridge." She pointed to the blood spatter on the walls and indicated how some of it seemed to originate from the ceiling. She directed his attention to the severed head in the bag and to the dismembered torso on the bed. "Nothing short of Hell could describe this scene, or the others." She pointed out the strange arterial spray pattern on the wall again and mentioned the lack of cast off. She then showed him the missing chunks of flesh on the corpse. He picked up right away on the lack of bruising or abrasions on the victim's wrists. They uneasily discussed the scene as they combed the room for evidence. However, they only found a few stray hairs. They documented blood splatter and the rest of the meager evidence they had found. They both printed the remainder of the apartment, finding only what they believed to be the victim's prints.

They had both decided that this was indeed the work of a serial killer. This was the fourth murder in three weeks, all of which had a matching M.O. The brutality of the murders was the calling card, along with the bite marks on the victim's neck and the large chunks of flesh that had been bitten from various parts of the body. Down at the precinct, they had deemed the murderer the Black Ridge Cannibal.

"It was him, Will. He's hit again. What the hell has come to Black Ridge? And who the fuck could do something like this?" Sam shivered as she spoke. She knew that a psychopath was loose in her town. One that apparently blended in well with the small town population, had extreme charisma and ungodly strength, and he had to be stopped quickly.

Detective Jameson turned to Sam and nodded. "This dude's a sicko for sure, a complete fuckin' whack-a-doo. You know, I've been reading some of those crime novels lately and even they don't get close to describing this kind of shit. I mean, Sam, did you notice that some of the arterial spray looks like it originated from the *ceiling* for Christ's sake?"

Her eyes drifted towards the pattern he was referring to, "Yeah, Will, I saw that, but I wasn't gonna say anything. I wanted to hear someone else say it."

They said little else concerning the scene during the next six hours. They spoke of family, friends, and anything else to try to get their mind off the bloody mess before them. They only spoke about their job when necessary. Neither of them spoke of the feeling that they were being watched.

After they had completed their investigation, Sam decided to call it a night. She collected her kit and all the evidence and loaded it into her SUV. She informed the on-duty officer that they were finished. He nodded, and called dispatch to let them know the scene was clear. Sam taped the door and headed wearily to her vehicle. She still couldn't shake the feeling that someone or something was watching her. Her eyes scanned the dissipating blackness around her, searching for any telltale sign of someone lurking in the distant brush. Nothing moved and not a sound could be heard over her escalated heartbeat. She fumbled with the keys to her Tahoe and quickly got in. As her hands touched the cold steering wheel, she sighed in relief to be out of the open night, especially after the recent events.

She started the vehicle and listened to it roar to life. Pulling the shifter into reverse then immediately into drive, she left the apartment complex in a hurry. It was early morning and she wanted to go home to wash the stench of death off her. She left the crime scene and headed toward the precinct to properly store the evidence she had collected. With that done, she headed toward home as fast as she dared drive. The morning light burned her eyes, causing them to water. The pavement blurred through her tears. The road twisted and crawled underneath the massive vehicle's tires, but she navigated through it with a genuine prowess. As she neared her driveway, she sped up, sliding her SUV into her parking spot as she had done every time for the last twelve years. As she opened the door, she could feel eyes moving over her body again, but she couldn't discern if it was malevolence or desire that she felt hidden in the cold prickles that slithered down her spine. She fumbled with her keys, found the house key and slowly approached the door with her sidearm drawn. *"Better to be safe than sorry,"* she thought to herself.

She quickly opened the door, keeping the weapon in front of her. She backed into a corner, efficiently scanning the room before her for any sign of a threat. Where her head turned, the weapon led the way. She cleared the house in a matter of only a few minutes before she returned to the fridge and grabbed a beer. Absentmindedly, she tossed the cap onto the counter and headed to the living room before turning on the T.V. and surfing through the channels. She came across a comedy about waiters and paused there for a moment. She took a long pull off the amber liquid and breathed a sigh of relief.

She went to the back door and unlocked the doggie door, then returned to the living room, kicked her shoes off and fell onto her couch. As she propped her feet up, her dog, a pure-bred German Rottweiler came bounding into the room. Sam smiled as he came into view and exclaimed, "Hi Mason baby! Did you miss me? Get your furry ass up here!" He plodded towards her and with one quick leap was on the couch with her. He smiled his goofy gin before laying his massive head in her lap.

As she began to pet him, she could feel the eyes moving over her again. This time, she could sense both the malevolence and desire behind them. She froze with fear as her faithful companion turned to look over her shoulder and issued a low warning growl. Sam could not move as fear consumed her. Mason whimpered, jumped off the couch and bolted upstairs, leaving her alone and defenseless. An odd sight indeed as Mason had been to every police training class in their locality in the year and a half since he had been a pup.

She only had a moment to ponder that thought before an icy hand brushed against her cheek. However, she could not turn her head to see who it was. It brushed a stray hair away from her face, gently tracing her cheekbone. The hands caressed her neck, squeezing ever so gently. As tender as the moment seemed, a sense of dread filled her body and the scent of blood filled her nostrils. She finally gained the courage to turn around. Only to find that once again, she was alone.

She began to question herself. "What the hell is going on? What is wrong with me? Am I losing my mind, had these crimes affected me deeper than I originally thought?" With shaky hands, she took another deep pull off her beer. Her eyes kept scanning the shadows that now seemed to creep at her from every corner. She knew she was alone, that there was no one else in the house. She had cleared every room and locked every door behind her. It was just in her mind. It had to be.

She quickly finished her beer, tossing the empty bottle in the trash as she crossed through the kitchen. She grabbed another from the fridge, mouthing the words, "*I'm a fuckin' loon,*" as she made her way upstairs. She entered her bedroom, again searching through the shadows as she then made her way to the bathroom. She turned the water on, adjusting it so that it was as hot as she could possibly stand and began to undress. Her clothes slid to the floor and she stepped into the shower. Again, she felt the eyes roaming over her body, but she ignored it. It was just her mind playing tricks on her.

It had to be, right?

She began to wash away the taint of the gruesome scene. She focused on the hot water washing over her body. She could feel the tension leaving her muscles as she washed away the remnants of the brutal murder scene she had just processed.

Between the hot shower and the cold beer, she began to relax a little. However, the feeling of being watched still gnawed at her. She kept telling herself that it was all in her mind. She closed her eyes as she let the water run through her hair and over her face. After twenty minutes, she turned the shower off and opened the opaque door. Her eyes searched the corners as she reached for the towel. As she began to dry off, she realized that she had not seen Mason since he had scurried from the living room couch. She wrapped the towel around her and began looking for her dog.

She stepped from the bathroom and quietly called for him. "Mason? Here boy. It's cool pal. There's no one else here. Where'd ya hide that big furry ass, huh?" Her mind began to race as she realized that Mason had *looked* at something behind her, something that had scared the hell out of him. "*Wait,*" she thought, "*is he even in the house?*" She began to doubt her sanity again. Had she actually unlocked the doggie door or had she imagined as well as the earlier incident on the couch?

She stepped into her study and a movement caught her eye. She immediately went on the defensive. Her hands poised to strike, her eyes searching for a target. Then she saw the telltale green glint of a canine's eye's reflecting light. It was Mason hiding in the corner like a scared little pup. She called to him again, and he still refused to move. When she approached him, he whimpered and she noticed as she got closer that he was shaking. As she reached out to comfort him, he growled viciously and snapped at her hand.

"What the hell is wrong with you?" She yelled as she stumbled backwards. "Fine, sit in here and freak out then. You're lucky I don't shoot your dumb ass." She stood, gave her hand a perplexed and somewhat angry look before returning to her bedroom to get dressed.

As she bent over to grasp her panties and pull them on, she felt a hand glide over her skin. However this time, she wasn't scared. She was excited, almost aroused. She closed her eyes and let the feeling wash over her. She could feel both hands now, sliding up and down her back, kneading her shoulder muscles, caressing her buttocks, sliding around to grasp her breasts. She could feel the throbbing heat of a man's excitement pressing against her.

A cold breath hit her neck. She shivered as cool lips pressed against her still steaming skin. She could feel the male presence shift his position so that he was now in front of her, still holding her tight and pressing his sinful need into her most intimate area. She thought she heard a faint whisper, like that of a sound carried on the breeze, "Sam. Who are you, my dark little flower?"

After debating for a brief moment, she forces her eyes open, and once again finds herself alone.

She backed up to a wall and slid to the floor. Her mind was racing again, her heart pounding as though it might burst through her rib cage. She felt dizzy and sick and excited all at the same time. Something was happening here, but what? Was she going insane? Again, the same questions beat at her consciousness. What was happening to her? What was this presence that she felt touching her?

It scared her, but it had seemed to caress her lovingly, almost passionately. Part of her wanted to dismiss it as mere fantasy, a daydream. Maybe it was the loneliness getting the better of her. But it felt so real. She shook it off and continued dressing. She threw on a pair of sweat pants, her sports bra and a thick hoodie and finally, her socks and running shoes. She went back to the study to check on Mason. He was still in his corner, but he seemed to have calmed down a bit. She made eye contact and gave him a command, "Mason, on guard. I'm going for a run."

She sprinted down the stairs, stopping long enough to open, close and lock the door. As she started down the road on her early morning five mile run, sliding her sunglasses into place as she went. She turned onto a deer trail off the road. It was a little tougher going than the paved road, but she didn't have to worry about oncoming traffic, or anyone trying to hit on her or check her out.

She did, however, have to worry about whatever was going on with her brain and about the killer on the loose in her town. Her mind went blank as she heard the birds start to chirp as the woods began to come to life. She kept an easy pace as she rounded a point and started up a hill. She ducked a few limbs as she sprinted up the first incline.

Halfway through her run, she began to feel the eyes on her again. She ignored the feeling at first, but it seemed to penetrate her soul, digging deeper and deeper. She began to run faster, her heart pounding in her chest, her lungs beginning to burn as she inhaled the crisp morning air. About fifty yards in front of her, she thought she saw someone hiding behind a tree, watching her. She could see that it was a very tall person, most likely a man, but she could not make out any features. As she quickly closed the distance between them, she prepared herself for a confrontation, but when she got within fifteen yards, he ducked out of sight. She slowed her pace, making sure she was ready for him if he attacked.

She reached the spot where he had been hiding and stopped. There was no one there and the only sound in the woods now was the sound of her labored breathing and the pounding of her own heart in her ears. Moving cautiously, she approached the tree where the mystery man had stood. She looked for signs of anyone having stood there but found no disturbed leaves nor any broken limbs or twigs. The forest floor was undisturbed.

She shook her head, sighed and mumbled to herself, "Get a grip, woman. You know weird shit happens with the shadows out here." He turned her attention back to the trail and began to run again. She topped the hill and started down. She slowed her pace so that she could listen to the sounds of the woods. She could hear the branches creaking overhead in the breeze, the birds were singing again, and somewhere in the distance, she heard a deer snort. The sun had made a full appearance now and was threatening to blind her, even with the sunglasses in place. She decided that her nature walk was over so she picked up the pace again and began to sprint towards home. As she rounded the last corner and her house came into sight, she wiped the sweat from her eyes. She could see Mason sitting at the living room window, watching her approach.

As she approached the house, the feeling of being watched had at last subsided. She was alone now. She unlocked her door and stepped inside. Mason immediately greeted her, wagging his cropped tail as hard as he could. She couldn't help but giggle. "Shake that ass, baby." She smiled at his display of happiness as she cautiously reached to pet him. But he made no threatening sounds, not recoiling as he had done upstairs. She scratched him behind his ears before heading back to the kitchen for a bottle of water. She opened it and drank deeply. She set the bottle down and did a few post-run stretches before heading back up to the shower.

After a quick rinse off, she returned to the living room to watch a little T.V. before trying to get a little sleep. For the next ten minutes or so, she could not pay attention to any of the shows. She decided to give it up and try to get some shut-eye before her next shift started. Quickly undressing, she made her way upstairs to her bedroom. She climbed into bed with Mason on her heels. He lay at the foot of the bed, giving her one last look before laying down his head. Sam pulled the covers up to her shoulders and was quickly sleeping soundly.

Chapter 2

HE WATCHED silently as the female detective exited her vehicle and gathered her kit. She was a fine specimen, perplexing though. Her soul was pure, but her heart was tainted. She bore the weight of the guilty but her soul marked her as an innocent. "Unusual indeed," he whispered.

He listened as she spoke to the officer at the door and gathered that her name was Sam. He moved through the shadows as though they were part of him, creeping closer to the apartment. As he drew nearer, he could smell his handiwork and wondered what the beautiful young detective was thinking. Did she know why the young woman had to die? Or perhaps she thought what everyone else did. That he was a brutal, sadistic, sick son of a bitch. Humans could be so narrow-minded. "*Everything is either black or white with them, no grey area to be found,*" he thought. He watched her from the shadows as she moved about the apartment, photographing everything and searching for evidence he knew she would not find. "*Maybe it's time I toy with her,*" he thought as a mischievous grin crept over his face.

He crept through the shadows, moving slowly and silently, watching his potential prey as he inched closer to the cop at the door. As he neared the edge of the shadows, he made eye contact with the police officer at the door. The man became completely oblivious to his presence as he walked right past him into the apartment.

Once inside, he slipped into the bedroom with Sam, who was intensely combing the room for anything to help her find the identity of who had done this. He couldn't help but smile when he thought about how close the killer that she was so desperately trying to catch was standing to her, and she was blind to it. He leaned forward, careful not to touch her, as that could break the spell, and sniffed her hair. She smelled of honeysuckle. He reached out and ran his hand through her loose hair and in the blink of an eye was swathed in shadows at the front of the apartment building, silently moving through the wooded area just beyond the property line. Even from this far away, he could still sense her confusion and fear as he heard her call to the officer at the door.

He watched her through the windows for several hours. He watched as her partner arrived.

He listened as they spoke of the details of his latest masterpiece and a malevolent smile crept over his face.

Soon enough though, Sam had apparently finished her investigation. She was loading her kit into her SUV. She looked spooked and he could smell the fear exuding from her. He watched as she surveyed her surroundings. The most likely assumption was that she was looking for whoever was watching her. At one point, she looked directly at him, their eyes briefly locking in a one-sided stare before she turned away. She didn't notice him standing less than twenty feet away from her.

She smelled of the young woman he had ripped apart just over ten hours ago. She smelled of death and fear, a combination that left him ecstatic. He started to move closer until she climbed into her vehicle, started it and sped out of the apartment complex.

He followed her on foot, an easy enough task as the surrounding area was heavily wooded and made it easy to stay out of sight. When she finally made it home, the sun had crested the wooded hills, making life a bit more difficult for him. He followed her into her home, quietly, sliding through the shadows as she cleared the house.

He had apparently spooked her.

But the best was yet to come.

She grabbed a beer and headed to the living room to turn on the TV before returning to the kitchen to unlatch the doggie door. She piled up on the couch and her dog lumbered into the room and curled up next to her. He moved closer to her, trying to decide if he should dismember her or if he should wait and get to know more about her. He could see the hair begin to stand up on the back of Sam's neck as the dog issued a warning growl. He couldn't help but smile as he made eye contact with the dog and sent it whimpering up the stairs. He stepped forward and gently touched her cheek, brushed aside a stray hair, and began to rub her shoulders. Even as his hands inched closer to her neck, he began to feel the urge to rip her head off. He released her and stepped back as she turned to see who had touched her. Even though she looked right at him once again, she remained oblivious to his presence.

He followed her through the house as she drank another beer and prepared for a shower. He watched her undress and he could sense her uneasiness. That wicked smile crept over his face once more as his eyes slowly drifted over her nude form.

She was actually quite stunning. Her body was toned, her muscles well defined, her breasts weren't large, but ample in size. He noticed a small butterfly tattoo on her ankle. Upon closer inspection, he noted that it had red and black wings. Her soul was what intrigued him the most though.

She bore one big black stain on an otherwise innocent life.

He allowed her to shower in private as he decided that he would rather seize the opportunity to find out more about her.

Looking around the bedroom, he noticed that the covers on the bed had been pulled back up, but not perfectly made. Her clothes were in the hamper, although barely. One of her shirts was hanging off the side of it, ready to slip and fall onto the floor with the slightest provocation. He peeked into her nightstand and found a .45 caliber Glock handgun and two spare, fully loaded magazines. Under her bed, he found a pump 12 gauge shotgun. Without removing it for closer inspection, he guessed it to be a Mossberg. A brief peek into her wardrobe showed him that she owned more pairs of jeans than dresses and preferred t-shirts to blouses.

On her dresser, he noticed a picture of what he guessed to be her at maybe eight years of age standing next to her father. He studied the picture for a moment before moving into the rest of the house. He found the study and immediately upon entering, spotted the dog cowering under the desk. He inwardly chuckled at the thought of this ferocious animal cowering before him like a small rodent staring into the eyes of a very large snake. He moved throughout the house, silently, disturbing nothing as he tried to gather some idea about why this woman intrigued him so. He attentively looked through her things until he heard the water in the shower cut off.

He crept back into her bedroom and waited for her. He watched her cross over the threshold of the bathroom, the light and the steam framing her silhouette, giving her an almost angelic profile. She sashayed down the hallway to the study where the dog was hiding. He heard her yell at the dog. When she finally returned to her room, she looked directly at him again, but never seeing him.

She dropped her towel and bent down to put on her panties. As she did so, he gently sild his hand over her back, caressing her body and massaging her shoulders, hoping to let her know that she was in no danger. Well, at least until he made his mind up about her. His hands slid around her torso and squeezed her breasts as he pressed himself against her buttocks. He kissed her neck, tenderly and passionately. He slid himself in front of her and almost kissed her on the mouth, stopping less than an inch from doing so. His eyes flickered over her beautiful face. When she held her breath with anticipation, it was enough to drive him mad with desire.

He moved closer and could feel her breath upon his lips.

"Who are you, my dark little flower?" he whispered

She opened her eyes and he was gone.

He watched as she backed into the wall and slid into a seated position. She seemed on the verge of hysterics. Again, a wicked smile played across his lips as he admired her semi-nude form. He inhaled deeply as the scent of fear began to intermingle with the scent of arousal.

She was *absolutely* intoxicating.

She composed herself quicker than he would have expected though and hastily got dressed. She set her dog to guard the house and quickly exited the house to go for a run. He was right behind her as she pulled the door closed.

He sprinted ahead of her so that he could observe her at a more relaxed pace. He could still smell the fear on her like the perfume on an exotic dancer. He could hear her breathing even from the quarter mile he had placed between them. He could hear the twigs snapping under her footfalls and with minimal concentration he could hear the pounding of her heart.

As she drew nearer to his position, he would move further down the path, finding a tree in which to sit or enough shadows to immerse himself and continue to watch her run. He did this for quite some time until he decided to let her see him.

Moving ahead of her once again, he found a large tree and stood behind it. He could see her as she rounded a corner. He locked eyes with her and whispered, "See me."

Her pace never faltered, but he could visibly see her body tense. As she came within just a few feet, he ducked out of sight and moved to another spot so that he could watch her. After a brief moment, he decided to allow her to finish her run in peace and returned to her house to wait for her.

As she returned home, he watched her as she unlocked the door and he slipped in behind her. He calmed the Rottweiler as he entered the house. She greeted her furry friend as he took a seat on the couch. She went upstairs and took a quick rinse off shower before retiring to her bedroom.

He crept through the house, as silent as a whisper and perched himself on the foot of her bed as she began to fade into sleep. He watched the rise and fall of her chest, listened to her rhythmic breathing and studied her intently. She seemed so pure, so innocent. He could sense that she had tried to live a good life, but something in her past had left an ugly stain upon her heart.

His eyes drifted over her body, examining every inch that was not covered by the thin sheet. Her hair was a coppery red, a beautiful contrast to her emerald green eyes and pale skin. He had been entranced with her eyes earlier in the evening and found that no precious gemstone, manmade or natural, could ever match the color of those beautiful orbs. He estimated her to be around five feet and eight inches tall with her hair reaching to her shoulder blades.

She was very slender and her facial features were exquisite. Her lips were a contradiction themselves. While her upper lip was somewhat thin, her bottom lip was very full. Kissable he had heard some men call mouths like hers. Her nose was narrow and slightly upturned, but not enough to seem "mousy." Her ears were slightly pointed at the tips and were adorned with several earrings in each ear, both in the lobe and the scapha. But her eyes were the most fascinating thing about her. They were big and showed not only an extremely high intellect, but also level of compassion he had not seen in an extremely long time. And although she tried to hide it, he could see the immense sadness locked away within.

As she slept, her mouth twitched and she whispered the word "mom." Her hand clenched at her pillow and her body tensed for a moment before relaxing again.

She shifted and the sheet fell from her chest, exposing a bit more of her. He noticed a small tattoo over her heart, a small cloud with a date and Mom inside of it. Yet another piece of the puzzle revealed to him.

He smiled as he surveyed her body draped by the sheet, the way it accentuated her body, the slope of her breasts, the curve of her hips and the rise and fall of her stomach. She was indeed beautiful. He found himself wondering what could have left such a stain on her yet did not taint her completely. What sadness dwelled within her heart and why did she call out in her sleep for her mom?

As he watched her sleep, his body told him that it was well past sun up, and that he needed to rest. His mind fell into a waking dream, reflecting on the previous night's events.

He forced himself to sit through yet another movie that perverted everything about him. However amusing the human misconception could occasionally be, this movie proved to be particularly disturbing as it completely destroyed everything about what he was. He had chosen his mark long before they had entered the theatre. During the movie, he could sense her arousal, and that only served to strengthen his resolve that she would be his next victim.

As the movie ended, the merciless one stood and followed the young woman to her car. As she pulled her keys from her purse, he lightly touched her shoulder. She gasped and turned to face him. He smiled sweetly and asked her for the time, their eyes locking for the briefest of moments, his mind creating an invisible thread between them, allowing him to see her memories and relive every dark deed and malicious thought.

She returned the smile and replied with the correct time, then moved to the passenger door and opened it for him. He entered the compact vehicle, which cramped his long legs, but he said nothing. She quickly opened her door and slid behind the steering wheel. Without a word between them, she started the car and put it into reverse.

She was wearing a short linen skirt and a lightweight blouse with just enough buttons left undone to allow a tantalizing peek at her cleavage. He smiled as he touched her thigh and moved her skirt up enough to see her panties. Her eyes never left the road as she shifted into drive and started towards her home. He reached for the radio and switched it on. His face blanched as a country ballad blasted from the speakers. He quickly changed the station to one known for playing only heavy metal. A dramatic and brutal rhythm of one of the more popular metal bands tore from the airwaves. He caught himself bobbing his head to the thrashing beat and smiled a smile of contentment.

They finished the drive to her place with only the driving beats of the music breaking the silence. As they arrived, he noticed that her apartment was in a very secluded area of the complex.

Perfect.

They made their way inside and she stood at the entryway to the bedroom, unblinking. He browsed her DVD collection, seeing several vampire movies, a few romantic comedies and a couple of action flicks. Upon inspection of her CD collection, he found only country music. "Well, there goes the mood music." He mumbled as he turned his attention to his intended victim.

He stood and took a step toward her. As he did, a sliver of light from a street lamp shone through a gap in the curtains and flickered across his murderous eyes.

In silence, she turned and moved into the bedroom. He followed closely behind. She began to undress. First, taking off the thin, silk blouse and then dropping the high-cut skirt to the floor. She slipped out of her shoes before removing her bra. He placed his hand on her shoulder to let her know that was enough. He pointed her to the bed, and as she looked him in the eyes, a single tear rolled down her cheek.

The merciless one could see the terror trying to find its way to the surface. She opened her mouth to speak, but nothing came out. Turning to oblige him, she reached to switch on the light and with lightning speed, his hand clasped around her wrist, almost crushing the fragile bones. A small whimper did manage to escape her lips. He roughly shoved her onto the bed and with a menacing whisper asked her, "That wasn't very nice, now was it? But, then again, you're not known to be very nice, are you?"

He dug his fingernails into the soft flesh of her thigh, piercing the skin and making her squirm against him. He swiftly pulled his hand towards her feet, tearing through the skin in the process. Again, her mouth opened, this time to undoubtedly scream, but still no sound issued forth.

He gazed deep into her eyes and spoke to her. "You know why I'm here, don't you?" Upon finishing the cryptic question, he leaned forward and sank his teeth into the soft flesh of her neck, piercing her carotid artery and he drank deeply, sucking against the skin to encourage the blood flow.

He stopped after a few seconds. He only wanted a taste, but he had taken enough to make her woozy. He climbed onto the bed, straddling her. He began to deliver blow after punishing blow to her face, chest, neck and shoulders. He could feel the bones cracking as his fist made repeated contact. As she began to black out, he stopped the vicious attack long enough for her to regain full consciousness. As she did come to, she mouthed the word "why?"

He grabbed her ribs and lifted her from the bed, flipping her limp body midair and slamming her against the ceiling. Her eyes instinctively closed against the disorienting movement. As she hit the ceiling, however, the shock of pain that wracked through her body forced her eyes open just in time to see her assailant lift himself off the bed to straddle her on the ceiling with nothing short of an unnatural grace. In his gravity defying pose, his coat and hair hung downward, giving him an almost comical appearance. If it had not been for the fact she knew that tonight was the night she was going to die, she might have laughed.

Her eyes widened in terror as the reality of what was happening hit her. He grabbed her throat and tore her flesh, severing the jugular vein. Blood spurted form the wound, painting the walls in crimson. He grabbed her right arm and clamped his teeth into her bicep, tearing out a chunk of flesh. He *bit her left arm and again removed another large portion of skin from her body. As her life rapidly slipped away, tears swelled in the corners of the young woman's eyes as she mouthed the words, "I'm so sorry."*

He released his grip on her and she dropped to the bed, her body bouncing like a rag doll tossed onto the unforgiving pavement. He chuckled dryly at the mental image before descending on her. He grabbed her left wrist and with a quick jerk, tore her arm from its socket and let it drop to the floor.

She managed a slight gasp and squeezed her eyes as tightly closed as she could.

He repeated the process with her right arm and tossed it haphazardly over his shoulder.

Tears flowed from her eyes as rapidly as water from a faucet. Her life was almost gone and she knew it. She forced her eyes open and looked directly into the eyes of her tormenter and whispered, "Forgive me."

A satisfied smile replaced the masque of rage he had been wearing. He had broken her, even though it had taken longer than he had expected. He leaned forward, kissed her on the forehead before pressing his lips to the torn jugular. He drank heartily, quickly ending her life.

He blinked rapidly as the memory faded and he found himself again in the beautiful young detective's bedroom. He had to rest. He slipped from the footboard and crept through the house, making no more noise than a spider crossing the headboard in the night. He left the house and moved quickly through the woods towards the old shack he had been using to shelter himself from the revealing light of the sun.

Chapter 3

SAM'S DREAMS were extremely vivid and somewhat perplexing. She dreamt of a tall figure, swathed in shadow. They billowed around him like living tendrils of smoke. He beckoned to her, calling her to come closer and closer, but he was never within reach. Sometimes, the smoke gave the illusion of wings on the figure, but the image was fleeting.

She tried to focus on his face, but the harder she tried, the more the shadows obscured him.

She awoke with a start as her phone ripped her from her dreams. She fumbled for her cell phone as she noticed Mason lying on the floor giving her a quizzical look. She swiped the screen on her phone to answer the call, placed it to her ear and mumbled, "What?"

It was Detective Jameson, Will, on the other end. "Hey Sam. I know we're supposed have another couple of hours before shift starts, but you might wanna get your cute little ass down to the lab. They've come up with some interesting shit, weird, but interesting. See you there in about an hour?"

"Yeah. Hour." She mumbled to him as she hung up. She rolled over onto her back and looked at the ceiling for a minute before sitting up and looking at Mason with sleep filled eyes. "Why do they think I have to be there for every little development?"

Mason lifted an ear and cocked his head to the side as if to respond to her question with one of his own. When she said nothing more, he dropped his head back onto his paws.

Sam slowly climbed out of bed and got dressed, warily surveying the room and waiting for the feeling of being watched to return. It didn't. As she made her way downstairs to make some coffee, she noticed that dusk was rapidly approaching. She led Mason to the back door and let him out, giving him a brief scratch behind the ears before making eye contact and issuing the standard of "On guard." She hurriedly collected her things and got on the road to the county lab.

It had only taken her just over thirty minutes to make it to work. She wanted to have time to consult with the coroner before she checked in with the lab. She went directly to the coroner's office. Dr.

Joe Yoshihara was on duty tonight. "Hey Joe, got any news on the female DB from last night?"

Doctor Yoshihara pulled back a white sheet that had been covering the body of the latest victim. "I don't know if I can tell you anything that you don't already know. There are multiple blunt force traumas. Her arms and head were disarticulated, multiple bite wounds. And take a look here on her thigh. It looks as though the murder stuck his fingers into her skin and yanked downwards, kind of like he unzipped her skin." He emulated the motion to demonstrate.

"What else can I tell you? All if this occurred pre-mortem. This poor girl went through hell before she died. The cause of death was blood loss. She bled out as she was being ripped apart. There are no tool marks, no bruising on the wrists or ankles to indicate she was bound and there were no fibers in her mouth and no trauma there either. So she wasn't gagged. We're still waiting on toxicology to report back, but I'm willing to bet it's clean." He looked at his shoes and she noticed that he was clenching his fist. "There is something else. It's over here on my desk."

He made his way to his desk and picked up a plaster mold. "Sam, I took this mold three different times and all three were the same." He handed her something out of a horror movie.

"I can make up another batch of plaster if you want and you can check it. But that's right, I'm sure of it."

Sam was holding a plaster mold of teeth. Most of them were normal although the maxillary canine teeth were elongated and very sharp.

Like Vampire fangs.

A cold chill ran down her spine as she considered the implications of all the evidence. She shook her head and handed the mold back to Doctor Yoshihara.

"Doc, did you find any trace we might have missed?"

"Here, I found two hairs, both light blonde in color and considerably longer than the victims." He held out a plastic bag with the two hairs inside. She could already tell they were the same color and length as the hairs she and Will had lifted at the scene.

She studied the hairs for a moment, letting her mind peruse the possible courses of action. "Well, this helps. I mean, there can't be that many people with hair this long and pale in Black Ridge." She turned and walked out of the room, her mind a million miles away.

As she absentmindedly made her way to her office, she stopped at the DNA lab and left the hairs on the supervisor's desk. She started to write a note when someone spoke behind her.

"Hey, uh, Detective, is this a priority?"

As the saying goes, Sam nearly jumped out of her skin. "Jesus, I didn't see you there."

The lab tech smiled, "Sorry detective. And my name's Levi, not Jesus."

Sam composed herself and chuckled, "Okay, Levi, thanks for the coronary and yes, these are priority. I need the results last week."

He reached past her and picked up the bag. "I'm on it." He turned his back and headed towards one of the various machines in the room that Sam couldn't name.

She left the lab and made her way to her office. Her mind was spinning with all the information she had just received. But one word kept clawing its way to the surface.

Vampire.

She returned to her desk and turned her computer on. As soon as it was completely booted, she brought up her internet browser and searched for unsolved murders involving disarticulated victims and got over thousand results. She clicked on the first link and began to read. It was a blog dedicated to vampire sightings and possible attacks over the years. Some of the attacks listed had occurred in the 1940's and hinted that the fact that these kinds of attacks have been happening since the beginning of recorded history. The most recent attack listed on the website was dated two months prior to the murders in Black Ridge. She sat for hours, going through her files, pouring over the internet and looking over her notes and photos of the crime scenes. She was looking for any discrepancies, similarities or anything she and Will might have missed.

After a while, everything began to blur together. She found herself unable to concentrate on the task at hand so she stood, stretched and decided a cup of coffee would do her good After pouring a cup, she found herself staring at the wall, thinking of the male figure in the woods.

Someone touched her shoulder and she quickly turned, dropping her hand to her sidearm as a small scream erupted from her lips. It was only Will. "Jesus, Will. You scared the hell out of me!"

He looked sincerely apologetic, slowly withdrawing his hand. "Damn, I'm sorry Sam. This shit's really getting to ya, huh?"

She shrugged, "Will, I want this son of a bitch off my streets. I mean, who's next? For all we know, he could go after a kid. I've been going over everything we have, I've been searching the net for any cases like this, and I've got squat. There's no pattern here and nothing to link the victims." She realized she had clenched her fist so tightly that her fingernails were cutting into her palms. She opened her hand and looked at the marks she had made. Apparently, this psycho *was* getting to her. She sat her coffee down, rubbed her palms together and looked at Will with a sheepish grin. "Let's go see if they have anything in DNA yet." She was already leaving her office as she finished the sentence. He fell into step behind her, following her to the lab.

The tech, Levi if she remembered correctly, looked up from his microscope as the two detectives entered. "Oh, hey, perfect timing. I was just about to call you. I've got the results on the samples you left me. Are these from something recent?"

Sam gave him a puzzled look. "Well, yeah. Why, what's wrong with them?"

"Well, there's nothing wrong with them. It's just, well, I've never seen hair this color on an adult, at least not without bleach. If a kid has pale blonde hair it changes and darkens as they get older. This is a natural color. But, with the length you've given me, there is no way this came from a kid. "

Will stepped up to the microscope and looked through it. "Holy shit, Sam, you gotta see this. What the hell? Okay, so we have a hair that is almost five feet long and perfectly blonde. Where the hell did it come from?"

Levi reached over and switched out the slides as Will continued to look through the microscope. "Here is what made it so strange. Look at the follicle. It was pulled from the scalp. See the epithelia?"

Sam made her way over and peeked at the sample. "So, what did the sequencer tell you?"

"Well, that the proud owner of this hair is male. Nothing else about the readout made any sense at all."

Sam looked up from the scope. "What does that mean?"

"I don't know how to explain it. The only part of the readout that made any damn sense was that it was male. The rest of it was gobbledygook."

"So, it was a degraded sample?" Will was scratching his chin, something he was notorious for when he was deep in thought.

"See, no, that's the thing." Levi stood sat down in front of his computer. "Look, the DNA doesn't even look human, but it doesn't match up to any known species. There is nothing like it in our database."

"Well, that doesn't help us at all. Did you get anything from CODU or NCIC?" Sam was crestfallen. She had been sure that the hair was going to be the key to putting this whack job behind bars.

Levi grabbed a stack of papers off the corner of his desk. "Actually, I got several hits. Four months ago in Coleen, Texas there were twenty-seven unsolved murders, all of which had a hair that didn't match any DNA on file. Eleven months ago in Auburn, Maine, sixty-seven murders. The hair only showed up at one crime scene there, but all of the murders were exactly the same. Fourteen months ago in Hopewell, Virginia there were thirty eight murders with hair like this being found at four of them. The list goes on and on." He flipped through the stack of papers. "Not all of the crime scenes had hair at them, or at least no samples were found, but every victim had been ripped apart and bitten."

Levi handed the list to Sam and Will looked over her shoulder as she skimmed through it.

"Sam, how the hell could one person do this? There has to be several of the psycho's working together. One person couldn't do this much damage to someone in that short of a time and not get noticed."

"Okay, explain to me how four or five or hell, even two people could have killed Cheryl in that little bitty apartment and left absolutely no evidence aside from some weird ass hair. It isn't possible." Sam shook her head in dismay, "Will, come with me. I nccd to see if we've got the toxicology back on Cheryl yet and I want to show you something. Thanks Levi, I appreciate you getting that done so fast."

Levi nodded and went back to the microscope, changing out the slides and starting work on another case.

She hurried down the hallway to her office where she hastily sat down, hoping that Will had not noticed how badly she was shaking. She felt as if she would drop straight to the floor if she had to stand for another second. "Look at this, Will." She showed him the website dedicated to vampire attacks as well as pointed out the discrepancies in the evidence as well as the lack there of. "Have you been to see Cheryl's body? Did Joe show you the mold?"

Will grinned. "Are you buying into this horseshit? The fucker has dentures, or had two fangs implanted. It's not a vampire. Bullshit like that doesn't exist. It's just some crap for under-sexed housewives with a severe bad boy complex to get off to. There is no supernatural phenomenon going on in Black Ridge. I promise you." He gave a hearty chuckle. "Fuckin' vampires in Black Ridge. Holy shit, I bet my dad's a werewolf. He's definitely hairy enough."

"Alright smartass, explain the hair, and what about the arterial spray from Cheryl's apartment? You and I both said it originated from the ceiling. How the hell did that happen unless the perp had supernatural strength? And while you're at it, explain to me how the victims were so brutally killed with absolutely no evidence to support that they were bound or gagged. You interviewed some of the neighbors and none of them heard a damn thing, did they?" Sam looked at her partner expectantly.

Will shook his head and gave a boisterous laugh. "Sam, you watch too much TV. If I were you, I wouldn't mention this crackpot theory to anyone else. They'll slap that cute ass of yours in a padded room in a New York minute. What we're dealing with is some sneak ass sons of bitches. And I promise you, every one of these motherfuckers are gonna pay for this. You understand me, partner? There's nothing supernatural happening, just some dickhead that's really good at covering their damned tracks."

"I pray to God you're right, Will. I really do."

Chapter 4

HE CAME upon the abandoned house as he traveled through the woods. The old shock looked as though no one had lived there for twenty odd years. He quietly stepped inside and without a sound made his way to the bedroom he had been using. The window had been boarded over, effectively sealing out the sunlight so he was sure to get some rest. Sleeping in the sunlight had never been one of his favored activities. It wasn't that it was painful. He just didn't care for it. He was more at home in the dark.

He took off his jacket and folded it into a makeshift pillow. As he lay down, his eyes began to droop before his head ever made contact with the somewhat uncomfortable pillow. His mind was already drifting through the past, settling on a memory from long ago.

He was following a young man through a city park. The vengeful one had read his soul and knew that he would be his next victim. The sun had long since set and darkness had embraced the trees and surrounding landscape. Only the security lights lit the path, and even they did little to hold the deepening night at bay. The young man in front of him kept glancing nervously over his shoulder.

The vengeful one decided that he had toyed with his prey long enough. With two long strides, he clamped his hand down on the young man's neck. A small yelp pierced the night.

As he turned his prey to face him, the young man released his bladder and began to beg for his life, pleading his innocence.

"Please man, don't hurt me. I didn't do nothing to you, man. Here, here's my wallet. It ain't much, just take it. I'll go home and I won't say shit to nobody. You got my word, man. I swear to God I won't say nothing!" Tears welled up in his eyes and flooded his cheeks, his voice cracked as he tried to persuade the predator before him to let him go.

The vengeful one stood perfectly still, his face an emotionless mask. He allowed his victim to process the fact that he was going to die. Slowly, he leaned his face closer to that of the young man. "Ben, you know why I'm here, don't you?"

The tears streamed faster and terror filled his eyes. He shook his head yes even as his mouth spewed forth more lies. "I didn't do anything, I swear to God I didn't!"

With a menacing whisper, the vengeful one calmed Ben. "Ben, you are going to stop screaming now. No one can hear you. Even if they did, they would only see you screaming into the air." He paused for dramatic effect. "They would see you as nothing more than a head case and as cold and callous as today's people are? No one would stop to help you."

The vengeful one's hand grabbed Ben by the throat, "This will all be over as soon as you do what you know has to be done." With his free hand, he grabbed his victim's wrist and snapped the bones like twigs. He sank his fingers into the soft flesh of the young man's forearm and tore it away from the bone. He hit him once in the sternum, sending him crumbling to the ground. He had heard at least a few bones break under the impact of his punch.

Ben was whimpering, his eyes rolling to show the whites as he started to lose consciousness.

"Stay with me, Ben. You're not getting off that easy." The vengeful one slapped the young man's face. As Ben came to, the predator leaned forward and bit a chunk of flesh out of his left bicep. Blood welled to the surface and began to pour from the wound, rapidly staining Ben's shirt.

Ben still tried to claim his innocence even though his voice no longer obeyed him. Only his lips moved, trying in vain to form the words that might save him.

Even though the sight before him was pitiful indeed, the pleas fell on deaf ears. A powerful blow answered the silent pleas, slamming into Ben's face, shattering his cheekbone. The vengeful one knew that the pain must be incredible. Had this pathetic excuse for a man convinced himself that he had actually done nothing wrong? The predator's foot slammed down on his prey's kneecap, dislocating the bones and shattering the patella.

Finally, Ben broke. With powerful sobs and giant tears, he began to plead again. This time though, his cries were for forgiveness. He had found his voice and he began to pray, asking to be forgiven for his sins and finally trying to strike a deal with God for his life.

The vengeful one leaned forward, softly placing his hand over Ben's mouth. "Your prayers have not fallen on deaf ears. You will be punished for your sins and death is your penalty. Take solace in the fact that your death will now be swift and painless." He leaned further forward, latching his mouth to Ben's neck. His teeth deftly penetrated the carotid artery. Blood spurted from the wound as his teeth were withdrawn. The predator sucked against the skin, swallowing the warm nectar of life as it poured from its previous host.

Night had fully fallen when he awoke from his dream. How many years had passed since he had taken Ben's life? How many had fallen victim to him in the time since then? How many before? Countless humans had fallen to his hands because of their own stupidity, greed and ignorance. He stood, stretched and dusted himself off.

Yet another would die tonight, and he would enjoy the kill.

He left his makeshift home and started towards the town. The trip was brief, taking him only a few seconds to navigate through the dense Arkansas forest. Every footfall landed on dried out twigs, dead leaves and other debris from the canopy of empty branches, but not a sound was made.

Soon he was looking at his next victim's house, a two story Victorian style home. He knocked on the door and after a few moments, an elderly man opened it. No words were spoken as the enraged one locked eyes with him. The elderly man stepped aside and allowed him entry. Once inside, the predator queried ever so softly, "Where is your wife?"

The old man simply nodded towards the stairs and spoke a single word, "Bed."

The enraged one lay his hand on the old man's shoulder and led him into the living room, stopping him by the recliner. With a malevolent whisper he asked the old man, "You do know why I'm here, don't you Frank?"

The old man simply nodded and closed his eyes. Without opening them, he spoke calmly to the man standing before him, staring at him with the promise of death in his eyes. "Forgive me for what I'd done. I only ask that my death atone for the terrible things I've done, and that those I've wronged can find peace now that I'm gone. I'm so sorry, please forgive me." A single tear rolled down his cheek as he began to recite the Lord's Prayer.

The enraged one was angry that the old man had given in so easily. He had inflicted more pain and suffering on people he loved and deserved to be punished for it. He deserved to suffer as his victims had. He deserved nothing less than hours of torture. But, he had repented. It wasn't his place to question it.

It still pissed him off, though.

As he thought about what should have been done to Frank, a floorboard creaked on the landing above them. He turned and locked eyes with an elderly woman. She blinked once, turned and retreated slowly into the bedroom she had shared with this monster for many years.

The predator leaned forward and locked his mouth to the old man's leathery neck. His teeth pierced the carotid artery with no problem and he began to drink deeply, rapidly draining the life from Frank. It only took a couple of minutes to finish the old man off.

After the last light of life flickered out of Franks eyes, the enraged one placed his hands on either side of Franks head and gave a violent twist. Franks head came off with a wet popping sound.

He carried the head to the front porch and placed it so it would be looking at whoever came up the steps. He secretly hoped it would be Detective Brae. What would she think of this scene? He returned to Frank's body and tore a sleeve from his flannel shirt and soaked it in blood. He returned to the porch and used the blood soaked rag to paint several symbols on the wall behind the severed head. After he had finished with the artistic endeavor, he turned his attention to the old woman that has seen him.

He made his way up the stairs and into the master bedroom where the old woman sat on the bed, a blank look on her face. He sat down beside her and gently took her hand. "Rosa, you have committed a terrible sin in allowing your husband to carry out his atrocities." As she blinked and looked at him, he continued, "Don't try to deny knowledge of what he has done, I know your every thought. I should punish you for letting those things happen, but consider tonight your lucky night. You get to live a little while longer. You will, however, spend your remaining time trying to make amends for what you allowed to happen. Do you understand?"

Rosa nodded with tears streaming down her face.

"When I leave, you will call the police. You will ask for Detective Brae. You will speak to no one but Detective Brae. You will tell her that your husband is dead and that you remember nothing else. And do not go downstairs. You will remain here for the police to arrive. Do you understand so far?"

Rosa gave him a brief nod.

"When Detective Brae questions you, your memories will be vague and you will remember nothing of this conversation." He stood and picked up the cordless handset for her phone. "Make the call."

Before he turned to leave, he touched her cheek with the back of his blood soaked hand, quickly leaving the house as Rosa began to dial the phone.

* * * * *

Sam had returned to her office and had been there for only a few moments when the phone rang. She picked up the receiver, "This is Detective Samantha Brae."

The voice on the other end of the line was shaky and solemn. "Detective Brae, I was told to call you. My husband's dead. He's been murdered."

Sam straightened in her chair. "Who told you to call me? Are the people still in the house?"

With an eerily calm voice, the woman replied, "A man told me to call you, a very handsome man. And no, I don't think he's still in the house."

"Alright, ma'am, I need your name and address. We will have officers there as quickly as possible but I need you to remain on the line with me, okay?" Sam was shaking so hard she knocked over the mesh pencil holder as she tried to retrieve a pen to write down the information.

"My name is Rosa De Lucca, twelve Davis Park Road. It's the last house on the left. You can't miss it. I'm just going to wait here in the bedroom till you get here. Will that be okay?"

"That'll be fine, Rosa. Stay where you are. We will be there as soon as we can. I'm going to transfer you to dispatch, stay on the line, okay?"

The line was silent for a moment before the woman answered. "Yes ma'am. I'll be here."

Sam pressed the proper sequence of buttons on her phone and informed the dispatcher that answered of what had transpired in the last couple of minutes before transferring Rosa.

"Rosa, this is Shawna. She will stay on the line with you until we arrive. I'll see you soon." Sam hung up her phone and with an explosion of movement, grabbed her coat and headed out the door.

She almost missed the entrance to Will's office as she virtually shouted, "Grab your stuff Will. We've got another one!"

Will was behind her in an instant, chasing her through the building to the parking lot. He was right on her tail as she slipped between two SUV's and opened her door. He sped around the next one and opened the door to his own vehicle. As Sam's vehicle sped away from him, the blue lights momentarily dazed him and the shrill scream of the siren caused him to flinch. He flipped on his own sirens and lights as he fell into line behind her once again.

Sam was almost frantic. Her heart was racing faster and harder than the powerful engine under the hood of her police issued SUV. They were closer to the killer than ever before.

According to thc woman who had called the station, the scene was less than fifteen minutes old, and with the ten minutes it would take her to reach the address Rosa had provided, they might even be able to capture this sicko. She picked up the handset for the police radio and called in for backup, giving only what information was necessary to insure a proper response.

The small town of Black Ridge seemed to come alive as sirens cut through the night and the strobe of the blue lights tried to chase away the shadows. Sam floored the vehicle, pushing it has hard as she could trying to cut the ten minute ETA down as much as she could.

Eight minutes and fourteen seconds after she had hung up the phone with Mrs. De Lucca, she pulled into the driveway of the latest crime scene.

As she pulled into the driveway, her headlights cut through the darkness, briefly illuminating what she thought was a man standing in the brush at the edge of the property. Two squad cars pulled in beside her, distracting her for a moment. When she turned her attention back, the figure was gone.

She clambered out of her vehicle, quickly drawing her sidearm. She motioned the other officers to follower her. She quickly and cautiously approached the area where she believed she had seen the figure. Against her training, her hands were trembling uncontrollably. She heard footsteps behind her and hastily looked over her shoulder. Two officers stood behind her. One holding his service pistol in both hands and the other holding a shotgun he had taken from the dash rack in his cruiser.

She suddenly remembered that Rosa was alone in the house with her husband's corpse. She called out to the officers, instructing them to keep searching and to get any other officers to help when they arrived. She immediately made her way to the house and skidded to a halt as she approached the front porch. A severed head stared at her from the porch and the bloody symbols on the wall caused chills to run up and down her spine.

Several more officers pulled in as she was choking back the urge to vomit. She forced herself to regain her composure and approached the front door, being extremely careful to avoid the blood pooling around the head.

The screen door was shut and latched but not locked. The front door was still standing wide open. She waved to some of the officers as they started to approach the steps to the porch. Most of them had their eyes locked on the severed head and almost failed to see the blood starting to run down the steps. At the last moment, they noticed Sam's frantic waving and stopped. They stepped to the side of the porch and avoided the steps completely. One by one they entered the house and made short work of clearing it.

They found the master bedroom where Rosa De Lucca was and passed the information on to Sam. She climbed the stairs with no small amount of trepidation. What would she say to this woman? How could she comfort her and grill her for information about the events of tonight?

Sometimes being a detective sucked ass.

She crossed the threshold of the master bedroom and found herself in a short hallway. She called to Rosa as she cautiously made her way down the hall. "Mrs. De Lucca? I'm Detective Brae. We spoke just a little bit ago. Are you okay?"

The feeling of being watched had started again when she arrived and began the search outside, but seemed to intensify in the bedroom.

"I'm okay dear. Come on in." The voice was weak and full of sorrow.

Sam moved further down the hallway, holding her pistol at the ready. The hallway opened up into a rather large bedroom. To her left was a king size bed, directly in front of her was a beautiful mahogany desk against the wall looking out a set of oversized windows. The room was lit only by a small lamp next to Mrs. De Lucca, casting eerie shadows around the room.

Sam holstered her weapon as soon as she saw the old woman sitting on the bed. Her back was hunched and she had obviously been crying. She was clenching the handset of her cordless phone to her chest. The small lamp next to her cast ominous shadows on the woman's face.

"Rosa, are you all right?" Sam was genuinely concerned for the woman. It was likely that she was in shock and Sam knew that could be a major problem.

Rosa looked up at Sam. Her eyes were puffy and red from crying and her bottom lip quivered as she spoke, "I'm fine dear, but my poor Frank. My poor, poor Frank." Tears rolled from her eyes as she spoke her deceased husband's name.

Sam laid her hand on the woman's shoulder and gave her a reassuring squeeze. "Rosa, I need to ask you some questions, I'm sorry. I know that this is probably the worst time, but it's important we do this while everything is still fresh in your mind. Do you understand?"

Rosa shook her head and her shoulders shook as she began to sob.

"Again, I'm so sorry. Can you describe the suspect?"

Rosa shook her head, "I'm sorry dear. I've been trying, but I just don't recall." She placed her head in her hands, the handset pressing awkwardly into her face and began to cry again.

Sam rubbed her back as she spoke reassuring words. "It's alright, Rosa. Try to calm down a bit. I know how upset you are, believe me. I know. But it's unbelievably important that you do your very best here, okay?"

Rosa gave a curious shudder before lifting her head and looking Sam eye to eye. "He was beautiful. I don't mean like a model or an actor. He was incredibly, sinfully beautiful." Although the woman was still visibly shaken, she took a deep breath and began to recount what she could remember. "I heard something downstairs. Frank usually watches TV until late before he comes to bed. But I heard something that didn't sound right. So I went to check on him. There was someone in the house, right next to Frank, but I can't for the life of me see his face. He was tall and had long hair, really long hair."

She sat for a minute before continuing. "I don't know why, but I came back to the bedroom and sat down here and called you. I didn't see Frank die, I didn't hear anything, but I know he's dead. I can feel it. He is, isn't he?"

Sam nodded and Rosa began to sob again. "Rosa, are you all right?"

Rosa grabbed a tissue from the nightstand and dried her eyes. "This is just so frustrating. I know my memory isn't what it used to be, but when I try to remember what that man looked like, it's like I'm staring into a void. There's just nothing there."

"It's alright, Rosa. Take your time."

The old woman jumped suddenly and looked at Sam again. "He had long blonde hair and blue eyes. The bluest eyes you ever did see. I... That's all I can remember, detective. I'm so sorry."

Sam smiled and gave her another reassuring squeeze on the shoulder. "You did great, Rosa. Now, is there anyone I can call for you?"

Rosa's eyes flooded with guilt, despair, anguish and sorrow all at once. Sam couldn't help but feel pity for the poor woman. "My daughter, Sarah, lives in Fayetteville, but we haven't spoken in over three years. I don't want to bother the poor girl. She's been through enough."

"Rosa, I'm sure that under the circumstances she would want to hear this from you, instead of someone else. If you would like, I can call her for you and let her know, but I'm sure she would rather talk to you."

Rosa gave her a weak little smile and patted Sam's leg. "Don't you worry, I'll call her in a bit. I'll get a motel room tonight so that you can do whatever it is you do here. Then I'll have someone come and clean all this up before I come back. I just don't have the strength to do it." With that, she looked at the floor and began to cry again. "If we're done here, I'll let myself out the back so I don't disturb anything."

"Well, if you insist on the motel, there's nothing I can do. I do need to get some pictures of you and I'll need to take the clothing you've go on. I also need to take a sample of the blood on your cheek."

Rosa blanched when Sam mentioned the blood on her cheek and slowly reached up to check and see if it was really there. Sam stopped her, "I'm sorry Rosa. I've got to take some pictures first. Let's get this over with so you can get cleaned up. Afterwards, I'll walk you to your car and have an officer escort you. It's just procedure."

"Okay dear. Do whatever it is you have to do." She stood and allowed Sam to take all the needed pictures. When the photographs were done, she slowly removed her clothing so that the detective could bag and document everything.

Rosa went to the closet and showed Sam the clothes that she wished to change into. Sam was more than willing to help Rosa remove her clothing without compromising it. She used an entire roll of film documenting every angle of the victim's current apparel. She then waited patiently as Rosa changed into the new outfit.

Sam took the clothes and placed them into paper evidence bags.

After all the evidence had been collected and Rosa had used the sink in the master bath to wash the blood from her face, Sam led them downstairs at Rosa's instruction. The camera flash was a little disorienting on the stairs, but they made it none the less.

As they entered the kitchen, Rosa pointed to her purse on the counter. Sam took several pictures before emptying the contents on the countertop. Every item was photographed before being returned to the purse. Once that was finished, they exited the house and Sam then followed the old woman to her car, a 1966 Oldsmobile Cutlass.

Sam was speechless when she saw the car. "Mrs. De Lucca that is one beautiful piece of machinery, my dad would have loved it."

Rosa smiled and ran a loving hand over the fender. "This was Frank's baby. He started working on it in '83 I believe. He's completely restored it and then some. I couldn't tell you what all he's done to it. I just know it is really fast."

Sam smiled. "It is a work of art, Rosa. Now, before you leave, let me make arrangements to have an officer follow you."

Rosa shook her head and paused as a helicopter flew overhead. "No dear. You don't have to do that. I don't want to be a bother."

"Not a bother at all, Rosa. I want to make sure you're safe, okay? Give me just a minute."

"Detective, are all the police as polite and as nice as you?"

Sam could feel the heat rising in her cheeks as she replied, "I'm afraid not, Mrs. De Lucca. I just have a little bit of an attachment to this case and a lot more compassion than most of the force."

The elderly lady gazed deep into Sam's eyes. After a moment, Sam wasn't sure if she was looking into Rosa's eyes any longer. Her eyes were now a shade of blue that seemed celestial even though she was sure they were hazel a moment ago.

"I see, little one. But, don't allow this... task to consume you. Do only what you need to do, and no more, lest you lose yourself to your job." The wrinkled face studies Sam with an almost cruel scrutiny, making her take a timid step back.

Rosa blinked several times before she spoke again. "I'm sorry dear, did you need anything else?"

Sam was sure of what she was seeing now. The old lady's eyes were changing from that incredible shade of blue back to hazel. She tried to read Rosa's expression, but the certainty and cruel arrogance that was there a second ago had been replaced with sorrow and anguish.

Sam was at a loss. This little episode had really shaken her, but she hid it well. "Give me just a moment, Rosa. I'll have an officer come talk to you before you leave."

Rosa gave another weak smile and opened her car door. "Thank you for your kindness, Detective. It's greatly appreciated."

Sam gave her a brief hug before taking her leave and made her way over to one of the officers that had just pulled into the scene. "Excuse me, Officer. I need someone to follow Mrs. De Lucca to a motel and report back with her location. I also need someone stationed no less than twenty feet from her at all times. The man that did this to her husband knows her face and we don't have him yet. I need this woman kept safe."

The officer called over another uniform and gave him the orders to follow and guard the newly widowed woman and to report back every half hour. Without any delay, the officer made his way over to Rosa, spoke to her for a moment before running back to his cruiser and pulling in behind the '66 Olds. Sam watched the two of them as they pulled out into the street and the tail lights faded into the deepening night.

* * * * *

Mrs. De Lucca watched the pretty detective speak to an officer. She waved as Sam gave her a quick glance over her shoulder and headed towards the house. A different cop approached her and asked her what motel they would be going to. Rosa only knew of one close, the Red Bud Motel. It was kind of a seedy joint, but the rooms were clean and it would do for tonight. She just wanted to go to sleep and forget that any of this had happened. She shifted into first gear and slowly released the clutch. The Olds surged into motion, bouncing down the unpaved driveway.

She cruised along slowly, enjoying the beautiful night sky and thinking of her Frank. Her mind quickly shifted to thoughts of the faceless man who had told her she was to spend the rest of her time making amends for the wrongs she had allowed to happen. Her mind drifted to the man's eyes, how cold and blue they had been. They were almost like staring into the artic sea. How could he have known about her past, about Frank's past? These questions and more began to eat away at her very soul. Had she done right by her child? Were the sacrifices she had made worth the price? Or had she failed as a mother?

She shifted into third, maintaining a speed of thirty miles per hour as she traveled over the unkempt road. It was once paved, many years ago, but time had taken a harsh toll on it. Pot holes had formed and scattered across it like a minefield, the edges of the road had long since crumbled away, yielding to the deep ditches that paralleled both sides, making it treacherous to navigate at night. She remembered back to when there had been markings, or, mayonnaise and mustard as she had always called the white and yellow painted lines, but only scant remnants of those markings remained.

She began to slow as she came to an intersection. It was a two way stop and the other two lanes were the ones who were cursed with the stop signs. After giving a brief glance both directions, she downshifted and accelerated across the intersection.

A bright light blazed through the driver's side window and tore her attention from the road ahead. She turned to see a truck bearing down her at an amazing pace. She caught a fleeting glance of the driver. Long blonde hair framed his face while his piercing blue eyes seemed to cut through the night and bear down on her soul. A gentle smile stretched his face as he closed the remaining gap between them. There was a split second before metal slammed into metal and her car blasted from the road.

The force of the impact rolled her car numerous times before it came to a rest on its roof in the hay field she had just passed. Her horn was going off and she could hear someone screaming. She could hear the engine revving over the screaming and she could smell anti-freeze and hot metal.

It took her a moment to gain her bearing and to realize that the person screaming was none other than herself. Her whole body ached and her heart threatened to pulverize her ribs it was pounding so hard. She squeezed her eyes shut and began to pray.

After what seemed like an eternity, she heard metal scraping against metal. It had to be loud because it was drowning out the ringing in her ears and although seemingly impossible, her heart began to beat harder and stars began to dance behind her eyelids.

She opened her eyes briefly to see flames dancing around the car, the sight of the ground over her head brought on a bout of nausea before the darkness claimed her.

Chapter 5

SAM TURNED her attention to the front porch. Her mind was still replaying the strange conversation with Mrs. De Lucca when she felt the eyes crawling over her skin again. She turned, slowly surveying the area, searching for whoever might be watching her even though she knew she would find nothing. She uneasily turned back to the task at hand doing her best to ignore the creepy feeling.

Either her mind was playing tricks on her, or the shadows were reaching for her, beckoning to her.

She shook her head and forced herself to focus. This scene wasn't as brutal as the last few, but it still had all the calling cards of the psychopath she was on the hunt for. The head that lay on the porch had been savagely disarticulated and placed in a position that would guarantee it would be seen by anyone approaching the front door. She had a theory that the killer was using this as a message for her. She had begun to believe that he was taunting her, using the heads to tell her, "*I see you, but you can't see me.*"

This guy was really pissing her off.

She returned to her SUV and collected her kit. She began searching for evidence after taking several hundred photographs of the porch and blood painted wall. As before, the only piece of evidence to be found was a single long blonde hair.

"I hate this son of a bitch!" she exclaimed as she held the hair in front of her face with a pair of tweezers, staring at is with complete disdain. Apparently realizing that she was extremely volatile, most of the officers around her stepped away from her and tried to pretend to be busy. She bit her lip and placed the single hair into an evidence bag.

She carefully picked up the head and examined the wounds. Partially obscured by the torn flesh was another bite mark. Her mind raced, spinning out of control as she considered all of the evidence so far. This was ludicrous. She forced herself back to reality and continued to examine the head. There was no bruising as far as she could tell and the torn flesh around the neck area was consistent with that of the other victims. After she had documented the wounds with photographs and notes, she placed the head in an evidence bag and had it sent to the coroner's office. Now she just had to patiently wait for the toxicology and autopsy reports.

She continued to search the porch for anything that might help them bring the killer to justice, even though she knew she was wasting her time. As she straightened, intending to venture into the house to continue her investigation, she could feel the phantom hand resting on her shoulder. She viciously brushed it away and strode into the house.

Will was standing by the recliner, finishing his examination of the body. He noticed Sam and gave a slight shake of his head. He hadn't found shit either. Her best bet now was the strange symbols painted on the front of the house.

She returned to the porch, allowing her partner to finish his investigation on the inside of the house. She instead turned her attention to the strange symbols. She took out her phone and brought up her web browser. She searched for satanic symbols and after several minutes of perusing the results decided that she was looking in the wrong area.

Sam was lost in thought as she stared at the weird markings on the wall. "The writing on the wall..." she murmured to herself. Her cellphone rang and pulled her from her musings.

The panicked voice on the other end cut off her usual greeting. "Detective Brae? This is Officer

Copeland. I was the officer assigned to Mrs. De Lucca."

There was a long pause and Sam could sense that the young cop was screwing up the courage to deliver some terrible news. "She's been in an accident. A truck came out of nowhere and hit her. She's being airlifted to St. Johns Hospital. She's in pretty bad shape, Detective."

The helicopter had arrived while Officer Copeland was informing Sam of what had happened, forcing him to shout to be heard.

"Was it a drunk driver? What the hell happened, officer?" Sam was shaken now. She had a feeling she knew what was coming next.

She could hear the sadness in his voice as he yelled into the phone, "I don't know. I saw the collision and I got to Mrs. De Lucca's car as fast as I could. She was hurt pretty bad and her door was so messed up I couldn't open it. I went to the passenger side door and managed to pry it open. After I got her to safety, I went to check on the truck but by then, whoever was driving it was long gone. I did find one thing, Detective, but you're not gonna like it."

Sam's patience was rapidly waning. "Spit it out officer, what the fuck did you find?"

"A really long blonde hair."

Sam dropped her phone and stood staring at the symbols on the wall. This psycho was trying to *tell her something. He had told Rosa to call her specifically and somehow made the woman forget what* he looked like. She knew it. He was leaving the heads for her, and now these symbols. She just had to decipher what it was he was trying to tell her.

She could feel the icy stare creeping over her again, the cold familiarity forming goose bumps on her arms and standing the hair at the nape of her neck on end. She turned, surveying the blanket of night that covered the area around them. Spotlights were pointed at various points in the woods and the helicopter searchlight blazed a path through the night, pushing back the shadows but revealing no specters of death hiding in the darkness, just as she had expected.

This *thing* wasn't ready for her to see him yet.

She angrily picked up her phone and checked to see if the officer was still there. He had apparently already hung up as the screen had already turned off. She gave it a once over to make sure it wasn't broken from the fall. She had lucked out on this at least. The screen remained intact.

Sam made her way inside the house and found Will. He was still in the living room searching for evidence. With a shaky hand, she touched his shoulder and relayed the news of Rosa's accident and informed him that she was leaving to go to the hospital.

He looked up at her and frowned. "You all right, Sam? You don't look so hot."

She gave him a weak smile. "Thanks for the compliment, ass. I'm fine, Will. I'm just tired of playing this bastard's game. I want to empty my pistol into his face and finally end this nightmare."

Her words were as cold as steel, cutting right to Will's heart. Samantha was never this angry or this emotional. Hell, part of the reason they had split up is because she was so damn distant. Apparently these murders were getting to her. It pained him to see her like this. He knew how generous and soft her heart was, how she cried at movies like Bambi and Titanic. She was the kindest and gentlest person he had ever met. She also had a fierce determination pushing her ever forward, causing her to strive for perfection in everything she did. Those were the qualities that had caused him to fall so deeply in love with her.

"I know what you mean, Sam. But we don't have enough to figure out who this asshole is, let alone find him."

Sam sighed heavily and said, "We don't even have a witness anymore. And to make matters worse, Officer Copeland told me that he found a single blonde hair in the cab of the truck. That fucker was driving the truck that hit Rosa, Will. He had this planned from the get-go. We played right into his hands."

Will's eyes looked as if they might pop out of his skull. "What? What the hell are you talking about?"

Sam sighed and flung her hands in the air. "I'm talking out my ass, Will. I don't know if it's the same hair or not. It's been sent to the lab for testing. I haven't seen the hair, but I just *know* it was our guy that did this. Don't ask me how I know, I just do. My gut says that this sick son of a bitch ran her off the road. Listen, I got to go. I'll call you as soon as I know something, okay?"

Will nodded his head and watched Sam leave. He strengthened his resolve and turned his attention back to the recliner, his hands moving slower, his eyes focusing more intently to find anything in the thick blanket of blood that covered the chair and the floor.

As Sam left the house, she climbed into her SUV and sped away from the gruesome murder scene. In her mind, she was going over all of the evidence she had collected so far. The fang-like bite patterns on the victims, the lack of physical evidence save the strands of hair and the fact that Rosa had been face to face with this guy and could not remember what he looked like. None of the victims were bound or gagged, but none of them had resisted or put up a fight. There were no defensive wounds to suggest otherwise. Her mind spun to the conversation she and Rosa had right before the bereaved widow had climbed into her car. What was with her eyes? Sam could see her eyes changing color again as if it were happing right in front of her.

"Yep, I've officially lost my fuckin' mind." She absently turned up the radio as Metallica's *'Until it Sleeps'* filled the interior of the large vehicle as she passed the scene of the accident. The emergency responders had already departed, leaving only the tow truck trying to pull Rosa's Cutlass out of the field.

Even with Sam driving well above the speed limit and the blue lights flashing away the night, the drive to the hospital seemed to take forever. The trees on either side of the road were a blur as her speedometer reached speeds above ninety miles per hour. She tried to release the accelerator knowing that these speeds at night were dangerous, but her mind would not allow it. The only witness was in the hospital in God knows what kind of shape and she felt as though she *had* to be there.

Her phone rang, interrupting the song on the radio. She pressed the answer call button on her steering wheel and Officer Copeland's voice poured from the speakers.

"Detective Brae?"

"Yeah, it's me, what's going on? How is she?"

The young officer hesitated for only a brief moment before responding. "She's in a coma. The doctor says she'll live, but there's no telling when she'll wake up. I'm so sorry Detective. I should have seen the truck and done something to stop it. It just came out of nowhere." His voice broke as he spoke and it was obvious to Sam that he was fighting back tears.

"Officer, you listen to me and you listen good. There was nothing you could have done, especially if this was our guy. This son of a bitch is damn clever and sneakier than a fox around a hen house. You can't blame yourself for this, okay? You said yourself that the doctors say she'll live." Her voice was firm yet full of compassion. She knew exactly what he was feeling. She knew he was going to blame himself to some extent no matter what she said to him, but she hoped that her words would alleviate some of the burden he was determined to carry.

"Thanks Detective, I appreciate it. I just wish there was something I could have done to stop this from happening." The sorrow in his voice was prevalent as he forced the words from his mouth.

Sam decided it was better to change the subject to help keep him from wallowing in self-pity and get his attention back on the task at hand. "What happened to the hair you said you found? Did forensics collect it?" Her voice had taken a lighter, more interrogatory tone with him, trying to ease him back into the seemingly impossible task of catching a killer at large.

As he spoke, more confidence came into his voice. "Yes Detective, forensics arrived a few minutes before the chopper did. We ran the plates on the truck as well. They came back to a stolen vehicle. Funny thing is, the report came in about the time we got the call to respond to the murder at the De Lucca house."

"Where was it stolen from?" Her voice more commanding that she had intended.

"That's where it gets weird. It was stolen from the Johnson's farm." He paused for a second, "It's on the other side of town. That's got to be at least a twenty minute drive. Mr. Johnson said that it was stolen by a tall blonde guy. Said he had really blue eyes."

Sam sighed as she remembered an old adage her Dad used to tell her. "*Never ask if it can get any worse, cause it sure as shit will.*" Apparently this also held true of weird. A twenty minute drive yet no evidence that there had been another car anywhere near the scene. They had been sure that the killer had been on foot. Rosa had told her during their initial phone conversation that she had called only moments after he had left. So how the hell did he get across town, steal a truck and get back across town in fifteen minutes? Unless he had a car nearby, that feat would be impossible. To travel that distance on foot would most *definitely* be impossible.

Apparently Officer Copeland was on the same train of thought. "Detective, when I was searching the area for a suspect, I didn't come across any tire tracks. Did you?"

"Nope, I sure as hell didn't. I'll call back to the scene and have the officers do a more thorough sweep of the area. Listen, I'm probably five minutes away from you. Let me call Will and get them searching for tracks and I'll talk to you when I get there, okay?" She didn't wait for him to answer before punching the end call button on her steering wheel once, then twice and telling her voice command prompt to "Call Will."

He picked up on the second ring. "What's up, hot stuff?"

"Cut the crap, Will. I need you to ask the search crew if they came across any tire tracks on the property. If not, I need ya'll to set up a search party and start looking for another set of tracks, something that doesn't belong out there. The truck that hit Rosa was stolen from the other side of town just minutes after Rosa called me. This guy had something nearby to help him get to the other side of town. I just don't understand why he would need the truck if he already had something there. At the speeds he would have had to hit to get to the Johnson farm to make the time frame add up, he's got to have a sports car or crotch rocket. If so, he won't have cheap tires on it. If we can find those tracks, we might be able to find this fucker."

"No, Sam, I didn't hear of any tracks. I'll go ask around though. If they didn't find anything, I'll get a search party going. You know how much I like to play with posse." When Sam didn't say anything, he continued, "Well damn, I was hoping to lighten the mood a little. But okay then. And I told you so, now will you admit there's more than one person involved?"

"Will, I'm telling you, if there was more than one person, we would have found more than just a few strands of hair. We'd have some kind of damned evidence by now!" Her whole body was shaking. She didn't know why she was so furious with him for refusing to acknowledge the fact that this was so far from normal that a duckbill platypus wearing a trench coat and strap-on would seem every day ordinary at this point.

"She punched at her stereo. The first blow missed the end call button so she swung again. Her hand stung, but her anger was far from abated. She swung the vehicle into the hospital parking lot and sat, staring into the black night surrounding her.

After a few moments of silence, she reached for the glovebox. After rummaging through the paperwork and odds and ends in the compartment, she finally pulled out a crumpled pack of cigarettes. As she anxiously stared at the pack, she carried on an internal argument. After finally convincing herself that one would be okay, she pulled one out and lit it. She gave a lazy sigh as she exhaled, the astringent smoke pouring from her lungs and seeping through her partially open lips.

She turned off the motor and sat in complete silence. With the keys pulled from the ignition, the dash lights had extinguished and the orange glow of the cigarette was the only light in the near perfect darkness inside the vehicle.

Her gaze drifted to the driver side window and she nearly choked as she gasped with lungs full of smoke.

A man with knee-length blonde hair stood less than a hundred feet from her, watching her. He was nicely dressed, and in the strange wash of the fluorescent streetlamp, he seemed to be a sickly pale. His eyes locked with hers and chills clawed their way up her spine.

A somewhat familiar sensation.

She threw her door open and as she slid from the driver's seat, she pulled her service pistol from free from the holster in one liquid movement. She pointed it center mass and shouted, "You, on the ground now!" When he did not move, she shouted again, her voice almost reaching a scream, "I said get the fuck on the ground! I will shoot you if you do not comply! GET DOWN NOW!"

She took a few steps towards the figure, not realizing that she had dropped her cigarette. Her eyes had locked on his face, his eyes in particular. The pale man never blinked as she continued her approach.

She was now twenty yards away from him and she could see the unnatural blue eyes staring back at her with perfect clarity. He was well over six feet tall with pale blonde hair that hung past his knees. His facial features were beautiful, enough to make her heart skip a beat and her breath to catch in her throat. His jaw line was slender, almost feminine but not quite. His lips were thin lines as he seemingly scrutinized her, like a hawk watching his prey. His nose was broad but not overly big for his face. There was just no possible way to describe the perfection that was this man before her.

While the man was incredibly beautiful, she could not tear her attention away from those eyes. They were the most vivid shade of blue she had ever seen. They made her remember a moment from her childhood. Her dad had showed her a sapphire and she had held it toward the sun, letting the most brilliant light shine through the depths of that beautiful blue gemstone.

Those beautiful blue orbs cut right through Sam, stripping her right down to her soul. The corners of his delectable mouth turned up, shifting into a partial smile as he cocked his head to the side. The movement caused the light to cascade across his eyes, causing them to glint at her like a cats eyes.

While that creeped her out, the only way she could have ever described this man was *angelic*.

She forced herself to look away from his eyes and take stock of the rest of the man. She needed to size him up in case he decided to resist arrest. He had broad shoulders and she could tell that he was very muscular even with the loose jacket hindering the view of his body. His clothing consisted of a black windbreaker type jacket, a white t-shirt, blue jeans and a pair of black boots. He stood with a grace and poise that seemed unnatural.

At last he spoke. His voice was calm and soothing and made Sam think of a choir. "You really shouldn't smoke, Sam. Those things will kill you."

"You think I give a shit what you think, psycho? I told you to get on the ground. I'm not going to say it again." Sam was focused now. She had pushed aside his surreal looks and focused on her job. This man, no matter how good looking, was a sick, sadistic murderer.

He took two quick steps forward and Sam did not hesitate. She pulled the trigger three times, the .45 caliber handgun bucking heartily in her hands. She expertly timed the pull of the trigger and all three shots would have found a grouping of a half an inch on a target.

But she had missed with all three rounds.

He was gone.

She turned in baffled circles trying to find him. She ran to the spot on which he had been standing a moment ago and found nothing. She searched the area and she found the spot her bullets had hit the rising embankment beyond, leaving great, gaping holes in the manicured grass.

She shakily holstered her pistol and gave one more turn, slowly surveying her surroundings. She found exactly what she knew she would.

Nothing.

She sat down on the pavement and held her face in her hands. Shame washed over her as she realized that she might actually be going insane. After all, she had heard how she was her mother's daughter all her life.

She heard footsteps rapidly approaching. She pushed herself to her feet and again drew her service pistol. She found herself staring down the sights at a cop running towards her.

He almost comically skidded to a stop just a few feet from her. "Holy shit, don't shoot!" He had his firearm drawn as well, but he was holding it pointed down at the pavement, both hands clasping the grip and his finger resting on the trigger guard. "I heard shots and I just knew it had to be you. What happened? Are you okay?"

Sam's face flushed as she tried to figure out how to explain that she had just shot a figment of her imagination. "I thought I saw something." Her voice quavered as she spoke. "He was there. I shot the son of a bitch three times in the chest from twenty feet away. I couldn't have missed." She glanced up at the officer long enough to see the confusion in his face as he looked around the parking lot for a body. "I didn't hit him. Or at least I don't think I did." Without looking, she pointed to the torn up grass by the light post where he had been standing. "I honestly don't know what happened. He was there then he wasn't."

The officer was visibly confused, but he said nothing. He just touched her shoulder and headed toward the hospital. As they walked he spoke softly, avoiding the topic of what had just transpired. "I'm Jim Copeland. It's nice to meet you, Detective." He turned mid-step and offered her his hand.

She took it with a look of gratitude. She didn't have to say anything, but she could see he understood. As they reached the emergency, she realized that she still had a white knuckle grip on her handgun. She forced herself to holster it before she entered the hospital. Officer Copeland led the way to Rosa's room and told her he would wait outside until she was finished.

Sam stepped into the room. A nurse was changing the bandages on the old lady's forehead. "How's she doing?"

The nurse replied without looking up from her duties. "It's going to be a tough road for her. She's got several broken ribs, her jaw was fractured and her right leg is broken but there was no internal bleeding, so that's a plus. We can't figure out why she's in a coma though. There's no concussion or brain trauma, surprisingly enough."

Sam moved to the side of the bed not occupied by the nurse and took Rosa's hand in hers. "I'm so sorry Rosa. We should have been prepared for this. I should have sent an entire escort with you or had you ride with one of our officers. I hope you can forgive me." Tears welled up in Sam's eyes and she nonchalantly wiped them away. She gave the comatose woman's hand a squeeze, "We're gonna catch this bastard, Rosa. I promise."

She returned her attention to the nurse. "I'm Detective Brae with the Black Ridge P.D. I need you or someone on your staff to call me the second she wakes up. She's an important witness in an ongoing investigation and I need her statement ASAP. I'm also gonna need her personal stuff."

The nurse nodded and finished tending to Rosa's wounds. She walked to a cabinet recessed into the wall and took down a plastic bag. She passed it across Sam without looking at her. "Leave a card at the nurses' station and I'll make sure that they know to call you if there's any change in Mrs. De Lucca's condition." With that, the nurse briskly left the room without as much as a nod.

Sam sat with Rosa for a while before she decided that she needed to get back to the lab and get back to work on catching the bastard responsible for this. She lightly kissed Rosa on the forehead before leaving the room. She eased the door shut and looked at Officer Copeland. She thanked him for staying with Rosa and let him know that they should have a replacement coming for him soon. He smiled and stretched back in the chair he had placed by the door.

Sam dropped her card at the nurses' station as she had been instructed and let the R.N on duty know the situation. They assured her that she would be the first to know if there was any change in Rosa's condition.

Sam returned to her vehicle and sat sullenly in the driver's seat. She glanced at the bag in her passenger seat containing Rosa's belongings. She shook her head and started the SUV. She backed out and rushed back to the Black Ridge police department.

When she arrived, she grabbed the bag and retrieved her kit from the rear hatch. She made her way to the evidence room, placed the bag on a large stainless steel table, her kit on the floor near the doorway and pulled on a pair of latex gloves.

She carefully opened the bag and removed the contents, spreading them across the large table. The first item that caught her eye was a small book with floral print on the cover. As she opened it, she quickly realized that this was Rosa's address book. She looked over the scattered items and realized that there was no cell phone to be found. So, she had either left it at home, lost it in the wreck or just flat out didn't own one.

Returning her attention to the address book, she slowly thumbed through the pages until she came across a page that looked like it had recently gotten wet. As she studied it, she realized that it wasn't just water that had stained the page. It had been tears. Taped to the page was a picture of a little girl, maybe eight years old with a name and telephone number written on the page above it.

Sarah.

Sam copied the number into her note pad and placed the book back on the table. She carefully examined every article of clothing and found nothing except Rosa's blood and broken safety glass. Nothing here would help her so she picked up her note pad, removed her gloves and withdrew her cell from her pocket. She dialed the number and awaited a response on the other end. After it rang three times, it went to voicemail.

Sam cleared her throat as she listened to the recorded greeting. After the obligatory beep, she started to leave her message.

Um, Sarah, my name is Samantha Brae. I'm a detective with the Black Ridge Police Department. It is very important that we speak with you as soon as possible. Please call me as soon as you get this message." After leaving her cell phone number and finishing her message, Sam looked at the clock and realized that it was 2:46 in the morning. Unless this young woman worked nights, she probably had her phone on silent. She thought to herself, "*Hurry up and wait,*" something her Dad used to tell her, something that he had picked up from his days in the Navy.

Chapter 6

THE VAMPIRE stood outside watching the cars approaching the house. He partially hid himself, waiting on Sam's arrival. He saw her Tahoe in the front of the pack heading down the driveway. Her headlights washed over him and he willed her to see him. It took her only a split second and she slid her SUV to a sudden stop. She clambered from the vehicle drawing her sidearm. He flashed a smile and disappeared into the shadows, making his way back into the house. Unseen and unheard, he returned to Rosa's room and took a seat at the desk.

He sat in the bedroom with Rosa as the police cleared the room and waited patiently for his dark little flower to show. He knew she would, she was obsessed with catching him. With minimal concentration everyone was oblivious to his presence.

Finally, Sam arrived. He listened to the banter between the two women and could not help but be pleasantly amused at how polite Samantha was. That was an incredibly rare quality these days. They stood as Samantha explained that she couldn't remain here for the evening and he then followed them to Rosa's car. As they exchanged their pleasantries, he saw an opening and could not resist. Placing his unseen hand upon Rosa's shoulder, he began to speak through her. He willed the old woman's eyes to change color as he gave his cryptic warning to Samantha.

After releasing Rosa from his psychic hold, he turned and left the two of them, a smug smile tugging at the corners of his mouth. He swiftly moved through the forest, his feet falling silently on the debris of the forest floor. He passed several deer that regarded him with little more than mild curiosity. It took him a matter of seconds to travel the distance across town.

As he came to the edge of the forest, he was looking upon a small farmhouse. His eyes fell upon a late fifty's model International pickup. "*They're not built like this anymore*," he thought to himself as he ran his hand across the cold steel fenders.

He approached the house, noticing movement through the curtained windows. He stepped onto the porch and opened the door as though he had every right to be there. A younger woman, maybe in her early twenties, stopped and looked at him. After a brief glance into his eyes, she returned to her business as though she had never seen him. He found the keys lying on the kitchen table and casually picked them up. As he turned to leave, an older gentleman stood at the doorway watching him. He started to speak, presumably to ask what the hell was going on, but the vampire waved his hand as if to dismiss him and the old farmer stepped aside and watched the stranger drive away with his old truck.

He drove back toward the De Lucca house at speeds that pushed the BD-240 engine to its limits. The old truck had been well maintained apparently as it accelerated rather smoothly and seemed to shift through the gears with no problems. It was nice to see that some people still appreciated their things enough to take care of them.

As he pressed harder on the accelerator, the aging engine gave a shudder of protest as the speeds continued to increase. Despite the continued protests of the old truck, the vampire continued on at speeds that would make most humans cringe or cry out in fear.

He parked the truck on the side of the road and cut the ignition. He opened the door and stood beside the impressive machine. It wasn't long before his sensitive ears picked up the purr of the police issue Dodge Charger and the Olds Cutlass. Soon after, he could see the headlights cutting through the darkness as he leaned against the International.

He climbed back into the cab and started the old truck. The engine roared to life and he shifted into first gear. He timed everything as the Olds came into view. He punched the accelerator to the floor as he dumped the clutch. The rear tires spun for a second before purchasing hold on the gravel road and lurching forward. Expertly shifting through the gears, the old truck gained momentum at an astonishing rate. As he neared the intersection, he opened the door and stepped from the truck as casually as one might step over a small puddle. In the blink of an eye he had entered the forest that lined the road.

As he moved into the thicker shadows of the woods, he turned to watch the two machines collide with an ear-shattering boom. The Olds flew from the road and rolled several times into a field across from him. The squad car slid to a stop a few feet from the truck and the young officer ran to the overturned car. He tried in vain for several minutes to get the driver's door open before moving to the passenger side. After the valiant cop had gotten Rosa to safety, he ran to the truck with his sidearm drawn and his flashlight searching for the driver.

Upon finding no one in the interior of the now battered old truck, he turned his light to sweep over the wooded area around him. The flashlight swept over the vampires face several times, causing him to flinch away from the incredibly bright light. The whole time the cop was searching, he had his head tilted to the side as he called the accident in through the mic he had attached to his shoulder.

The vampire smiled as he heard the ambulance sirens in the distance. They were too far away for the cop to hear, but he could hear them as clearly as if they were only a few hundred feet down the road. He turned back towards the De Lucca house and within seconds he was standing at the edge of the property, watching Samantha again.

For some reason, he could not get this woman out of his mind. She had gotten under his skin. He, who had walked the Earth since Adam and Eve had tasted of the forbidden fruit, had become enamored with a human female. He had seen a countless number of women, some good and some bad, but he had never before become entranced with one. It was ridiculous.

He watched her study the symbols he had left for her on the front porch. As she photographed it, he slipped through the shadows like the deadliest of snakes and placed his icy hand on her shoulder. She angrily brushed it away and he chuckled as he sat on the step beside her.

She was such an attractive woman. What would it be like to kiss her? Would she…

Angrily he muttered to himself, "*This has to stop. You know where it will lead.*"

Samantha's phone rang and after speaking to whoever was on the other end her face went as white as a sheet before turning an intense red. He watched as she dropped her phone and he saw the rage twist her features as she bent to snatch it back up. She surveyed the outside scene before rushing inside.

He hesitated as she tore out of the driveway. He wanted to follow her and he had several hours before sunrise, but he was afraid. Not afraid of the sun, that couldn't hurt him, but of his feelings for her. At last, he gave in and in the span of a breath was pacing her speeding vehicle along the highway.

As she pulled into the hospital parking lot, he made his way down the hill and stood under a security light not too far from her Tahoe. She sat in the SUV for a few minutes before lighting a cigarette. It was then that he spoke to her, "See me."

Samantha nearly choked as she caught sight of him. She jumped from her vehicle and pointed her gun at him. She shouted her commands and he could smell the fear emanating from her. She was terrified. He tried to give her a disarming smile, but that only served to set her on edge. So, he tried a small joke. "You really shouldn't smoke, Sam. Those things will kill you."

He had to touch her. He had to smell her hair. He took a step forward and she opened fire.

He saw her finger tense as she started to pull the trigger. He blinked and was standing a fair distance to her right, hidden by the blanket of darkness around them. He had pushed too far and she had taken action. She was still convinced that he was a cold and brutal killer.

He just had to be patient. She would learn the truth of the world soon enough. He sped off, back to the shack he had been using as a home. As he entered the ramshackle house, he took off his jacket and made his way to the back of the place. He settled down on the floor again and closed his eyes, hoping to dream of Samantha Brae and those intoxicating eyes.

His dreams came swiftly and he dreamt of a young woman, although it was not Samantha Brae.

The remorseful one sat in her house, awaiting her arrival. She had just finished her aerobics class and would be returning home at any moment. He heard her car pull into the driveway and shortly after, the rasp of a key sliding into the deadbolt. As she entered, he stood and approached her. Her eyes filled with terror as she watched him draw nearer. He spoke softly and the tension quickly dissolved from her body. "You have been difficult to pin down, Susan. Do you know why I am here?"

They young woman stared at him with glassy eyes and shook her head no. He slammed his fist into her torso, sending her sailing across the room. She landed on the hardwood floor with a thud. Her gasps for breath and pitiful cries did nothing to stop him from taking the few short steps to close the distance between them. He clasped his hand around her throat and with inhuman strength, lifted her from the ground, holding her face to face with him. He could smell the cheap wine on her breath. Her eyes were filled with tremendous terror as she stared into the ice blue orbs that were stripping her to her very soul.

He threw her across the room again, sending her crashing over the couch. She somehow found the strength to force herself to her feet and stood defiantly facing her attacker. The remorseful one slowly walked towards her. She stood her ground as he approached. She took a swing at him, her fist solidly connecting with his jaw. He smiled as she jerked her hand back, cradling it against her chest. He was actually impressed at how strong her will must be to defy him like she was. In the, too many to count, years that he had walked the Earth, only a handful of his victims had found the will to fight back. She then tried to kick him in the crotch. He shifted to his left, letting her foot swing harmlessly through the air before grabbing her ankle. Holding her leg at waist height, he brought his elbow down on her knee. Susan's face contorted in pain as her leg bent impossibly backward, shattering bone, tearing muscles and tendons in the process. With one fluid movement, he brought his hand back up, his fist connecting with the underside of her jaw. Her head snapped backwards and she lost consciousness. He grabbed her by the hair and dragged her through the house to the bedroom.

While the unconscious woman lay on the bed, he slowly undressed her, preparing the stage for what was to come. He sat on the edge of the bed waiting for her to regain her senses.

As her eyes began to flutter open, she tried to move in vain as her hands and feet had been secured to the bed frame. She was laying spread eagle on the bed, clad only in her bra and panties. Her attacker was sitting right beside her, looking away from her. The realization that she was going to die hit her like a ton of bricks and she began to cry. Her mind reeled as her life flashed through her thoughts. Several memories seemed to repeat, forcing her to cringe.

The remorseful one could sense that she was now conscious. Without looking at her he spoke, "Finally with me again, Susan?" His question was more of an observation she realized. He slowly shifted on the bed, his unnatural blue eyes locking with hers. "Have you figured out why I am here?"

Tears rolled down her face as she nodded, "I'm sorry, I'm sick and I couldn't help myself."

The remorseful one flew into a rage. His voice rattling the windows and threatened to shatter her eardrums. "You always have a choice in matters such as those. There is no excuse for what you have done. And tonight, you will pay for all of it!" His voice then grew dreadfully quiet. "But, you have another choice. You know what you must do to find mercy in all of this."

Her face turned red as the realization of what he wanted hit her. "Never." She whispered through clenched teeth.

The remorseful one drew his hand back and drove his fist into her ribs, breaking several of them and cracking her sternum. Susan yelped in pain as he grabbed her arm, digging his fingernails into the soft flesh of her bicep, slowly dragging his hand towards her elbow, shredding the flesh and muscle in the process. "This can end quickly, Susan."

Blood poured from her wound as he removed his fingers and placed his hand on her side. His fingers began digging into the flesh around her shattered ribs. She began to scream and he locked eyes with her. He dominated her will and her mouth closed without ever making a sound. She shook her head as she refused to meet his demands.

Again he slammed his fist into her sternum, the thick bone exploding under the tremendous impact.

Her resolve broke under the excruciating amounts of pain. "Oh, God, I'm sorry. Forgive me! Please, God, forgive me. Just make it stop! Dear God in Heaven make it stop!"

He had known she would break. They all did, it just took some of them longer than others. However, she had broken far more rapidly than he had expected. He gently placed his hand on her cheek and leaned forward to whisper in her ear. After what needed to be said had been said, he leaned over and sank his teeth into the carotid artery. He drank deeply, and as her precious life force filled him, her pain was lessened as she went into shock. As she neared death, he stopped and grasped her cheeks, giving a great twist. Her body went limp and her life was snuffed out. He carried her head into the kitchen and placed it on the table.

He looked down at the bloody mess his clothes had become. He sighed and left the house. The night was overcast now and no stars could be seen in the sky. Even the moon had been obscured by the clouds. He slipped through the shadows, calling them to envelope him like a cloak and left Susan's house slowly, thinking about the depravity of humankind.

As he awoke, he could tell that dusk had fallen although the room had no windows. He stood and stretched. He gave his surroundings a once over and quickly decided that this was his last night in this hovel. Tonight he would find something a bit more lavish.

His mind turned to his dinner. "The world is full of choices. Let's go down and check out the buffet, shall we?" He gave a quiet chuckle as he spoke to himself. He picked his jacket up off the floor and headed towards the door. He gave one last appreciative look at his humble lodging before stepping out into the deepening night.

Chapter 7

SAM HAD just finished her shift and was heading home as her cell phone rang. She didn't bother to look at the number before she answered. "This is Detective Brae," her voice in a monotone as she spoke her greeting.

The voice on the other end of the line spoke softly at first. "Detective, this is Sarah De Lucca. You called me earlier this morning. I'm sorry I'm just now returning your call. How can I help you?"

"Ms. De Lucca, the reason I called," her voice caught in her throat as she tried to tell the woman about the tragedy that had befallen her parents, "Ms. De Lucca, your mother has had a very serious car accident and your father was murdered. I'm so sorry."

There was no response for several seconds before the voice on the other end calmly replied, "Dad's dead? Did mom do it?"

"No, ma'am, we have no evidence to suggest that your mother had any part in it. I can't say very much about it as it's an ongoing investigation, but I don't believe that Rosa had anything to do with it."

"So what happened to mom? Is she gonna be okay?" While still eerily calm, Sarah did seem at least a little concerned for Rosa's wellbeing.

"I sent her to a motel while we finished our investigation at her house. On the way there she was broadsided by a stolen vehicle. Her car rolled several times and she was pretty badly injured. She's in a coma, Sarah. She's at St. John's hospital."

"I'll go see her today. How was Frank killed? I hope that bastard suffered." Her words grew louder and Sam could hear the anger and pain in her voice. "I hope that fucker suffered until the very end. Tell me he didn't die easy."

Even though Sarah's voice never cracked, Sam could tell that she was crying. "Like I said, I can't say a lot about the case right now, but I can tell you that his death was pretty brutal." After almost a minute of silence, Sam had to ask if she was still there.

"Yeah, I'm here." The emotions in those two words were too numerous to count. After another pause, "Detective, I'd really like to talk to you, face to face. Would you be willing to meet me for coffee this morning?"

Sam looked at the clock on the car radio and with a resigned sigh, "Sure, I just got off work, where would be good for you?"

The young woman gave Sam directions to a coffee shop in Fayetteville. Sam turned the vehicle around and headed south before ending the call. Sam was exhausted and wanted nothing more than ten days of sleep, but this woman may have information that would help break the case.

As she entered the college town, she remembered why she had decided to live in a small town. The traffic here was hell. Everyone was bumper to bumper, even at six o'clock in the morning. They were cutting each other off, vying for spaces, waving their middle fingers at each other and shouting profanities through closed windows. Sam frowned and tapped her brakes as a Toyota swerved in front of her, nearly clipping her bumper. She smiled and waved at him as she flipped her blues on then off. The driver apparently got the idea because he slowed down and began driving a bit more cautiously.

Sam pulled her Tahoe into a parking space at the coffee shop in which she was supposed to meet Sarah. As she entered the building, a young woman waved to her. Sam held up a finger to let her know it would be a moment. She approached the counter and ordered the largest cup of Kona blend they had.

She then moved to the booth that Sarah had chosen and slid into the seat.

She offered her hand to the woman, "Sarah I presume? It's nice to meet you."

Sarah took the offered hand and shook it gently, "Likewise. Thank you for coming to meet me, Detective."

Sam held up her hand, "Please, call me Sam."

"Okay, thanks for meeting with me, Sam. I wanted to explain my outburst. I know it couldn't have sounded good after what had happened to Frank."

Sam noticed that she grimaced as she spoke her dad's name. "Well, to be honest with you, Sarah, I had toyed with the notion that you might have done it. Apparently there's no love lost between you two."

"That's why I wanted to meet with you. I wanted to get this out there and get it off my chest. You're a complete stranger, but I feel I can trust you. Besides, it was gonna come out anyway during your investigation, might as well get it over with." Sarah took a deep breath before continuing. "When I was growing up, Frank loved me a little too much. Mom knew about it, but she never did anything to stop it. I told her over and over and she would just tell me to stop being silly, or she called me a liar. Once, she slapped me and told me to stop making these filthy things up. So, when I finally got away from them, I had planned on never going back. I got married to a great guy, then I got pregnant and that's when it all went downhill."

A tear fell from Sarah's eye as she continued her story. "My ex decided that it was okay to use me as a punching bag shortly after we found out we were gonna have a kid. I only put up with it for seven months, which was way too long, but one night when it got really bad, I got his gun and shot him. I had never even held a gun to that point. I wanted to shoot him in the dick, I really did, but I shot him in the foot. We split up and I filed for divorce. He managed to hide everything from the court, our savings account, his 401k, the bastard even sold my car to a friend of his for ten bucks just so I wouldn't get it. He left me with absolutely nothing but the clothes on my back. I had nowhere to go so I gave up and called Mom. She was ecstatic that I was coming home."

The tears had begun to flow steadily down her cheeks now. "Frank never said a word to me except for the day I got home. He told me that it was my fault and I probably deserved the ass beatings. Mom heard it and never said a word. Well, the day came that my daughter was born. I still didn't have any place to go after the hospital released me so I continued my stay with mom and Frank. I was there for another three years trying to pay off the attorney, the fines I got for shooting my ex even though it was self-defense and I even had to pay that asshat's medical bills. Anyway, I picked Hailey, my daughter, up from daycare one day and went home. Frank was waiting just inside the front door. He punched me and knocked me out cold. When I came to, I searched the house for him. I was going to kill him. I couldn't find him or Hailey anywhere."

Sam was in shock. Her only words came out in a choked whisper, "Oh, dear God no."

"He had her in the tool shed. When I opened the door, he had his pants around his ankles. I snapped. I grabbed a hammer and threw it at him. I don't know what else I threw at him, but I know I threw a lot of things. I hit him with something and knocked him on his ass. I wanted to kill him, but Hailey was crying out for me. I grabbed her and ran. That was the last time I saw him. I went to stay in the battered women's shelter for a couple of months before I had the money to get a place of my own. Haven't seen or spoken to those two since."

She paused, wringing her hands together and taking several deep breaths, "I've moved on with my life. Hailey is thirteen now and has forgotten that day in the shed. I've left that shit in the past where it belongs and haven't given it another thought, until last night."

She reached into her purse and pulled out her cell phone. She dialed her voice mail and handed the phone to Sam. "I saved the message. Just listen."

Sam placed the phone to hear ear. The system gave her the time and date of the message before allowing it to actually play. It was left late last night, minutes after Sam had received the call from Rosa. It was Rosa's voice that came over the phone. "Sarah dear, it's your mom. I'm calling to tell you that your father is dead. He was murdered tonight. I'm so sorry dear. I should have stopped him, I should have taken you away from him, but I was terrified that if I said anything he would hurt you even worse, maybe even kill you. I was a coward and a terrible mother. I love you so much, baby. I want you to know that not a day has gone by where I have regretted not doing anything. I should have given my life to stop him. I don't know if you can ever forgive me, Sarah, but I hope you can. I love you so much, so very, very much. If you can't, I'll understand. Just give that precious grandbaby of mine a kiss for me and tell her that her grandma Rosa will always love her."

Sam handed the phone back to Sarah as the message ended. She sat in silence as she chewed over her next words. "Sarah, I don't mean to pry, and if I'm out of place, just tell me to shut the hell up and I will, no hard feelings. You need to go see your mother. She could use all the support and love she could get right now. I'm not saying this as a detective that needs your mom's testimony, but as a woman who knows what it's like to lose their mom. Take your daughter to, she needs to know her grandma."

Sara sat for several minutes before placing her head in her hands and openly sobbing. Her shoulders were shaking from the force of the emotional outburst. Sam slid around the horseshoe shaped seat and placed her arm around her neck.

At first, Sarah flinched before turning and wrapping her own arms around Sam's torso and squeezing tightly. She cried for several minutes before sniffling and sitting herself upright again. She used a napkin to blot the tears away from her eyes as she asked Sam for the room her mother was in. Sam pulled out her notepad and hastily scribbled a note along with the room number. "Give this to the officer at the door and he should let you in. If you have any trouble, tell him to call me and I'll take care of it. But Sarah, I need your phone. I need to log it into evidence." Sam reached into her pocket and pulled out a stack of nicely folded cash. She counted out three hundred dollars and handed it across to Sarah. "Take this and get a new phone."

Sarah pushed the money away. "I'm okay, really Sam. I've got enough to get a new phone."

Sam gave her best stern "not going to be messed with" look and spoke as gruffly as she could, "Okay, this is how it's going to work. You are going to take this money and get a new phone or I am going to have every cop in the county pull you over and issue a ticket for being stubborn."

Sam couldn't help it, she felt a connection with this woman and wanted to help her. As Sarah giggled, Sam had to smile.

"Alright, alright. I didn't know I was dealing with a dirty cop."

"That's dirty *detective* to you."

Both women broke out into a heartfelt laughter. Soon after, they said their goodbyes and left the coffee shop. The sun had risen high enough to give Sam problems with her vision. She pulled on a pair of extremely dark sunglasses to help ease the stinging daylight from her eyes. She drove home without too many problems from traffic.

When she finally pulled into her driveway, she was beyond exhausted. She slowly exited her vehicle, making sure that she had all of her belongings and the cell phone she had bought from Sarah. She didn't want to take a chance of something happening to it before she made a copy of the message.

She called Will as she unlocked the front door and greeted Mason. After several rings, it went to voicemail. "Hey, got some new evidence but I'm too damn tired to bring it in. I'll log it in tonight."

She went to the refrigerator and grabbed a beer. After tossing the cap into the trash, she went upstairs and turned on her shower. Her mind drifted to the strange feeling she had the previous night, but she quickly discarded the thought as she undressed and stepped into the water, the almost scalding water doing wonders to unknot her tense muscles. She completed her hygienic duties as quickly as she could before letting the water rush though her hair and down her back.

She stepped out of the shower feeling a little better, her mind still going over the conversations she'd had over the last few hours. She wrung the water from her hair and wrapped it in a towel as she dried her body with another before wrapping it around herself. Mason was already lying on the bed with his eyes closed as she entered the bedroom to get her clothes. She picked out a pair of boxer shorts and a light weight t-shirt to wear.

After dressing, she went downstairs and turned on the television. She finished her beer and returned to the kitchen for another one. As she twisted the cap off the second bottle, she realized that she had not felt the strange presence since the previous night. She shrugged her shoulder, believing it to be nothing more than her mind temporarily losing grip with reality. She had lost her mother to dementia only a few years before and she feared that she would go the same way.

She thought about her mom for a few moments before returning her attention to the television. She surfed through the channels, not for anything specific, just trying to keep her mind off of less desirable events. She drained the second beer quickly enough and turned off the TV. She was too tired to focus on anything on the television and her mind kept trying to return to events that she would rather not think about. She slowly climbed the stairs to her room and crawled into bed. It didn't take long before she was sound asleep, her dreams filled with images of the beautiful blonde haired man and the carnage he was leaving behind.

* * * * *

Will's phone belted out the mellow sounds of Barry White's *'You're the First, the Last, My Everything.'* The ringtone he had programmed for Sam.

It had been a couple of years since they had dated, and he knew, without a doubt, that it was his fault that they were no longer together. His devotion ran deep and his love for her was boundless. His heart would remain forever loyal to her.

Too bad he was the only one that knew it.

During the time they had dated, he had felt things for her he had never thought possible. He had grown to love her and that scared the hell out of him. After his dad's luck with women, he was terrified to put himself out there emotionally and he knew it.

He turned to the bottle for the courage to tell her this, and ended up a blubbering drunk on every date they went on. While on shift, he was totally professional, strictly business. But after hours, when they got together, that was a totally different man. There were actually two dates that Sam had to carry him out of the restaurants. It wasn't like he deliberately tried to get wasted. He just wanted to get loose enough to tell her how he felt about her, but ended up screwing everything up in the end.

One night, he tried to explain to her why he acted like he did while totally sober and everything came out all wrong.

"Sam, I like you, a lot, but I like the bottle more. I mean, you like to drink, don't ya? So you know how good it feels to get that buzz. And I just feel like I can't talk to you unless I've got that drink in my hand."

As the words ran through his head for the billionth time, he placed his head in his hands and closed his eyes.

"You're so fucking stupid, Will." He lifted his head and grabbed the bottle of Dewar's scotch off the bar. Not bothering with the glass, he pulled the cork and took a large pull straight from the bottle. With a sigh of appreciation, he grabbed a highball glass and filled it with the stiff drink.

He picked up his cell and listened to the message Sam had left him. Part of him had hoped beyond all hope that she was calling to tell him how much she missed him and wanted him back. Nope, no such luck. She had turned up more evidence. Well whoopty-do for her. He shook his head and took a sip of scotch.

"You shouldn't be that way." He mumbled to himself. "She's just doing her damn job." He couldn't help but wonder if this might be the crucial piece that set him and Sam on the trail of the psycho nutbag that was terrorizing their town.

In the living room, he sat down in his brown leather recliner and kicked his feet up. The poor old chair had seen better days and to be honest, it looked like hell. The leather had cracked and faded due to negligence. The thing creaked and moaned as he sat down in it and he considered throwing it out and getting a new one, but dammit, this one was just too comfortable to get rid of. He might consider it when it completely fell apart.

He glanced around the room, thinking to himself that he should tidy up a bit. The room was coated in a thin layer of dust. Newspapers and junk mail cluttered the coffee table. Glasses, some empty and some half full, crowded the entertainment center, bookshelves and end tables. Some of his clothes were scattered around the room. But this was a bachelor pad, right? No need to clean it up yet. Not until Sam was back in his arms.

That train of thought lasted all of ten seconds before he turned his attention back to the glass of scotch in his hand. Shifting his weight to get comfortable elicited another groan of protest from the old chair. He retrieved the bottle of scotch as he guzzled down the remnants of the highball and poured another. As he tried to focus on the western he had selected while flipping through the channels, his mind kept wondering back to his beautiful partner and what he could do to win her back.

Chapter 8

SARAH SPOKE with the officer at the door to her mother's hospital room and showed the note that Detective... Sam had written along with her identification. He never said a word but nodded his head in the direction of the door.

Her hand trembled as she quietly opened the door. While trying not to squeeze her daughters hand too hard, she took the first few steps towards the broken old woman that lay in the bed. She slowly made her way into the room and saw her mother's horrible condition. Her face was swollen and bruised, tubes ran down her throat, an I.V. was stuck in her left arm, a pressure cuff encircled her right arm and a tube was wrapped behind her ears and under her nose to provide oxygen. If it wasn't for the rhythmic rise and fall of her chest and the insistent beeping and steady hum of the machinery, Sarah would have thought her dead.

She moved to the side of the bed and reached down to touch the winkled hand that lay on the white sheets. Her mom's hand was warm and her fingers twitched as their hands touched. Sarah looked at her face, hoping to see those hazel eyes looking up at her, but Rosa's eyes remained closed.

She ushered Hailey to the edge of the bed. She squeezed her hand tight as her daughter stood by her side. "Hailey, this is your grandma Rosa."

Hailey looked at the bruised and battered woman for several minutes before asking her mom, "She's in a coma, isn't she? When will she wake up?"

A tear rolled down Sarah's cheek as she answered, "Well, baby, yeah, she is in a coma. She was in a bad car accident and her brain is pretty much saying you better sleep for now and heal. We don't know when she'll wake up. We just have to pray and be here for her."

The young woman studied her grandmother for a few minutes longer and asked her mom "Isn't there anything the doctors can do to wake her up?"

Sarah could see the pain in her daughter's expression. "No, honey, there isn't. They don't know why she's in the coma in the first place. They said that there was no brain trauma, no sign of any kind of damage, so they don't understand and can't give her anything without knowing what they need to be treating. They could make her worse."

"Okay, mom, what can I do for her?"

"God, you're an amazing kid. You know that?" Sarah was genuine in her compliment. Here was a woman that Hailey most likely didn't remember ever meeting and yet she was going to do whatever she could for her.

Hailey went to the other side of the bed and pulled a chair up next to the rail. She opened her Kindle and selected a book by Sara Shepard and began to read aloud to her Grandma.

A smile crept over Sarah's face as she listened to her daughter. She sat down across the room from the two and wondered if maybe this reunion wasn't long overdue.

* * * * *

Sam got out of bed slowly. She had awakened to her alarm blaring an eighties hair band. She stood and stretched before she walked to her dresser and turned off the alarm. She went to the bathroom and ran through her morning routine. After she was dressed and somewhat ready to face the day, she went downstairs and poured a cup of coffee. She let Mason into the back yard and sat down at the dining room table to finish her coffee and watch the squirrels play in the trees.

She put her dishes away and locked the doors. As she walked towards her vehicle, a cold chill ran down her spine. Mason was watching her through the privacy fence that surrounded the back yard. He gave her one single bark as she walked by him. She knelt down by the fence and looked him eye to eye through a crack in the planks. "Mason, on guard." She unlocked her SUV and climbed into the sizable vehicle. After buckling her safety belt, she started the engine, slid the shifter in reverse and backed out before starting in the direction of the precinct.

As she entered the police department, she was trying to form a mental list of things to tell Will. It seemed as though she could not think of half of what she wanted to tell him about last night. She reached the evidence storage sooner than she would have liked.

As she unloaded the new evidence, she finally got things straightened out in her mind. She hurriedly walked down the corridor to her office where she found Will already waiting for her.

"So, you got some new evidence? What'dya find?" He gave her his best 'sexy smile' as she entered the room.

She almost rolled her eyes at him.

"You ready for this? I spoke with Mrs. De Lucca's daughter last night. Turns out that Frank was a pedophile and was molesting her. Rosa knew and didn't do anything about it. God knows why, I would have cut the bastards balls off. Anyway, Sarah ran away and got married, her husband beat her, so she split and moved back in with Frank and Rosa." Sam's voice cracked with rage as she continued the story, relaying every detail to Will. "So, I'm thinking, what if the other victims had skeletons in their closets? It's a long shot, but what if?"

"Fuck it, let's start digging. It's the best lead we've got at the moment." Will grabbed his cup of coffee before heading to his office to start his own research. Sam already had her head buried in the computer screen and was paying him no never mind. As he started to leave, Sam spoke. "Thanks Will." He glanced over his shoulder to see that she had not looked away from the screen. He mumbled, "Anything for you," as he left her office and was sure he was out of earshot.

Sam was searching through the county database, looking for any criminal records on the other victim's backgrounds. Several hours into her shift, things started to fall into place. While none of them had been convicted of anything, some of them had been charged. The first victim, Lawrence Robinson had been charged on two counts of rape and four counts of murder. Due to a technicality, he was not convicted and was released. She found that all but one of the victims had been charged but either never tried, or they had gotten off on a technicality. The only one that she couldn't find anything on was Cheryl Henderson.

It seems that they had finally found the connection between the victims. Maybe Cheryl was just a coincidence. One of those wrong place, wrong time type things. Her killer was some sort of vigilante, killing those who had committed horrible crimes and had walked away from the justice system without as much as a slap on the wrist.

The phone rang, interrupting her train of thought. She gave a frustrated sigh as she picked up the receiver. "Detective Brae speaking, how can I help you?"

The voice on the other end was one that she didn't know, but he identified himself as Officer Whitney. His voice had an extremely somber quality as he delivered his message. She now had a new twist in her investigation. A twelve-year old child and her mother had been murdered. The brief description of the crime scene seemed to match the MO of the rest of them. His voice cracked several times while delivering the disturbing news.

"Thanks officer. We're on our way." Sam's hand shook as she hung up the phone. She had thought she had started to understand the killer and she had even allowed herself to believe that she had found the reason he was killing.

Only to have the murderer spit in her face yet once again. This time, he had murdered a child. Her mind spiraled as she tried to think of any reason he might have taken the life of someone so young. She could feel the heat rising in her cheeks as she became violently angry. She closed her eyes and pounded her fists against her desk as the tears rolled down her cheeks.

She took a couple of minutes to compose herself before leaving her office. She dashed to Will's office. "Grab your shit, he's killed two more. This time, he killed a kid."

He sighed deeply and shook his head, "It was only a matter of time. Sam, we *have* to catch this son of a bitch before somebody else dies. And I'm not gonna try to take this fucker alive. He's a damn dead man." Although his face contorted with anger as he spoke, his voice remained strangely calm.

Chapter 9

THE VAMPIRE stood on the edge of a cliff, watching the cars on the streets of Black Ridge below. He could see the white hot glow of the people driving, he could see them sitting in their homes watching television or reading a book. He watched as one woman started her bath. He watched a man split several pieces of wood before carrying them back inside his house and stoking the fire.

And he watched the blue lights of the police cruisers speed through town. The red lights of the ambulances followed closely behind.

There was no joy to be found in him tonight for he knew exactly where they were headed. He turned his head slowly to one side and then the other, observing his surroundings and thought to himself, "*Well, this is a tad bit cliché isn't it?*" A remorseful smile flickered over his lips as he turned, slowly making his way down the hills, through the trees and toward the town. He could not stop thinking about Samantha Brae. He tried to push her from his mind, but even the events of tonight could not tear her from his mind.

His mood was funereal even though he had fed well. His steps were slow and deliberate. He was taking his time to observe nature and to revel in the beauty of the night. As he walked, he began to whistle a melancholy tune he had first heard centuries ago.

He listened to the wind rustle the leaves, several of them falling to the ground before him. Only a scant few leaves remained attached to the branches, but the cold air and long nights were quickly taking care of that.

He smiled softly as the cold night's breeze stung his face, and he inhaled sharply through his nose as the crisp smell of the cedar trees filled his senses. Coyotes howled and yipped in the distance stirring the dogs in a nearby neighborhood to start howling with them. Such beauty filled the night, even with such tragic happenings.

He looked to the sky and determined that sunrise was still a couple of hours away. His pace never changed as he began his search for a place to call home during the daylight hours. He made his way into Black Ridge, careful to remain wrapped in shadow.

It took a while to find a suitable house on the edge of town with only one occupant, an elderly woman who cheerfully greeted him. He was shocked to see her awake at this hour. With another glance to the sky, he estimated that it was 5 o'clock. She smiled sweetly as she turned, motioning for him to follow her inside. As he stepped inside, the acrid smell of wood smoke and the aroma of freshly baked biscuits filled his nostrils.

She returned to her seat in front of the television, the weatherman was giving his forecast for the next seven days. She craned her neck around to look at him, forcing him to realize that he was being rude. He removed his jacket and stepped slowly into the living room. His eyes drifted across numerous likenesses of Jesus Christ, along with several Cross' and Crucifix's. Her gaze never faltered as he moved gracefully around the room, her wise old eyes never straying from his and never showing one ounce of fear. He gave her a pleasant smile as he sat down on the couch across from her. Her voice shook as she spoke, not out of terror, but from the countless years that had taken their toll on her. "What brings you to this old woman's house this time of morning?"

His voice was still young, unaffected by time, deep and comforting. He replied, "I'm trying to find a place to rest my weary head, ma'am. The Arkansas cold has been extremely unforgiving tonight."

Her smile seemed to brighten even more as she responded, "You are more than welcome to stay here and rest your bones. You got a name?"

His icy blue eyes never faltered as he spoke to the old woman. "I never really had a use for a name. I hope that won't be a problem. How should I address you, though, ma'am?"

She chuckled softly, "Call me Velma. And it don't bother me in the least bout your name. I'll just call ya Mister. Alright, weather's over. Let me show you to your room." She stood and made her way through the house with amazing agility. She showed him to a room that was lined with shelves, and each shelf was filled with various fabrics. "Pardon the mess. I been sewing a quilt for my great-grandson, though I'm not sure I'll ever get it to him. My fingers just don't want to cooperate anymore."

He gave her a genuine smile. She was so full of life.

She quickly removed the bolts of fabric that were strewn about the bed and smoothed the blanket back down. "You ready to turn in?"

"Yes ma'am. I've had a very eventful night."

"Okay, well, if you need anything, I'll be out in the yard most of the day." She turned her head in the direction the emergency vehicles were going earlier. "Make yourself comfortable, I won't bother nothing, not till you're ready to get up anyways. Need another blanket?"

He turned down the bed and upon feeling the already impressive weight of the quilt already on the bed, smiled again. "No ma'am. This one will be more than sufficient. Might I trouble you for one more thing, though? If it's not too much of a bother, I'd like to take a shower."

Velma let out a boisterous laugh. "Stink do ya? Well, I'll have to charge ya for that. It'll cost ya a whole quarter."

He wasn't sure if she was serious or not so he reached into his pocket.

She laughed even harder and slapped his hand. "Get your fool hand outta your pocket. For being such a good looking boy, you're none too bright are ya?" She continued to laugh as she motioned for him to follow her. She showed him the bathroom and pulled some towels and wash cloths from a cabinet. She reached under the sink and retrieved a bar of soap, a straight razor and a shave cup. "These were my husbands, God rest his soul. Kept them here just in case. Feel free to use them, might wanna strop that razor though. Strop's over there." She pointed to the wall behind the door. "Gonna leave you to it. Sleep tight, Mister."

She left the small bathroom as he turned on the water and waited a few seconds for it to get hot. He began to wash, reveling in the feeling of being clean once again. After he had finished bathing, he stepped in front of the bathroom mirror and lathered up with the badger hair shave brush. The shave soap was a sandalwood and vanilla mixture, a traditional scent that brought back many memories. He stropped the straight razor and gave himself a smooth shave. Not that he needed to, his facial hair didn't grow like humans did. It took him almost a year to get five o'clock shadow. After washing his face off, he used the aftershave on the side of the sink. It was bay rum, another one of his favorites from days past. He cleaned up the mess he had made and returned to his room. He slid into the bed and pulled just the sheet over him. Within seconds, his mind was off and racing and he was once again chasing down victims from long ago.

* * * * *

Sam spoke not a word as she turned and left the office. She knew he would be right behind her as she left the building. She quickly made her way to her vehicle and climbed inside. A long and solemn sigh escaped her lips as she prepared herself to make her way to the latest crime scene. Her mind was unwilling to accept this new revelation in her case. As she started the engine, her hands began to shake again. She tried in vain to steady herself as she backed out of her parking space and turned the SUV towards the latest crime scene. She caught a glimpse of Will entering his vehicle in her rearview mirror as she left the parking lot.

Her drive to the crime scene was a solemn one. The radio seemed to mimic her mood as a melancholy song by Katra poured from the speakers. She pulled into the driveway of the house of the two latest victims. A man stood outside speaking with an officer in an exceptionally slurred voice. He kept wringing his hands together as he attempted to speak.

She gave another great sigh as she collected her kit. She walked past the grieving man, trying to keep her eyes on the ground in front of her.

As she approached the door, she asked the officer about the man and was informed that he was the husband and step-father of the decedents. She shook her head as she pulled on her gloves and cautiously stepped inside. The house was a disaster to put it mildly. Clothes were strewn about the floor, at least a quarter inch of dust adorned the ceiling fan and the couch was torn, tattered and stained with so many different things it would take a lifetime to discern the source of each one. As she took another step into the house, the pungent aroma of cat urine made her gag.

She moved past the mess in the living room and walked into the kitchen, her camera splashing the walls with the blue-white glow of the flash. There was not much difference in this area of the house. Dishes were piled in the sink and on the countertops. Beer bottles and cans had fallen out of the trashcan and lay across the floor with a variety of potato chip bags, pudding cups and other refuse. She forced herself to walk further into the house, resisting the urge to vomit the whole way.

She came to the child's bedroom first. As she stepped inside, something was definitely wrong here. She scanned the room with her camera, documenting everything that she saw.

There were no clothes on the floor, the floor was vacuumed and everting appeared to be dusted. Several potpourri jars adorned the dresser along with a small TV. Even with the jars of scent on the dresser, she could still make out the underlying smell of ammonia. She carefully approached the dresser and pulled out one of the drawers to find that all of the clothes were neatly folded and sorted. The only thing that really did not jive with the rest of the room was the busted door frame.

She wondered what this little girl must have had to endure as she began her search for evidence. As she combed through the room, the feeling that something was seriously amiss with this whole scene increased to a scream inside her mind.

She heard Will speaking the officer at the door and wondered how many nights this little girl had lain awake, listening to her parents fighting. She heard his footsteps approaching the bedroom.

As he came to the door of the bedroom, he spoke softly, "this is one hell of a mess, even before you make it this far in, huh?"

She nodded in agreement, but dared not speak for fear that her voice would crack and reveal just how emotional she actually was. He asked her if she wanted him to take over, apparently he had noticed that this bothered her more than she was letting on.

Sam shook her head so he turned and headed to the master bedroom without another word. As she went over the room, something, or the lack of, caught her attention. "Where are the hairs?"

She finished collecting what evidence she could find in the little girls room and reluctantly headed to the master bedroom. She had tried to mentally prepare herself for what lay ahead. She knew that the two dead bodies were in that room. She knew that one of them was a child. She kept repeating to herself, "You can do this, Sam. Suck it up and do your job."

When she stepped into the room, she sucked in her breath and immediately regretted it. The smell of ammonia and death hit her like a ton of bricks. But that wasn't the worst of it. The woman's body lie on the bed and Will was stooping next to her, collecting evidence. The child's body lay at the foot of the bed in a crumpled heap. It took all the self-control she could muster to calm down and keep herself from running from the room in tears.

"Will, did you find any hairs in here?" She asked in a voice just above a whisper.

Will answered in an equally hushed voice, "Not a one. Something feels different about this one. Know what I mean?"

"Yeah, I had the exact same feeling. Need any help in here? She looked around, grimacing at the condition of the room. What little carpet was visible was stained. The rest of the floor was covered with clothes, trash and various other things. The bed only had a comforter on it, partially hiding the yellow stains on the mattress. The smell of urine grew stronger as she approached the bed. Candles had been burned without any kind of catch for the melted wax. They appeared to have become a part of the dressers and nightstands. Beer bottles lined one of the nightstands, leaving room for only the single candle. An older CRT style TV sat on a stack of milk crates at the end of the bed, the screen looking as though it had been dragged along the cement sidewalk. The plastic casing was broken and battered as well. There were holes in the sheetrock as well, making a polka dot pattern on almost every wall in the room. Sam shook her head in disgust.

As for the woman's body, the head had been disarticulated and lie on its side in the middle of the bed. She was wearing a pair of sweat pants and a t-shirt. That also struck Sam as odd. None of the other victims had been wearing more than a pair of panties or underwear.

Her attention snapped to the head. Its position was all wrong. "Will, did you bump the head?"

He shook his head and replied, "Sure as hell didn't. You know me better than that. I entered, saw it in its current location and snapped a buttload of pictures. Then I came over here and I've been going through this crap since then." He made a grandiose gesture with his hands as he finished.

Sam turned and stormed from the room. She yanked her gloves off with quick, jerky movements as her anger boiled over. The second glove hung up on her fingers and she gave it a violent tug, tearing the latex and letting part of it snap back onto her hand, pissing her off that much more. She grabbed the first uniformed officer she saw. "Who the hell has been in the house? Somebody moved evidence and failed to notify me. I want a list of everyone who stepped inside that damned house and I want it twenty minutes ago!"

The officer gave her a look of shock and fear before he turned and ran to another officer. He hastily spoke to him, pointing back to Sam and shaking his head a couple of times before running to one of the squad cars and started making calls from his cell phone while referring to a note pad the other officer had apparently given him.

The second officer turned and gave her a baleful glare as she approached him. He smiled as she closed the distance and extended his hand. Sam accepted the gesture and squeezed just as tight as she could manage.

His tone betrayed the smile on his face, "Detective, you had questions about my men?"

"I did, officer. How many of your men went inside the house?"

He cocked his head and his eyes shifted to the right. She knew then that he was trying to remember. If his eyes had shifted left, he would have been trying to concoct a lie. He reached up and stroked the barely visible stubble on his face as he spoke. "Three, there were three of us that went in. We were extremely careful not to touch anything. We checked the bodies and after seeing the condition of them, we decided not to check for a pulse and risk contaminating any evidence you guys might be able to collect."

"So, none of you bumped any of the bodies and you moved not one damned thing?"

The officer looked as though she had slapped him, "Now, you listen here, *detective,* I've been a cop for fifteen years. I've been offered promotions and desk jobs and turned them all down cause I'd rather be out here doing the real work. I didn't touch a fuckin' thing and if you think one of my guys did, you're an idiot. If you think one of us tampered with the evidence or compromised a crime scene, then spit the accusation out and be done with it!" As he spoke, spittle flew from his mouth and he clenched his fists tightly enough to cause his knuckles to turn white.

Sam sighed and shook her head. "I'm sorry officer. I'm not accusing anyone." She lowered her voice, "It's just that the woman's head is lying on its side. It wasn't posed like the rest. It doesn't fit with the other murders. The first thing that came to my mind is that someone had bumped it. You're *sure* no one did, right?"

The officer shook his head, his posture visibly relaxing, I'm sure. Like I said, we cleared the scene and after seeing the bodies, we knew it was a moot point to check for a pulse. It was pretty damn obvious they were dead. Now, Charlie Sheen over there might have bumped it, but I don't think you're gonna get any clear answers from him tonight." He indicated the husband who sitting on the curb cussing at a nearby officer for not letting him go get another beer.

She thanked the officer and turned back to the house. Her mind was spinning over the possibilities. She turned and watched the only survivor of this latest attack. He was stumbling all over the sidewalk. One of the officers grabbed him and forced him back to the curb.

Having seen enough, she turned back to the house and walked back to the master bedroom. She stood in the doorway, staring at the head.

This made no sense. From her forensic analysis, the head was laying where it was dropped directly after it had been severed. The victims were wearing too many clothes, and someone was left alive again. This was the second time that the killer had deviated from his normal pattern but it just didn't sit right with Sam.

Her radio cut through her train of though. The officers outside were arresting the step-father for assaulting an officer. She pulled her radio from her hip and aske the officers to photograph his clothing and have him change before he was transported to jail. The officer that responded seemed a little more than perturbed at her request.

Sam gave no hesitation with her response, "I don't care if you have to strip that drunk son of a bitch right there in the street and take him in naked, those clothes don't touch the inside of a squad car. Got it?"

He agreed and the radio went silent.

Her mind was racing again, vivid images of the last few scenes running through her head, crisp and clear in her mind's eye. Something about this scene just didn't add up. There were too many discrepancies. And her gut told her that this was all wrong. She had never ignored a gut feeling and she wasn't about to start now.

* * * * *

The vampire woke up around five pm. He listened carefully and could not hear any sound inside the house. Velma must still be outside. After he finished dressing, he opened the front door, the fading sunlight stung his eyes and the bitter cold nipped at his exposed flesh. His breath came out as bright white plumes against the crisp air.

He could hear the thump of an axe not too far from the house. He turned in the direction of the sound and made his way to the chopping block where Velma was splitting wood. The woman was easily in her eighties and here she was, splitting each log with the strength and vigor of a woman half her age.

He smiled as he approached her. She gave another great swing of the axe and split another piece of wood expertly in half. "Well, my goodness, Mister. You clean up nicely!" She gave him a slight chuckle as his smile widened even further, revealing a little more of the secret hidden behind his lips. The old woman didn't seem to notice.

"Would you care if I did some of those for you? I mean, you did extend the hospitality of your home to me this morning. Here I am a complete stranger and you allowed me the use of your beautiful home. This would be the least I could do for you."

"Oh, hogwash Mister. I didn't do nothing that anyone with half a heart wouldn't have done. But, if you really want to, I suppose I ain't gonna stop ya. I do gotta admit, you're a bit of an angel, aren't ya?"

His breath caught in his throat for a split second. He quickly recovered and took the axe from her. It was heavier than he had expected. She gave him a sweet, albeit knowing, smile as he rested the axe on his shoulder.

"You ever swung an axe, Mister?"

He chuckled lightly, "More than you could ever imagine." He stacked two logs on the chopping block. He lifted the axe from his shoulder, placing his right hand near the head and dropped it to a resting position behind his right hip. He then spun his arms up over his head, his right arm lifting the weight of the axe high in the air before sliding down the handle to rest against his left hand. The muscles in his arms corded as he slammed the blade home, splitting both logs perfectly.

Velma laughed. "Well, Mister, It looks like you know what you're doin', so I'm gonna leave ya to it."

He nodded to her as he stacked two more pieces. He continued his pace as Velma began picking up and ricking the pieces that had already been split. He finished the two rick of wood in a matter of minutes. There were only three more logs left when he stopped and looked at Velma. "I should have asked if you needed any kindling."

"I could use some, yes. That would be nice."

He picked up one log, and using only one hand, he slammed the blade against the wood, shaving off quarter inch pieces at a time. He noticed that Velma was now watching intently.

He finished all three logs in just under five minutes. He thumped the blade of the axe into the chopping block, sticking it here. He started gathering up the kindling and set it aside in a wooden box. He then began helping Velma finish ricking the wood.

He dusted off his hands as they finished and a satisfied smile crept over his face. He looked to Velma and noticed that her face had taken on a somewhat mystified look. After all, she had just watched him split two rick of wood in less than a half an hour, a job that would have taken her at least two days.

Velma noticed him looking at her and gave him a reassuring smile. "Alright, Mister, now that that's done, let's go have us some dinner. Well, I guess I'll be feedin' you some breakfast! She laughed again and hurried back inside. She stoked the fire before ambling into the kitchen.

The vampire followed her back inside and basked in the warmth of the wood stove. She busied herself with breakfast which left him some time to think. He wanted to see Samantha again tonight, but with the latest murders, he didn't think she would be in the mood for his games, even if she didn't know he was playing them with her.

He didn't get to daydream about his red headed obsession for very long. Velma called to him from the kitchen letting him know that the food was ready. He stepped into the kitchen to find that she had fixed ham, eggs and toast as well as some spiced cider to help chase away the cold. She sat at the table already holding her cup. She had prepared his plate and had it waiting for him at the head of the table.

He smiled as he took a sip of the steaming cider. It tasted amazing. He had almost forgotten how nice some of these small pleasures in life could be. It had been quite some time since he had even allowed himself to enjoy the company of a human being.

They made small talk for a while before Velma caught him off guard. "You're no like the rest of us, are ya Mister?"

He stared into his cup as if the answer would magically appear in the brownish beverage. He finally resigned himself to the fact that she would know if he was lying and nodded. He already knew that he could trust her.

"And you've got something to do with the terrible happenings around town, don't ya?"

Again, he slowly nodded.

She stood slowly and made her way to his side. Lightly, she put a hand on his shoulder and gave him a little squeeze. "Sometimes, our life's tasks aren't what we'd like 'em to be. And sometimes, even though what you're doin' is right, it just don't feel that way."

The vampire was dumbfounded. He thought to himself, "*How could this woman know so much about me, just from looking at me?*"

As if reading his mind, "I've been around for a long, long time, Mister. I've seen things that most folk only dream about."

He gave her a smile as he stood and gathered his things. As he neared the threshold, the old woman gave him a hug. "You come back her in the morning if you need a place again. You might be a monster to some of them uneducated folk, but I know that heart of yours. You'll always be welcome under my roof."

He returned the hug before silently making his way out into the familiar night. His thirst was not so strong tonight, but a snack wouldn't hurt.

Again, his mind turned to Samantha.

He made his way back into the woods, traveling towards Sam's house, quickly and quietly slipping through the brush. He passed several houses during his trek through the forest, some of which still had a few lights on. Others were as black as the night around them. In only seconds, he had made his way to Sam's.

He stood in the shadows of the trees only a few hundred feet from her front door. Her house was black, save one light in the kitchen area. He assumed that must be for her dog, Mason. She was still at work. He quietly slipped into her house, making his way to Mason. The brute of a dog softly nuzzled his hand as he approached. The vampire knelt before the dog and gave him a vigorous scratch behind the ears. After a few moments, he looked into the animals eyes and the dog went to the couch and lay down.

He stood and surveyed the house a little closer. She had beautiful cutlery in the kitchen area and for the most part, everything was in its proper place, except for a dirty bowl, spoon and a glass in the sink. He moved throughout the house, not caring if he made any noise, his footsteps landing heavily against the hardwood flooring.

He wondered around, casually browsing at Sam's things. He perused through her belongings trying to get a sense of why he was so attracted to her and what was with the dark spot on her heart. He found a set of wedding rings, but no marriage license, no clippings from the newspaper, no pictures, nothing. That was rather odd, but he decided that the rings must have belonged to her parents. He finished looking through her things and returned downstairs to have a seat on the couch and wait. He knew that he had work to do, but it would have to wait. He could go no longer without seeing this amazing woman again.

Chapter 10

SAM FINISHED her work at the latest crime scene finding nothing aside from the mess these people lived in. Her mind frantically trying to push her conclusion from her mind, yet she was unable to do so. She had searched every inch of the house, turned over every pillow, cushion and pile of laundry in the house. She had picked through enough garbage to overflow a landfill. She had even crawled around on the disgusting carpet looking for any hairs that might not belong to the victims.

And she found nothing that matched her killer.

Frustrated, she loaded her kit and few articles of evidence into her SUV and hurried back to the coroner's office. When she reached the precinct, she hurried to her office and stowed all of her collected evidence behind her desk. She locked the door as she left and briskly made her way to the morgue. As she pushed through the cold steel doors, a shiver ran down her spine. She knew what she going to hear and a part of her wanted to run the other direction, but she forced herself onward into the room.

She wasn't familiar with the doctor on duty tonight. She thought his last name was Cole. He seemed to know her well enough. "Ah, Detective Brae, good to see you! I would continue with the pleasantries, but I'm sure you just want to know my findings. So, here we go. I have to tell you though, I'm not much liking what these wounds are telling me." His light British accent caught her a bit off guard and she found herself fumbling to speak.

He moved around the autopsy table so that he could begin his report. "Here, on the mother, I forget her name, "Look here, Detective." He picked up the head and tilted it so that she could see the wound. "If you look here, this tissue was cut after she was already deceased. It looks to have been done with a serrated blade of some sort..."

Sam's eyes shot open. She felt as if she had been struck by lightning. "Sorry Doctor, did you say *cut?*"

"That I did, Detective. You see here, the edges of the wound are smooth with small ridges. This tells me that the blade was sharp and serrated. Also, take a look at this." He sat the head down and pried the victims eyelids open. "She has petechial hemorrhaging, indicating that she was strangled, and that, my dear Watson, is the cause of death." He gave a wry smile, "I took a mold of the tool marks and left it lying on my desk. Moving on, there are defensive wounds on her hands, looks to have been quite the scuffle. Several remodeled injuries to her ribs, jaw and arms tell me that she had been abused regularly for the last two years at least. I have to say, Detective, this doesn't add up at all. The only thing in common with the other murders is the decapitations. And even they were done incredibly sloppily."

"Sam studied the wounds for a moment before asking the question she was dreading. "What did you find on the little girl? Did you find anything?"

Doctor Cole's face paled as he spoke, "I haven't done a full workup yet. I am having a bit of trouble forcing myself to start the autopsy. I can tell you this though. She has a lot of the same marks. Petechial hemorrhaging, her hyoid is broken and it looks as if the same blade was used to remove the head. There aren't any defensive wounds though. That in itself tells me that she didn't see the attack coming." His eyes were shimmering as he forced himself to point out what the wound patterns had told him. "I'm terribly sorry, Detective. I didn't mean to get all misty eyed, it's just, well I've got a little girl myself and I can't imagine what kind of monster would do this."

Sam's face had been tightening in to a scowl has he walked her though the evidence. "I don't want to imagine it, but I have a damn good idea *who* the monster is." She turned and her stride spoke of the determination that was now driving her. She strode through the corridor back to her office. She was so consumed with her anger that she forgot she had locked her office door and slammed into it as she tried to push through it. She balled her fists at her side and stood there, immobile as she tried desperately to regain control of her anger before she lashed out at the door. As calmly as she could manage, she fished her keys out of her pocket and unlocked the door. She called Will as she stepped into her office.

"Hey, head back to the last crime scene. We've got a murder weapon to find. I'll bet you a bottle of that expensive ass scotch you like that the dad did it." She hung up before he could respond and snatched up the evidence. She was almost virtually running as she made her way to the evidence storage. She impatiently waited as the evidence clerk checked everything in.

When all paperwork was signed and everything was kosher, she tore out of the building as fast as she could and returned to her Tahoe. She slammed the door behind her and cranked the engine over. She slammed it in gear and burned rubber out of the parking lot. The rear tires of the massive SUV spun the complete distance of the parking lot before finding purchase as they made contact with the asphalt highway. The speedometer quickly rocketed past 80 mph as Sam raced back to the crime scene.

She slid the vehicle into the parking spaces in front of the house and rushed back inside. She began searching in places that would seem to be out of the way or hard to reach. She racked her brain for any ideas as to where the knife used to severe the heads of the latest two victims might be.

As she walked through the house, she saw something that she had not noticed the last time through. On the back of the refrigerator, near the wall, was a miniscule smear of blood. She did her best imitation of a strobe light using the camera's flash. She used her flashlight to peer behind it and saw something crammed into the coils. Several more pictures documented her find before she pulled the fridge away from the wall.

There was a white towel, stained with blood, stuffed between the coils and the back of the refrigerator. She removed the towel and carefully unrolled it. Hidden in the folds of the blood stained cloth was a bread knife. The blade was approximately 10 inches long, extremely sharp and serrated the entire length. She documented the grisly find with another several photographs. As the flash lit up the room, she noticed several fingerprints in the blood on the handle. She lifted the prints and secured them in an envelope before bagging the knife.

As she finished processing the kitchen, Will stepped into the house. He gave her a puzzled look. "What the hell is going on? Did you find something?"

She held up the bag containing the knife, "There are prints all over it. Now, we just have to see who they belong to. But, I'd be willing to bet dollars to donuts I already know who's they are. Come on, let's get this shit back to the lab and see if we get a hit."

"Sam, I don't understand. Didn't the same psycho do this? Or do you know something I don't?"

She explained the coroners finding to Will, effectively bringing him up to speed.

"Oh, shit. You think that piece of shit did this?"

"I sure as hell do, Will." Sam's face portrayed a myriad of emotions. She might not have the evidence to track down her serial killer, but she could get at least one piece of shit off the street.

Will shook his head, "What could cause a man to kill his family? I get the wife thing, especially after the ordeal with my ex, but your own kid? Jesus...."

They both took to their vehicles and headed straight to the precinct. Once there, they wasted no time getting to the lab. They had the on duty technician run the prints for them, and in a matter of minutes the printer spit out the results. The name on the sheet was Preston Billings. The picture showed a less disheveled version of the drunk they had arrested earlier in the evening.

"I knew it, Will. I didn't want to believe it, but in my gut, I freaking knew it." Sam's face was crestfallen as she considered the evils that her fellow man was capable of committing.

She called the chief of police and filled him in on the situation. He listened intently and gave a momentary pause before informing Sam that he would call the prosecuting attorney just as soon as they hung up. They would have charges filed against Mr. Billings before the sun came up.

Sam made her way to the holding area of the jail and approached the drunk tank. The door was heavy steel with a two inch thick Plexiglas window. Holes had been drilled in a circular pattern to allow officers to speak to the prisoners without having to open the door. She had to yell to get Preston's attention, and when she finally did, he stumbled to the door. She informed him that he was also being held for two counts of murder and read him his Miranda rights. He probably already had his rights read to him, but she was taking no chances. The video cameras in the cell would show that even inebriated, he knew his rights. She asked him three times if he understood before she got him to shake his head and give her the finger. He spat on the window of the door before returning to his bunk and passing out.

Sam silently thanked God that there was a door between them. She would have loved nothing more than to bash his skull against the wall until his brains coated the cinderblocks.

She left the drunk to his solitude and walked down the corridor to the observation desk. It was a raised station, circular in shape with monitors lining the entirety of the desk. Every angle of every cell was being recorded, 24 hours a day, 7 days a week and 365 days a year. If a camera went down, the inmates were moved to another area until repairs could be made. The only privacy the inmates got was the semblance of it in the bathrooms.

She informed the two jailers that Preston Billings was also being held for two counts of murder and that once he sobered up, he should be moved to solitary confinement.

She left the county jail after bidding Will a good night and headed back to her office. She tidied up a little bit before calling it a night. She had made no progress on the serial killer's case, but she did manage to solve a double homicide. That particular case was far from over, and she would probably be back to the house in which the murders were committed looking for evidence, but she knew that she had already gotten enough evidence to put this scumbag away for life, if not earn him the chair.

She drove home with the radio off. The sun was starting to rise causing the world to take on shades of blue and black as the darkness reluctantly lifted. Her mind was completely blank as she negotiated the corners at breakneck speeds. Soon she pulled her SUV into her customary parking spot and she could see Mason peeking at her through the curtains of the living room window. Finally, she found something to smile about. No matter how shitty her day was, she always had a faithful companion to return home to. She had someone, albeit a furry someone, who depended on her and loved her unconditionally.

As she hurried to the house, she could hear her four legged friend whining through the door. She unlocked it and stepped inside, gently nudging the large dog away from the entrance. Mason bounced with happiness as she scratched him behind the ears. He nuzzled his nose against her palm before loping through the house to the couch. He plopped down and turned to look at her.

She grinned at him, the horrors of the day temporarily forgotten. "Just a second, you impatient butthole!" He chuffed in response and laid his head on his paws, eyeing her as she went to the kitchen. She grabbed a beer from the fridge and downed it before she even stepped away from the fridge. She grabbed another and returned to the couch. Mason made a small growl chuff sound which she interpreted as *"finally."* She turned on the TV and flipped through the channels. She absently kept changing them while she drank her beer.

After she had drained the contents of the bottle, she decided that she had to take her morning run. She went upstairs and changed into her athletic apparel before descending the stairs and setting her Rottweiler to task of guarding the house.

As she stepped from the house, the feeling of being watched returned. While it left her a bit on edge, she found something comforting in the feeling as well.

Her feet slapped against the moist earth and crunched dry leaves with every step. The noise unnerved her as it could mask the sound of someone's approach. She refused to show fear, and she absolutely repudiated the idea of being intimidated by a mere feeling.

Her pace did not slow.

The stinging smell of frost assaulted her nostrils along with the pungent aroma of rotting wood and the musky scent of the forest. A thick fog had rolled in, obscuring visibility severely. She was only able to see a few feet ahead of her, heightening her sense of unease.

The sun had begun to peak through the trees, trying to burn away the thick brume that hung in the air. Her senses were in overdrive. Every rock, every tree and brush had become a possible ambush point. The feeling of being watched continued to grow stronger with every step she took.

The fine hairs on the back of her neck stood on end as she rounded a corner in the trail she had been following and her pace did slow. Maybe fifty yards away was the crest of a small hill. Standing at the top of the hill was a figure silhouetted against the rising sun. The fog still obscured any details about him, but she was sure this was the man from the hospital parking lot.

She had slowed her run to a walk as she cautiously withdrew her handgun from the pocket in the front of her hoodie. She held the pistol at her side, finger on the trigger. As she brought the weapon to bear on the figure in the mist, she blinked.

He was gone.

She climbed the small hill at a moderately brisk pace, keeping her weapon trained ahead of her. Her head and firearm tracked as one as she searched the area for any signs that someone had been there. She searched for a few minutes before telling herself that it had been a trick of the light, even though she knew deep down that it was not.

She finished her run. The whole time the hair on the back of her neck and arms stood on end. She could feel the eyes moving over her body as she returned to her house.

She fumbled with her keys and unlocked the door with tremulous hands. As she entered the house, she frantically shut the door behind her. She slammed the deadbolt home and engaged the security chain. The sensation of someone watching her did not diminish as she moved throughout her house. She kept looking over her shoulders, using her peripheral vision to scan the room behind her. The shadows seemed to move as they slipped to the edge of her vision. She would stop and turn to face the imagined movement before chastising herself for being stupid.

A grown woman, who possessed some serious firepower no less, was jumping at the shadows.

Mason lay on the floor watching her twitchy movements with mild curiosity. She checked the entire house, leaving every light on behind her. She even checked the attic and left the light on as she descended the retractable ladder.

She knew she was being ridiculous but couldn't stop herself from continuing her paranoid actions. Finally, she forced herself to accept the fact that it was only her and Mason in the house. She kept telling herself that she was being stupid and she had nothing to freak out about.

She went to her bedroom and gathered up the clothes, a pair of men's sleep-shorts and a sports bra that she would wear to bed and a couple of towels. She laid her clothes on the counter in the bathroom. She hung the towels on the hook on the back of the door and began to undress. She turned on the Pandora app on her phone and connected it to a small, bulbous Bluetooth speaker she kept in the bathroom for when she just wanted to relax.

As she shut the door, she heard Mason chuff as he lay down in front of the door.

Sam plugged the tub and turned the water on, waiting for a moment for the hot water to start flowing from the spout before adjusting the temperature to her liking. As the water began to fill the tub, she went to the sink and began methodically removing her makeup. A few minutes into her ordeal, she took a bag of Epsom salts from under the sink and poured some into the quickly rising bath water.

As she finished removing her makeup, the tub had filled to the perfect level and she quickly moved to turn the water off. She tested the temperature with her toes before stepping in. It was hot enough to turn her skin red, just the way she liked it.

The faint smell of lilac filled her nostrils as she slowly immersed herself in the piping hot water. She lay back in the tub, reveling in the feel of the water caressing her body.

She cleared her mind, forcing herself to relax. The music, although playing at a very low level, was exactly what she needed. For a blessed few minutes, she forgot about the murders, the shadowy figure in the wood and the ever present eyes that slithered over her body.

In this moment, she was the only person in the world.

After she finished bathing, she stood, pulled the plug and drained the water. Her hands found the faucet and quickly turned the knobs. Hot water poured from the faucet before she pulled the diverter plug to engage the shower. Sam washed and conditioned her hair before shutting the water off and stepping from the tub. She grabbed her towel and quickly dried herself off and wrapped the towel around her torso.

The steam had clouded the mirror and the smell of lilac hung strong in the air. She stood before the mirror staring into the blurred reflection as she began to brush her hair.

Something about the reflection was off. She studied herself intently before locking eyes with the ghostly image. It was not her fierce green eyes looking back at her, but the icy blues that haunted her dreams. The eyes of a man she had shot outside of the hospital. The eyes of a killer.

She slashed her hand across the layer of condensation on the mirror and looked again. The same blue eyes stared back at her from the reflection of her face. However unnerving this was, she couldn't tear her gaze away. Deep within her mind, she could hear a voice. It was seductive, alluring and pleading. The voice was strained and the words were garbled. Even though she couldn't understand what was being said, she knew that the next time she came face-to-face with the blonde haired man, she wouldn't be so quick to shoot him.

Finally, with an exorbitant amount of willpower, she tore her gaze from the mirror. She gathered her clothing and left the bathroom. She stepped over the sleeping form of Mason and went to her bedroom to begin dressing.

As she let the towel fall to the floor, she could feel the eyes roaming over her naked body. She forced herself to ignore them pulled on the sleep-shorts.

Mason got up, shook, and took a running leap onto the bed. She watched him with a smile as she slid the sports bra on. She felt a familiar breath on her neck. Her body tensed as she fought a mental tug of war with herself.

Her desire won out and she reluctantly gave in. Her mind was still spinning with the implications as she laid her head back, almost certain that she was resting against a shoulder.

With her head was resting against an invisible body, she started to analyze the situation and quickly thought better of it. She told herself to just enjoy the moment.

Standing there, grasping the edge of the dresser in an effort to remain grounded, she started to open her eyes, but the feeling of lips pressed against the bare flesh of her neck felt sinfully good. She could feel hands sliding down her bare arms, gently caressing and kneading the taunt flesh of her forearms, leaving a tingling trail of pleasure in their wake. A passionate sigh slipped from her lips as a faint whisper brushed past her ear, the words somehow seducing her farther into this intoxicating bliss.

"What is it about you that is so enslaving? Why am I drawn to you like the proverbial moth to

the flame?" the words whispered in a thousand different voices.

She exhaled as she gave herself to the entity in the room. She knew that if she opened her eyes, the feeling would flee from her just as it had before and she didn't want this to ever end. The hands now ran over her breasts, lightly brushing over the tightened points of her nipples. Shivers ran down her spine as she attempted to answer the questions with some of her own. "I don't know why. Who are you and what do you want from me?"

The whisper of a thousand voices answered her. This time it sounded closer. *"I only want to know you, my beautiful Samantha. And I want you to know me."*

Powerful arms wrapped around her, the hands caressing her body again. He was pulling her against him as he pressed his body against her. She could feel his thickening manhood pressing oh-so-gently against the top of her buttocks.

She fought the urge to gyrate her hips against his erection.

The kisses continued to leave a blazing trail around her neck. One feather-light kiss after another drew her skin tight and her arousal began to perfume the air. She needed him now and to hell with the consequences. Her knees were beginning to go weak with her painful desire.

After too brief a time, the sensual torment ended. There was a light kiss on her cheek and she knew she was alone again.

She gave a sharp shout of exasperation before she opened her eyes. She slowly surveyed the room. Once again, she found herself alone and doubting her sanity. Reluctantly she turned and climbed onto her bed, pulling the covers up to her neck. She had thought about watching the TV for a little while before turning in, but tonight she couldn't wait to see what dreams would visit her.

She closed her eyes and thought she felt a hand brush a stray hair away from her cheek as she drifted off into the black void of sleep.

He came to her again, this time though, he was defined. She could see him clearly. His hair flowed past his buttocks, almost reaching the bend of his legs. His piercing blue eyes locked on her, stripping everything away from her. Her pride, dignity and her deepest and darkest secrets were left exposed. As she looked into those icy blue orbs, memories that she hoped to never have to face again came clawing to the surface. Memories of the abuse she had suffered at the hands of her ex-husband. Memories of the broken bones, of the multitude of bruises and cuts she had tried to explain away to friends and family. Memories of the excuses he had given her for his actions. And the memory of the child she had lost due to his beatings. As her knees grew weak, the blonde haired man was there, his arms wrapping around her waist. He held her tight as she regained her strength. She looked up into his eyes and for the first time, the pale blue eyes emanated warmth she had not noticed before.

A thousand voices in unison whispered in her mind, "Is it because it was never there, or because you refused to acknowledge it?"

The question shocked her. She was an incredibly perceptive person. She noticed things that most people would normally remain unseen. But she knew the answer to his question even before he had asked it.

She had simply refused to look.

His hand touched her face, his cool skin jerking her from her thoughts. She locked eyes with him again, this time peering deeper. She could see the violence and clandestine rage behind them, she could also feel the immense strength in the arms that held her and she knew that he could kill her in the blink of those baby blues. Yet, she was not afraid anymore. She touched his face, her fingertips gliding over his flawless skin.

He leaned forward and she knew he was going to kiss her. His hand cupped her chin, tenderly lifting and pulling her toward him. Instinctively she started to pull away but then reminded herself that this was only a dream and gave in to her baser desires.

This man, this… thing was a predator. Even though she was dreaming, she knew that this was the man responsible for every murder in Black Ridge. And here she was dreaming about him.

He was a brutal murderer and a vicious killer.

But, his face was so gentle, so otherworldly and full of compassion.

His lips pressed against hers. Shivers of anticipation and pleasure racked her body as she shared the most passionate kiss in the history of ever with her dream lover. She screamed in her mind, "This is a dream, dammit! Stop thinking and just go with it!"

He spoke to her, his voice just above a whisper, "Samantha, what has marked your soul?" His lips touched her cheek, her jawline, her neck. His breath felt hot against the sensitive area. "Something has drawn me to you, and I am still not convinced that you are not to be one of my victims. I have to know what happened to you."

She felt his teeth press against her neck, pressing harder with each beat of her heart. As the pleasure became a starburst behind her eyes, she felt as if he would puncture her jugular vein, he stopped and kissed her again.

His hands slithered down her back, grasping her buttocks and lifting her into the air. She wrapped her legs around his waist, grinding herself against him as her hands explored his chest.

One of his hands, she was unsure of which as it happened to fast for her to comprehend there had even been a movement, tore her shirt away from her body. Her heart raced in her chest as she kissed him again.

When she opened her eyes, she was lying on her bed, alone. She gave a loud moan of frustration as she stood and looked at herself in the mirror. Her eyes fell on two small beads of blood. The skin had barely been punctured leaving a small bead of crimson adorning each wound.

Chapter 11

THE VAMPIRE was exhausted. He had not fed tonight and he hadn't slept very well. He could feel his power waning. He would have to feed again and he definitely needed his sleep, but he could not bear to pry himself away from the lovely red headed woman that lay before him.

He watched Sam slip into the dark waters of sleep. He gently brushed a stray hair from her face as she drifted off. He lightly touched her thigh through the blankets. So many thoughts ran through his head. He could have her, he could make her his, but somewhere deep inside, he wanted her to know him. To understand what he was and even love him. He prayed for her to want him. Even though he knew that he was destined to live a life of solitude, the tiny flicker of hope had already burrowed inside his heart and continued to grow with each second he spent with this uncanny woman.

He watched her sleep for a short while before the need for sleep overpowered him. He stood and leaned forward ever so lovingly and placed a tender kiss on Samantha's cheek. As his lips touched her skin, his thirst threatened to destroy his willpower. The feel of her blood pounding against her skin, beating against his lips pushed him to the brink of his limitations. He tenderly brushed the hair away from her neck and pressed his lips to the soft flesh of her throat. His lips peeled away from the dagger-like teeth and he pressed them against the pulsing vein. He pressed harder, his teeth starting to puncture the smooth skin.

The reality of what he was about to do hit him like a brick to the face and he jerked away from her. Where his teeth had pressed against her skin two tiny crimson gems bedecked her alabaster skin.

He could taste her life's essence and knew beyond all shadow of a doubt that she was not intended to be his victim.

Then what was she to be to him. That tiny seed of hope seemed to blossom then, taking root in his heart. Maybe she was to be the one he would spend eternity with. A smile twisted the corners of his mouth as he briskly left her room.

He left Sam's house and made his way through the forest, quickly finding the abandoned shack he had been using as a home. It was too late in the day to try and make it back to Velma's house. He was simply too weak to make the trek across town. As he bed down for the day, his last thoughts were of Sam as he drifted into another dream of yet another life he had snuffed out.

He sat in a small and grubby biker bar watching his intended prey. He watched the man joke with his friends, tormenting the waitress and becoming increasingly violent. He had earned the moniker "Slaughter" from his cohorts for slaughtering hundreds. He apparently believed that everyone deserved a bullet, no matter their age, creed or color.

Earlier today he had stabbed a woman and her infant to death in their car for nothing more than parking too close to his motorcycle.

The enraged one had already decided to play with his food tonight. He would humiliate this monster in front of his friends before he died. Slaughter's thoughts crept into his mind, disgusting and disturbing things that made him shiver with anticipation of the kill.

He finished his beer and made his way to the jukebox. Inserting a dollar gave him a two song selection. He selected "Come on" by Mushroomhead. He smiled as he thought about how appropriate this song would be for the coming fight. He turned and with a wicked smile and the promise of violence playing across his face, made his way across the crowded bar to the psychotic biker.

The enraged one deliberately slammed his shoulder into Slaughter as he passed him. The biker immediately grabbed him by the jacket and spun him around. The biker had unsheathed a hunting knife and thrust it at his latest 'victim' as he growled insults for the crime of bumping into him.

Effortlessly, the vampire batted the blade away from him, the knife slicing harmlessly through the air. Fueled by whiskey, beer and a demented need for violence, Slaughter's temper exploded. He hacked feverously at his intended target, every swipe of the blade flying innocuously though the air.

The vampire released a quick jab, catching the berserk man square in the chin.

The biker stumbled backwards, but was quick to catch his balance. He lunged forward in an attempt to tackle his new enemy. The vampire sidestepped the clumsy attack, grabbing the man's leather jacket and using the momentum of the attempted tackle to slam the man into the wall.

Instead of pressing the attack again, he had apparently had enough humiliation. He threw the knife at the blonde man and pulled a pistol that had been poorly concealed beneath his bulky leather jacket.

In less time than it took to blink, the vampire crossed the room and clamped his hand on the slide of the semi-automatic pistol. Before he had time to disarm the violent biker, he had squeezed off a round from the .40 caliber handgun.

The vampire had underestimated the man's ruthlessness.

At this point blank distance, Slaughter didn't need to aim. The discharged round struck him in the chest, throwing him off balance. As he lurched backwards, he ripped the smoking pistol from the biker's grip.

Angry and now injured the enraged one reached forward and rapped the butt of the pistol against the biker's forehead, knocking him unconscious. With blood pouring from the gaping wound in his chest, the vampire quickly forced his way out of the bar.

He slipped into the shadows and watched as Slaughter's friends quickly dragged him out of the bar. As they laughed and made jokes about the fight that had just taken place, two of them loaded the unconscious biker into the bed of a nearby truck. They continued to crack their jokes as one of them climbed into the cab of the truck. The rest of the bikers climbed on their respective motorcycles and sped out of the parking lot.

The vampire knew that he must feed soon. He struggled to follow the speeding pickup, his powers draining from him as rapidly as his own blood.

The truck stopped and the driver kicked his door open and quickly slid from the seat before sprinting to the door of what must be the MC's clubhouse. For a brief moment, he was alone with his prey. The rest of the club had not arrived and judging from the roar of the exhaust, he estimated them to be ten minutes away. They had to have stopped somewhere.

In the blink of an eye, he was standing in the back of the pickup next to the still snoring biker. He thought about waking him but the pain in his chest was beginning to become unbearable. He lifted the man's head and sunk his teeth into the carotid artery. It was a matter of seconds before the psychotic man's life was at an end. Even with the intense pressure forcing the blood from the wound, the vampire spilled not a drop of the precious liquid.

After the man's body began to cool in his grasp, he gripped the sides of the biker's head and tore it from his neck. He carried the bloody head to the hood of the truck and positioned it so that it was staring at the entrance to the parking lot. As the rest of this man's MC entered the property, this would be one of the first images to greet them.

As he awoke, his hand absently rubbed his chest. He looked to one of the dirt encrusted windows and noticed that the sun had already set. He dusted himself off and started a leisurely stroll to the jail.

He had pressing business with one of the inmates.

Chapter 12

SARAH HAD been at Rosa's bedside for several days. She had done everything she could think of to help her mother though this even though the doctors had told her that there was nothing to do but wait.

She was trying to do the right thing by her mom, but she could only spend so much time at the hospital. She had already missed too many days of work and Hailey had missed way too much school. So, Sarah had made arrangements for Hailey to stay with her best friend until this situation sorted itself out. Sarah had decided that she would go to work and when she got off work, she would return to the hospital. Hailey would stay with her friend and go to school. Sarah would pick her up and bring her here on Fridays after school.

As if reading her thoughts and sensing her internal conflict, Rosa's eyes fluttered. Sarah nearly leapt across the short distance to the bed and pressed the call button, summoning a nurse. Apparently they had noticed the variance in the readings of the many machines monitoring Rosa. Several nurses came bustling into the small room and began tending Rosa even before the old woman had her eyes fully open. Sarah had moved as close to the bed as the crowded room would allow and watched intently for her mother to show any further signs that she was coming out of the coma.

As Rosa's eyes opened, Sarah could see the fear and confusion in them. She spoke over the nurses to try and calm her mother. "Mom, you're in the hospital. You had a pretty serious accident. Hailey and I have been watching over you along with these nurses. You're okay, just let them work."

Rosa turned her head toward the voice and the tears began to roll down her cheeks as a smile of pure joy lifted the corners of her mouth.

Half an hour after Rosa woke, the doctor entered the room and began going over her charts and monitors. The nurses had just finished with their work and all but one left the room. He checked Rosa's vital signs, her reflexes and checked for feeling in her feet and hands. He gave her a few simple psychological tests as well. He turned to Sarah and nodded. "She's going to be fine. I want to keep her here for a while, mainly because of the broken bones, but we also want to keep a watch for any internal damage or signs of mental trauma, just to stay on the safe side. All of her stats look good though, which is promising. I'll be back periodically to check on her." He gently touched Rosa's foot as he left the room with his nurse in tow.

This was the first time Rosa and Sarah had been alone together since the elderly lady had regained consciousness. Rosa finally tried to speak to her daughter, but her voice came out as a guttural whisper. "Sarah baby, I'm so glad you're here. I've got..."

Sarah cut her off by placing a finger against her lips. "Mom, we'll have plenty of time for this later. Save your strength. You're gonna need it in a bit. Hailey is on her way here now. She can't wait to see you."

The tears poured forth from the old woman's eyes as she mustered the little bit of strength to squeeze her daughters hand. Sarah told her mom about her life and tried her best to fill her in on the comings and goings of her life since she had left home ten years ago. She kept her mother enthralled with her stories until her daughter arrived.

As Hailey entered the room, she ran to her grandmother and hugged her with such a fierce gentleness that the battered woman in the bed gave a small gasp before trying her best to return the embrace. A virtual river of tears ran from her eyes as she held the grandchild she thought lost to her.

Rosa cried out of sheer joy. She had her daughter back in her life and she was hugging the granddaughter she had missed for so very long.

* * * * *

Sam made it to work a little early. She wanted to speak to Preston Billings again, now that he had time to sober up. She knew that he had already been informed of the new charges being brought against him, but she wanted to know why.

She arrived at the jail a full hour before the start of her shift. She reasoned with herself as she made her way down to the holding area, trying to convince herself that killing this dirtbag with her bare hands was a very bad idea.

After a brief discussion with the jailers on duty, she locked her sidearm in a small lockbox that was attached to the cinderblock in a small secure room leading into the detention area of the jail. Afterwards, she was shown to Preston's cell. He had been placed in solitary confinement to keep him safe. Once word of what he had done got out, every inmate in the jail would be itching to kill him.

Or worse.

The heavy steel door swung open smoothly and Sam stepped inside of the small concrete cell. Preston lay on a thin mattress on the floor.

Without looking up, he spat out a single word, "What?"

Sam stood silent for a moment. She was fighting the overwhelming urge to start stomping on his skull. "I have to know Mr. Billings. Why? Why did you kill them? What the hell did they do that was so bad they deserved to die?"

Preston chuckled almost manically as his bloodshot eyes crawled over Sam's body, drinking in every curve. "You ain't got a clue, do ya bitch? That fuckin' wife of mine, always on my ass cause I don't make enough money. That whore could spend my whole damn paycheck in less than an hour and not pay a single fuckin bill! And nag, Jesus Christ could that bitch nag. It was never ending! You didn't do this, didn't do that, this isn't right, that's fuckin crooked. Blah, blah, fuckin' blah. You can only step on a man's balls so many times afore he snaps. She had it fuckin coming!"

Sam was biting her lip now. "What about your daughter? What the fuck did a thirteen year old girl do to deserve to die like that?"

Preston was visibly agitated by her words. "*Step*-daughter you mean. That little skank acted like she was too fuckin' good for us, always walking 'round with her nose in the air like her shit don't stink. Oh, and the money that little bitch wanted! All the damned time! I need this, I need that. I was doing everything I could to support that stupid whore I married and her stupid fuckin' daughter wanted everything else I had. I just couldn't do it anymore! I figured that if I made it look like that other psycho's work, ya'll would leave me the fuck alone. Figured you'd pin it on him."

Sam was shaking with rage, but before she did anything stupid she left the cell and slammed the door as hard as she could behind her. It was a futile gesture, but just exerting the force to slam the unwieldy door made her feel a little better.

She wanted to bash his face against the wall until he was reduced to nothing more than a pile of mush. She wanted to kick him, beat him, cut him... She wanted to *hurt* him. It was people like him that reminded her why she took this job. She wanted to make the world a better place by helping to take the worst of the worst off the streets. In the past, crime had not been a huge problem in Black Ridge, but in the last couple of years, it had been getting worse. And now they had a rash of murders with virtually no leads to follow.

Sam tried to harness her anger, she needed to focus it. She had another murderer to catch.

Chapter 13

AS THE vampire approached the entrance to the Black Ridge precinct, the moon had begun to peek through the clouds. He knew his prey would be heavily guarded, but that didn't worry him at all.

He paused and listened to the coyotes in the distance for a moment before approached the automated bullet proof glass doors that led building. The doors opened into a small entry way with another set of automated doors just inside. As he stepped through them, he noticed the room was fairly good sized, with plastic chairs in rows and along the walls. Printouts of wanted persons were placed in shadow boxes on the wall and posters against drunk-driving and texting while driving plastered the rest of the wall.

A cork board caught his attention and he moved to stand before it. As he looked over the pictures of the missing children on each of the seventeen flyers, his heart filled with despair at the thought of what each of these little ones might have endured or might still be going through. He grew angry at the lack of compassion in human society now.

That turned his thoughts to Preston.

He approached the two inch thick safety window that protected the two officers on duty. The officer sitting at the window greeted him as he approached. A sweet smile adorned his face as she gazed into her eyes. "I'm here for Preston Billings."

Her voice was monotone as she answered, "Please proceed through the metal detectors and into the next room."

The second officer jumped up from her desk and rushed across the room. "No, you wait a second buddy. Visiting hours are over. If you want to see somebody, schedule a visit for tomorrow and be here early." She turned her attention back to the first officer, Sanchez according to her name tag, and began to speak softer, "What the hell are you doing?"

The vampire rapped two knuckles against the thick glass effectively gaining the second officers attention. "I'm here for Preston Billings." He gazed deep into her eyes and watched as they clouded over.

"Please step through the metal detector into the next room."

While it was fun to mess with the minds of humans, he could ill afford the time it took to alter the perceived reality of everyone in the precinct. He closed his eyes and extended his will throughout the building. He sensed every lifeform within and forced his way into their subconscious. No one in the jail would see him, he would be nothing more that the flicker of movement in their peripheral vision.

The second woman, Officer Wilson her nametag informed him, came into the room as he passed through the metal detector. He motioned to a door on the far wall and moved to open it. He followed close behind her, his invisible link to her guiding her actions. She led him deep into the holding area.

When they reached the holding area for felons, she spoke, "These are the felony pods. Mr. Billings is being held in solitary because we were afraid he would be assaulted if we placed him in general population. You have a nice night."

"Hold on officer. What about surveillance cameras? Are there any here?"

"The only cameras in the building right now are in the general population pods. Do you need anything else?"

"No, officer, I do not. You have yourself a fine evening."

Officer Wilson left him standing at the end of a hall looking at a room with hallways cutting away in the center of each wall. In the center of the room there was a raised platform with a circular desk on it. Three jailers sat in chairs watching various monitors and talking amongst themselves.

Each corner of the room had a door with tinted windows in it. These must be the doors into the "general population" holding areas. He could see down the opposite hallway and there were several more doors set into the cinder block walls.

The vampire smiled as he approached the circular dais. He concentrated his will on the closest of the three jailers. Through the mental link, he found that his name was Ronnie Turenbul. He forced his will into the jailers thoughts, making him an extension of the vampires own body.

Ronnie turned and left his station, heading down the right hand corridor. At the third door, he stopped and pulled a loaded keychain from his belt loop. After selecting the correct key, he opened the door and left it open as he returned to his station.

The vampire stepped inside the small room and knew instantly that his Samantha had recently paid this man a visit. He looked at the man with a cruel scrutiny as he began to stir. Preston seemed no worse for the wear. He silently commended Samantha for not losing her temper, although he had to admit to himself that he was more than a little surprised.

Preston had sat up on the floor, looking around with bleary eyes. "What the fu…"

The vampire clasped his hand around his throat and lifted him from the floor. Preston kicked to no avail as the hand clasped around his neck increased the pressure. The pain was immense. Preston's eyes felt as if they might pop right out of his head. He swung his fists wildly, connecting several solid punches. And every one of them landed harmlessly on his assailants face.

A solemn look adorned the vampires face as he caught Preston's fist mid-swing. He started applying pressure and listened as metacarpal bones snapped like toothpicks in his powerful grip.

Preston started to scream. The sound was pitiful, his voice trying to push through his constricted esophagus.

With a small shove, the vampire threw Preston into the concrete wall. His head bounced off the wall with a hollow thud and he fell limply to the mat he had been laying on just a few seconds earlier.

The vampire stomped downward, the sole of his boot smashing a kneecap. He kneeled before Preston and lifted his face to address him eye to eye.

"Do you know why I'm here?"

Preston nodded.

"I want you to know that usually, my victims can earn a painless death. Not you. No, you will suffer for hours before I allow you to die."

He grabbed one of Preston's fingers and gave a quick, violent twist. The finger came off in his hand with a sickening sound. Again, Preston tried to scream only to find that he could not. He no longer had control of his own voice. His eyes rolled back in his head and he started to go limp.

The vampire touched his head and his eyes fluttered open. "Oh, no. You're not getting away from me that easily. There is much more for you to endure before your time on Earth comes to an end."

He dropped the severed finger and snapped Preston's wrist backward. The bones cracked like brittle twigs. Tears welled in the broken man's eyes as he tried to plead for mercy.

His lips moved, but nothing came out.

The vampire drove a fist into his ribs, fracturing several of them with the powerful blow. Preston gasped for air and winced as the movement wracked his body with excruciating pain beyond what had already been inflicted on him.

He was struck in the face, again and again. He heard his jawbone shatter under the weight of one of the blows. His eyes had begun to swell shut from the repeated punches. He flailed his one good hand in front of him, trying to ward off any more attacks. That proved to be the ultimate exercise in futility.

The attacker dug his fingers into the weeping man's thigh, digging his fingers deep into the flesh. Preston's eyes were trying to roll back, the whites of his eyes rolling into view for a millisecond before his iris' rolled back into view. The man was trying to pass out, but the vampire's will held him solidly in the moment.

With a lightning fast movement, the vampire ripped his hand downward, shredding the flesh with the maneuver. The violent one stood, wrapping his hand around Preston's neck and lifting him from the floor. He slammed him against the wall hard enough to crack the mortar of the bricks. The attacker used his knee to shatter Preston's shin. He grabbed Preston's un-mangled hand and ripped it from his wrist, blood spurting from the new wound.

"To kill is one thing. To kill a child because you are too selfish to provide for her is entirely another." His voice shook with rage as he spoke. He slammed the child-murderer against the wall again and again. He lifted the mutilated felon higher in the air before slamming him down to the floor by the still open door. He slid forward and drove his fangs into the soft flesh of his victim's neck.

He could feel the warm liquid against the back of his throat. He could feel its essence worming its way through his body. He stopped drinking for a moment, staunching the flow of blood with his fingers. He lifted his head and looked at the ceiling and closed his eyes. He reveled in the feeling of his power returning to him.

He withdrew his fingers from the wounds on Preston's neck. The vampire knew that he had precious few seconds before he bled out and his fun would come to an end.

He gripped Preston's biceps and with hardly any effort, tore both of his arms from their sockets. The vampire dropped them and initiated a brutal assault on his face.

Before Preston could bleed out and die, the vampire grasped the man by both cheeks and made a great wrenching movement with his head. It came loose, the flesh tearing and partially obscuring the puncture wounds.

As the head tore free, the dead man's heart gave a couple last pumps, spraying the last little bit of blood across the walls in the cell.

The satiated one placed the severed head at the door of the cell, facing the dais and the three jailers.

He stood for a moment. Mingling with the coppery aroma of the blood was Samantha's fragrance. Something about this mixture unsettled him. This was a combination of scents that he knew he never wanted to smell again.

He closed his eyes and stood perfectly still. He cleared his mind and pictured the woods outside of Velma's house.

Chapter 14

SAM'S MIND was spinning as she sat down at her desk and switched on her computer. She kept thinking about the strange symbols the serial killer had painted on the front of the De Lucca house. Knowing that this could be a break in the case, she decided to find out what it meant.

She started her search on the internet by typing in occult symbols. After seeing the extensive result list, she clicked the filter for images and started scrolling through the pictures trying to find something remotely like the bloody image left in the wall. It would take her hours to cypher her way through all of this.

Her eyes began to burn so she leaned back in her chair and stretched. She glanced at the clock and realized that she had already been staring at her computer screen for over an hour and had not heard from Will.

She dug her cell phone out of her pocked and dialed his number.

When he answered, his speech was slurred and incoherent. "Yeah, whaddya wan?"

"Will, its Sam. You're late and I need some help in here."

"Oh, fuck! How late?"

She could hear him shuffling around in a tizzy. She imagined him rushing around his room looking for his pants and giggled. "You're an hour late, Will. I'm looking for something on that symbol on the wall at the De Lucca place, but I'm coming up with nada."

Will grunted and cursed as he stubbed his toe against something while hopping around on one foot trying to pull his pants on while holding the phone between his ear and shoulder. "Dammit that hurt! Hey, Sam, why don't you call that egghead with the university? You know, the guy that's head over heels for you, the language guy."

"Not funny asshole. I hope you stub the other toes."

As she started to hang up, she heard Will cussing another piece of furniture. She laughed aloud as she touched the end call icon. "Apparently wishes do come true." She laughed for another couple of minutes before regaining her composure.

She picked up the handset for her office phone and pressed the speed dial she had programmed for the U of A main office. The county sometimes used consultants from the college for various cases. So, Sam figured that a case this high profile and this strange would definitely warrant some outside help even though the little town of Black Ridge didn't have the funding the county did. Hopefully the Chief wouldn't tear her a new one over this.

When the receptionist answered, she politely asked to be transferred to the language department.

After several rings, a male voice came over the line. "This is Dr. Nellis. Can I help you?"

"Dr. Nellis, hey, this is Sam. I've got something I need your help with."

"Ah, Sam! How are you, my love? Well, I hope! How have you been? You know, I've been thinking about you a lot lately and I think...."

Sam hated to be rude, and interrupting people was probably the rudest thing a person could do in her opinion, but she couldn't let him prattle on about how well they would be together for an hour like he tended to do. "Don, hey, pay attention. This is urgent. I'm going to send some images to you on your secure email. Can you take a look?"

He was definitely irritated now. She could hear it in his voice. "Sure, sure. Send it over. You know, all work and no play makes Sam a dull girl."

"Sorry Don. I don't mean to seem coarse, but I need to know what the hell I'm looking at here." She tried to keep her voice apologetic to appease his over-inflated male ego. Don Nellis had been chasing her since high school. Now both of them were in their early thirties, he had gone on to college and went to work for the linguistics department. After only a year of college, she dropped out and went on to become the youngest Detective in Black Ridge history.

The line was silent for several minutes while Sam worked to upload the photos from her camera onto her computer and send them to Don.

"Okay, got it. Let's have a look."

There were another few minutes of silence, presumably while Dr. Nellis looked over the graphic images she had sent him.

"Sam, you still there?"

"Yeah. Do you know what in the hell that is?" Sam sat straight as an arrow in apprehension.

"I do. Would you meet me for dinner to discuss it?"

"Doc, I can't. I'm in the middle of a case. I'm sorry, I just don't have the time."

"Oh, okay." She could hear the despondence in his voice. "Well then, I can tell you it's Enochian. Before you ask, Enochian is supposed to be the very language of the angels and even of God. Now, there is quite a bit of skepticism about it. Anton Szandor LaVey is mostly given credit for documenting the Enochian Keys, but according to my research, he's not the one who discovered them. You see, in 1582, John Dee, with the help of a seer named Edward Kelly, supposedly made contact with the angel Uriel and..."

Here she went, being rude again. "Professor, I'm sorry. I don't need to know the history behind it, only what it means."

Clearly agitated, he continued, "There's no clear codex, or well, no official one to help with translation. But, from what I know of the language this says *The guilty are punished so the righteous may thrive.* And that may not be the actual translation, but it should be close. I mean, this has never been accepted as an actual language, so..." His voice drifted away as he spoke.

"So, you're telling me that this is a language that no one actually speaks, and you can't learn in a college course? It's kind of like Klingon then? Or Elvish? Something you would have to learn from the internet?"

"No, no, not at all. Well, kind of. Okay, for the most part. What I mean is, you can buy books that will teach you how to write some Enochian, and you can even learn some chants and basic words, but nothing like this. I mean, this is written with structure. Whoever wrote this *actually* uses this as a language. They went beyond anything I've ever seen."

Sam was flabbergasted now. Her killer was some kind of wacked out vigilante that could read and write a language that wasn't a language, a language of angels no less. Sam began to laugh as she bid the doctor a farewell and hung up the phone.

Now she had Angelic language written in blood on the wall of a dead pedophiles house. This case just kept getting weirder and weirder with every passing second.

She went over the facts in her head. This vigilante was killing people who had either been acquitted of violent crimes or who had at least committed some atrocity or another, he was apparently self-educated, crafty and unbelievably stealthy. And her vigilante killer was unperceivably strong.

She stood, intending to go to Will's office to await his arrival. An officer further down the hallway called out to her as she rounded the doorway, "Hey, Detective? Chief wants to see you in his office, now."

She sighed and walked the short distance from her office to the hallway that led to the Chief of Police's office. She gave a light rap on the door and got the customarily gruff response, "IN!"

Chief Bill Robinson was in his late fifties and had been the Chief of Police in Black Ridge for over twenty years now. He knew everyone in the town and was on a first name basis with most of the residents. He was an incredibly fair man, level-headed and usually calm.

She had wondered on several different occasions what the Chief had looked like in his prime. Even in his fifties he was a handsome man. His short white hair was combed back making her think of the late Christopher Lee in his roles as Dracula. She started to smirk at the thought but quickly dismissed it. He was over six feet tall and a bit on the round side from too many years of sitting behind a desk. And he was usually in a downright jovial mood.

Tonight was a different story.

The Chief was fuming when Sam stepped into the office. His bright red face contrasted greatly against his snow white hair. "Sit down." he said as he unceremoniously gestured to the chair in front of her.

She did as directed without a word and awaited the apparent oncoming tirade. He paced back and forth behind his large oak desk, his hands clenching and unclenching at his sides. "Did you go see a prisoner tonight?"

"Yes sir, I did. Before my shift started I went to see Preston Billings. I wanted to know why he killed his wife and step-daughter. Why? What's going on?"

"Preston Billings is dead and according to the jailors and the log book, you were the last one to see him alive. Now, I don't want to think that you had a hand in this, but it looks bad, Sam. It looks really bad. Tell me everything that happened."

Sam was shaking now. The news rattled her to her very core. She told the Chief exactly what had transpired in the cramped cell, and relayed the conversation word for word. "I don't know what to say, Chief. I didn't kill the bastard."

"I know, Sam. I know. But this just became a State investigation, since all eye witness accounts say that you were the last one to see him alive. This doesn't look good. We didn't even have any visitors today, Sam." He ran his fingers through his hair and gave a sidelong look at her. "I'm sorry, Sam, but I need you to turn in your badge. I've had to call the state boys in on this one. You're suspended with pay until this is all cleared up. Go on home and rest up, drink a beer or whatever, but go on home."

Sam was shaking. "How did Preston die? You can at least tell me that much, can't you?"

Chief Robinson nodded. "He was torn apart just like the others. I know you didn't do it, that you physically couldn't have. But, just to keep the masses happy, I gotta do this."

Sam shook her head in disbelief. She knew her vigilante had done this. She just didn't know *how* he had done it. "I understand, Chief. I don't like it one bit, but I understand." She pulled her badge loose from her belt and gently placed it on the oak desk. She turned and graciously left his office.

As she walked through the corridors towards Will's office, she was trying to figure out how exactly someone could get into the jail, into the most secure area of the jail no less, and rip someone to pieces without any of the guards noticing. It just wasn't humanly possible.

Vampire.

"And here I am back to this bullshit." She mumbled to herself as she knocked on the door frame. "Hey, just thought I'd let you know I'm headed home. I'm on suspension."

"What the fuck are you talking about? Are you serious?" Will jumped up from his seat and had his best 'I will save the day' face on. "What the fuck happened?"

Sam explained the situation to him. "We're off the case for now. State Troopers are gonna take over until they figure out what happened in the jail."

He stepped around his desk and hugged her. It felt good, but not right. "It's okay, Will. I needed some time off anyways. This shit was just getting too crazy for me and was starting to get to me. You saw that first hand."

"I know it was bothering you, Sam. Don't mean I gotta like it. It's a chicken shit call on the chief's part." He stuck his hands in his pockets and paced back and forth. She could see the anger simmering just below the surface and knew that if she didn't leave soon, her anger would just fuel his into something uncontrollable.

"Listen, I'm going out tonight. I'm gonna clear my head, and I'll start my own research on this sneaky fuck tomorrow morning. Okay? We'll get this guy. I may be down, but I'm not out yet."

He placed his hand on her shoulder, "You call me if you need anything or come up with something, okay?"

"You got it partner." She gave him another hug then left the precinct. She climbed behind the wheel of her Tahoe and sat there for a moment, letting the reality of what had just occurred sink in. She clenched her hands around the steering wheel before starting the massive vehicle and leaving the parking lot.

She drove home in silence. It was just her and the drone of the engine. This was the perfect time for her to think, for her to put her thoughts in order and try to make sense of everything that had happened over the last few weeks.

She slid her vehicle into the drive with her usual fervor. After unlocking the front door and giving Mason a brief rub down she went upstairs to change her clothes.

Her selection of attire included a pair of blue jeans, a Metallica concert tee and her leather jacket. She clipped her concealed carry holster inside her jeans, next to her right hip. Placing her police issue handgun in the dresser, she withdrew her Glock and slipped it into the holster. After what had happened with her ex-husband, she would never go unprepared again. The world had just gotten too crazy. Eighty year old women raped in broad daylight, children abducted from busy restaurants, teenagers carrying high capacity semi-automatic weapons into schools, not to mention the vigilante psycho that was tormenting her town. It was a violent world and she planned to be armed when disaster struck.

As she started to leave the house, she gave the big Rottweiler a brisk rub down and left him with the command sequence "On guard."

She clambered back into the SUV and fired up the engine again. As she pulled out of her driveway, the tires kicked up gravel before giving a short squeal as they grabbed the asphalt.

Now she turned on the radio and cranked the volume to maximum. She turned off her cell phone and dropped it inside the center console. She was off duty tonight and did not want to be disturbed.

She made her way to the interstate and turned south. She accelerated heavily as she merged into the flow of traffic. She did not lift her foot as she matched the speed of the traffic already on the road, instead pressed harder, coaxing the behemoth vehicle to go faster.

She was angry, hurt, depressed and in a hurry. She flicked her turn signal lever and merged into the left hand lane, pushing her speedometer to eighty-five miles per hour.

After a forty minute drive, she finally reached Fayetteville. The traffic was as she expected, bumper to bumper. She maneuvered the SUV through the crowded streets until she came to Dickson Street. She finally found a place to park and as she exited the vehicle, she unclipped the concealed carry holster and stowed it and her pistol in the glovebox, then walked to one of the many bars known to have local bands play.

As she came to the bar in question, the thrashing beat of the double kick already had her bobbing her head. She paid the cover charge at the door and stood a few feet from the stage letting the bass beat against her body. She singer, a young man with long dirty blonde hair and covered in tattoo's was doing a great job of getting the crowd involved, even instigating a mosh pit on the dance floor.

It only took her a few seconds to figure out the gist of the song. It was about snitches and keeping their mouths shut. She smirked at the irony. Here she was, a cop, moshing to a song about not talking to the cops.

She stayed at the front during their set, ordering a beer from the waitress who was fighting her way through the crowd. The band finished up and started removing their equipment from the stage. Sam made her way to the bar. As she sat down, a friendly voice called out over the din of the room. "It's been awhile, Sam. How've ya been?"

Sam returned the smile, although she could only manage a halfhearted one. "I've been better Zach. I've been a hell of a lot better. Hey, throw in a shot?"

Zach laughed, "Anything for a pretty cop. You never know, might get me out of a ticket someday. Whatcha having?"

"I think I need a little Comfort tonight."

Zach let loose with another laugh and replied, "Well, darling, I think my girlfriend might be a bit upset over that one."

Sam's smile became a bit more genuine as she chuckled. She estimated him to be in his early twenties, maybe ten years her junior. As he returned with the beer and the shot of Southern Comfort whiskey, he held up his hand as she pulled her cash from her jacket pocket.

"Nah, sweetie, these are on me. Looks like you need them pretty badly tonight."

This time her smile was genuine. "That obvious, huh?"

He nodded and turned to tend the other patrons. For a bartender so young, he did an excellent job and was always polite. She picked up her shot and tossed it down her throat, grimacing as the bitter liquid burned her throat and left a trail of fire down her digestive system. She chased it with her beer, downing over half of it in a matter of seconds.

She intended to get sloppy drunk tonight.

A hand touched her shoulder and she jumped in surprise. It was the singer from the previous band. "Damn, you drink like a pro, lady. Can I get you the next one?"

"Thanks, I'm just here for the beer and metal. Nothing more, okay?"

"Hey, I'm here for the same. Besides, don't you know it's bad luck to refuse a free beer? Means you won't get your buzz on as fast." He gave her a broad smile and offered her his hand. "I'm Kole. That's my wife over there with the rest of the band. You look like you need some company tonight, so I figured I'd offer our services. A bunch of screw ups to help you cheer up."

Sam couldn't help but laugh. He was trying to be friendly and she expected him to be another misogynistic asshole. She took the offered hand. "I'm Sam, and I'd love some company, thank you."

She waved to get Zach's attention, lifted her beer in silent salute, her way of letting him know she was moving. He smiled and nodded acknowledging the gesture.

Kole gathered his drinks and they made their way to the band's table. She pulled up a chair as Kole introduced her to the rest of the band. The conversation was lively and thanks to the drummer, a screwball named Tristen, she laughed hysterically several times. The whole band was incredibly nice and didn't seem to mind that she was a cop. Actually, she found herself to be the focal point of some incredibly dirty jokes throughout the night.

After her sixth beer, she called it quits and ordered a glass of water. Even though she had entered the bar wanting to get sidewalk licking drunk, she now decided against it. Nothing good ever came of it. She ventured into the mosh pit. Had she not had seven total beers and a shot of whiskey, she would not have dared join in the fray.

But, she did and knowing the whole time that she would pay for this in the morning.

She made it through two full songs before she had to give it up. She tapped Kole on the shoulder as she left to let him know that she was done. She worked her way through the frenzied crowd to the bar. Since she had entered, the place had really filled up. Looking around, Sam estimated the bar to be close to their capacity which was two hundred people.

She caught Zach's attention when she finally reached the bar and ordered a Coke. After several minutes, Zach returned with a martini glass that contained a dark red liquid.

"What the hell is that?"

"It's called a Vampire Kiss. The gentleman at the end of the bar sends his regards."

Sam nearly fell as she pushed away from the bar to get a look at the man that sent her this drink. She scanned over the bars patrons and saw no one that caught her attention. Zach was giving her a concerned look when she returned to the bar. "Everything okay?"

"Who sent me that drink, show me!"

Zach looked down the bar and when he apparently didn't see the sender, he climbed up on one of the shelves and scanned over the crowd. He hopped back down and yelled, "I don't see him."

"What did he look like? This is important, Zach!"

"He was tall, maybe six feet. Whitish blonde hair, maybe down to his butt, black coat, looked like one of those gothic rock guys." Zach shrugged as he finished his vague description.

"What about his eyes, did you see his eyes?"

"Yeah, Sam, I saw them. They were creepy ass blue. Why? What the hell is going on, Sam?"

Sam slapped a fifty on the bar and began forcing her way through the bar causing some of the patrons to spill their drinks. She apologized as she kept forcing her way toward the door.

As she stepped outside, she gasped as the cold night air hit her with brutal force. As she acclimated herself to the freezing temperature, she scanned the streets. At this hour, most people were either at home or inside a warm bar. There were very few out on the sidewalks and none of them matched the description Zach had given her.

Then something struck her. That watched feeling had returned, stronger than it had ever been before. She wanted to run to her vehicle and go home where she had a big ass dog and a boat load of firepower to help overcome whatever this was. Yet, another part of her wanted to return to the bar and see if he came back.

Sam decided on neither. She returned to her vehicle and collected her handgun and tucked it back into its proper place inside her waistband. Then she started walking to the eastern end of the street to one of the nicer motels on the street.

She tried to keep her pace nonchalant and tried to use her peripheral vision to seek out any threats to herself so that she didn't draw attention to the fact she was actively looking for someone.

As she entered the lobby of the motel, she could almost feel the presence of whoever was watching her. She casually glanced over her shoulder and saw that there was no one there.

She paid for her room and took the key from the clerk. Her room was on the second floor so, rather than try to navigate the stairs in her somewhat inebriated state, she took the elevator. When the doors closed, she reached out, touching the doors with her left hand and the back wall with her right and then walked forward keeping her hands in contact with both surfaces.

She felt ridiculous, but she knew that she was dealing with something out of the ordinary.

Vampire.

That word kept screaming at her from the back of her mind. Once she had made it to her room without incident, she placed her handgun into a drawer near the bed and flopped down across it.

She wasn't quite drunk enough to get the spins, but the room did seem to rock back and forth as she closed her eyes. She didn't drink very often and hated it when she made it to even this point.

Try as she might, she could not get the room to stop moving and the concentration it took trying to accomplish such a feat drained her completely.

Within minutes of lying across the bed, she had drifted off into a world of slumber.

And the dreams of her long haired stalker were soon to follow.

Tonight, he motioned to her, beckoning her to come closer.

And she obeyed him.

Chapter 15

THE VAMPIRE followed Sam into her motel room and watched her fall asleep. He smiled as she began to snore ever so lightly. He stood beside the bed and brushed the hair away from her face. His hand glided gently down her cheek, brushed ever so lightly against her neck and rested on her shoulder. He leaned forward and kissed her on the forehead, his lips lingering against her warm skin for a moment longer than they should have. He could not help himself. He wanted to kiss her on the mouth, to share a moment of passion with her, but he felt a little like a creep at the moment. He was in her room, uninvited and having impure thoughts about her as she lay unconscious before him. "Yeah, just a little creepy, dude." He whispered to himself.

He pulled a chair to the edge of the bed and sat down, taking her hand in his. He closed his eyes and began to concentrate deeply.

He reached out, beckoning her to come closer. She walked towards him, albeit it cautiously.

She stood before him, holding his outstretched hands and staring deep into his eyes.

"Hello Samantha."

Sam blinked as he spoke her name. The sound of his voice was so soothing to her, and hearing her name roll from his tongue made her quiver. It took her a moment before she could find her own voice to respond. "And what should I call you?"

The vampire leaned forward and kissed her hand, keeping his eyes locked with hers. "Forgive me Sam. I have apparently forgotten my manners. I am Michael."

Her cheeks flushed as his lips touched her skin. She felt like a schoolgirl with her first crush just realized. "No last name? So, are you like Prince? Or Cher?"

Michael laughed heartily. "Actually, yes, something like that. I was never given a last name. I have only ever been Michael." He released her hands and moved behind her, brushing her fiery red hair away from her alabaster neck. He gently traced his fingers along the contours of her skin, along her shoulder and up her neck before lightly brushing against her ear.

She shivered violently with the pleasure of his touch. His touch was so tender, so caring. A complete contradiction to what she believed him to be. "You are a killer, aren't you?"

"In the black and white world you live in? Yes, you would call me a killer. But I am so much more if you would only ask what you really wish to know."

"What are you? Are you a vampire?"

Michael walked to stand in front of her, smiling broadly revealing the elongated incisors. "I have been called many names, Nosferatu, vampire, obayifo, asema, callicantzaros, drakul, archfiend. These are just some of the names I have been called. But they are names given to me out of ignorance, out of fear and misunderstanding. Yes, I drink blood to sustain me. No, I am not quite human, although closer than myths and legends would have you believe. I have lived thousands of years and I have seen things that even your imagination could never fathom."

"Wait, you're telling me that vampires are real? How many are there?" Sam's face betrayed her excitement, fear and confusion all too well.

"To be honest, like me, there is only one. There are others though, maybe two, maybe ten thousand. I don't know." Michael's tone suggested that there was a long story here, but one that he was a bit hesitant to share.

"What the hell do you mean, you don't know? How can you not know if there are more vampires? Don't you sense each other? You know, like some psychic link or some crap like that?"

"You watch entirely too much TV, young lady. If only it were that simple. I have felt them, my brothers and sisters, but I have never met them. I know they are out there but they avoid me. I believe they fear my judgement. If only things were as simple as the movies made them out to be, or at least as romantic." His tone had become dark and brooding, instilling her with a fear that she couldn't explain.

He gingerly touched her chin and lifted her face so that she was looking at him. "I smell your fear, Samantha. Do not fear me, for I will never hurt you. I cannot harm you. That is something else that has baffled me, and perhaps, the reason behind that will be revealed to the both of us in time."

The scenery around her changed and she found herself standing in the middle of a forest, dense and green. The sun shone though the canopy of leaves far above them and the wind rustled the branches causing the shadows to dance across the forest floor. A light fog hugged the ground giving this place a mystical feeling. She studied the flora for a moment and realized that it was unlike any she had ever seen. "What is this place?"

"This is where it all began. This," he gestured around him, "is the Garden of Eden." Michael looked around, beads of crimson forming in the corner of his eyes as he turned his eyes to the tops of the trees. He seemed to bathe in the sunlight.

Sam could only stare at him for he truly was a spectacle to behold. Her mouth wide with astonishment and wonder at what he had just told her.

"You are dreaming, my beautiful Samantha, and through that dream, I could bring you here, to my memory of this place. This is where I fell and began my life on Earth." He paused for a moment, "I am the Archangel Michael, servant of our Lord God."

Sam gasped in bewilderment. She could not find any words. She watched him intently as he prepared to tell her his tale. Apparently a sad one, for before he began, a single, crimson tear rolled down his cheek.

"I should say that I was once the Archangel Michael. Now, I am only Michael, although I am still a servant of God. For over seven millennia I have carried out his will. After Lucifer rose against my father, a great battle threatened to destroy the Heavens. Many of my brothers and sisters died in that war. The recollections of the battle with my fallen brother have been greatly tamed since they happened. Millions of angels perished during that conflict. It raged on for a thousand years before I fought with Lucifer and helped cast him out of Heaven and into Hell at my Father's behest. After the *conflict had ended, I realized that I had only delayed the inevitable. Lucifer would raise an army and someday attack Heaven again."*

Michael walked over to the biggest tree in the garden. "I spoke to my Father and asked him to place angels on Earth so that Lucifer would not succeed in his plan. He refused, so I asked him to send me. I explained that I loved him so much that I alone would defend his creations, his children. To this request, he agreed. I have tried to be a shepherd amongst a flock of wolves and guide you humans from Lucifer's clutches. I must now admit that you humans are much more susceptible to corruption that I originally thought."

He sat down and leaned against the mighty tree and Sam noticed that the bark was almost golden in color.

Michael's face reflected his somber mood. "He told me that to protect you, I should throw myself from the Heavens. And so I did, not knowing what the consequences would be. I assumed that I would remain an angel, or that I might become human, not this creature bound to darkness and trapped somewhere between the two worlds. I am now cursed to walk the Earth alone, feeding from the wicked in order to sustain my powers. I move through the shadows so that you will not be afraid and so that I would not become hunted."

He paused and laid his head against the tree, closing his eyes and inhaling deeply. "As for others like me, the book of Enoch has been my only clue to their true existence. Like I said, I have felt them, but believed that to be angels walking amongst mankind and that I was cursed with the human's limitation to see them, or, at least I did until I stumbled across the works of Enoch. You see, Enoch was Noah's great grandfather. He wrote that two hundred angels fell from grace, "taking wives and conceiving giants who would devour the land and drink the blood of man.

By giants, he meant indestructible men, or, as half angel, half human. So, you see, after those 'giants' conceived, and their children and so on and so forth, there could be millions of 'vampires' walking the Earth. Although their blood will be extremely diluted and their powers have suffered greatly as their Angelic heritage has been bred out. Even so, many of them are not a threat to you, they just know that they are different. Some actually develop a taste for human blood. Now, please understand, this is all only speculation on my part. I do not know any of this for certain, this is just a theory."

Sam stared at him wide eyed as he spoke, his voice almost taking shape in front of him, playing out the scenes he spoke of. When he finished speaking, it took her a moment to soak in what he had said. "Wait, you are an Angel? You're a psychotic killer. That's sure as hell not what bible school taught me about angels."

"You are correct. Most angels are benevolent. However, if you remember, it was angels that destroyed Sodom and Gamorrah. Angels have always done God's wet work. I was once called the Sword of

God, but, well, that was a long time ago. Now, I am only a servant, walking the Earth and passing judgments that your laws will not and named a vampire out of ignorance and fear."

"This is crazy, absolutely bat scat insane! I am dreaming that I am having a conversation with a psychotic murdering angel that drinks human blood. I'm calling bullshit." She turned to walk away, she wanted to wake up and leave this demented dream, but had no idea how to. Everything was so real. She could smell the trees around her, could hear cicadas in the trees, crickets chirping nearby and birds calling out from the treetops. She was sure she could hear a babbling brook in the distance. As she looked over her surroundings, she began to wonder if this was indeed a dream.

"Again, you are right, Sam. It is crazy, believe me I know. But seven thousand years of living this craziness has shown me that it's real enough. If I don't consume blood, I will eventually die, or cease to exist. Well, I think that is the case. To be honest, I've always been a little afraid to try and fast. It goes against everything that I am."

"An Angel, you mean. So, if you're a vampire, what happens if you step into sunlight? Do you burst into flames or sparkle? Which is it?"

Michael laughed, "Well, I sure as hell don't sparkle. Come to think of it though, I was quite fond of gold lame shirts in the seventies." He laughed again at his own personal joke. "As for bursting into flame, well, I can only venture a guess as to how that started. I'm sure you've heard of xeroderma pigmentosa? It is a disease that causes a severe allergy to ultraviolet light. In extreme cases, a person suffering from XP could blister if exposed to sunlight. And since I do most of my hunting at night, I'm sure people put two and two together to get five. Victims of XP were blamed for my kills in the early black ages because they were different. I saved as many as I could, but I couldn't help them all. Some of them even begged me to let them die. That was a sad time in history."

Sam studied him for several minutes, looking for any indication that he was lying, and found none. "For some weird ass reason, I believe you." She had begun to wring her hands together, something she had not done since her mother was alive. "So, what did you mean by you couldn't hurt me? You said I'm somehow special. What the hell does that mean? And I swear to God, if you tell me that I'm a fuckin' half fairy or half unicorn, I'm gonna drive a wooden stake soaked straight up your tune tweeter!"

Michael gave out a great guffaw. "Now that is a term I have not heard yet, and I thought I knew them all!" He laughed for several minutes, his laughter proved infectious and soon Sam was laughing hysterically with him.

After they finally calmed themselves, Michael wiped his eyes and turned back to Sam. "It's a little hard to be serious following an outburst like that one, but I promise, I will try." He fought another bought of laughter before he could begin again.

"Samantha, I must reiterate, you watch too much TV. No, you don't have any magical blood running through your veins. As for being half unicorn, isn't that illegal in Arkansas? Listen, you aren't that much different from most others, but something about your soul called out to me. Now, this part is harder to explain. You see, when I hunt, I see most humans as bright stars against the night sky. They are following a Christ-like life. Now, the wicked, the murderers, rapists and child molesters I see differently. They are pure blackness in the dark. They seem to pull the night into themselves. You, on the other hand, are not pure white, yet you are not a shadow either. When I hunt, I see everyone in either black or white, never grey. You however, I see as both, shadow and light."

"So, you can't hurt me because I'm light and shadow? What kind of crock are you trying to feed me here?"

Michael sighed, "Let's take an atheist for example. Say this man or woman has led a good life, helped their neighbors and has done right by mankind, they will appear as a burning beacon of hope to me. If not, if they have cheated their neighbors, murdered, raped or what have you, they appear as a stain or impurity."

"So, wouldn't it be easier to hunt in the daylight if you don't burn or sparkle or whatever?"

"No, simply because everyone appears as shadows in the daytime. The innocents are easier to see in the night. The souls of the wicked are stained by the evil of their actions. You see, crimes are mostly

committed at night, under the cover of darkness because they believe that no one see's the terrible things they do. However, in the black of night is when they are the most vulnerable to me."

Sam nodded as his words started to make sense to her. "Okay, I think I understand. So, why the hell am I both? I don't get it."

Michael stood and moved away from the golden tree to stand beside her. "Walk with me." He brushed his hand against hers, sliding his fingers over her palm. Part of her wanted to yank her hand away from him, but she found herself intertwining her fingers with his.

They walked hand in hand through the most beautiful forest she had ever seen. "Samantha, something in your past has marked your soul, but not stained it. Something happened that you did not want to."

Tears immediately sprang to the corners of her eyes. She knew exactly what he was referring to. "My mom." Her words were solemn and full of pain and sorrow. She had struggled to put the events of that night behind her, and had almost succeeded. Yet, here it was again, violently digging and clawing its way to the surface of her thoughts.

Looking at the beautiful young woman over his shoulder, Michael could see the crushing pain in her eyes as the tears formed. He stopped and turned to face her. He gently and lovingly wiped a tear away as it started to roll down her cheek. "Samantha, I'm *sorry I brought it up. I sincerely apologize. I didn't realize how painful this memory must be."*

Sam looked at the ground as she spoke. "No, it's okay. I haven't told anyone about what happened that night. Not even the police. I think they figured it out on their own, though. I just couldn't force the words out." Her legs grew weak as she spoke and she found herself seeking comfort in this strange man's arms.

He held her tightly as she buried her face in his chest. He could feel the tears spilling down the front of his shirt as she began to cry. "Samantha, let's not do this now. Tomorrow night I will visit you at your house and we can talk further. Dawn is coming and I must rest. You will also need your rest because I have a feeling that your hangover is going to be a nasty one."

She lifted her head and wiped away the tears. "Alright, I'll be waiting. Just do me a favor, okay? None of that sneaky vampire shit."

He smiled as he began to fade from sight, "It's a date."

Sam was alone in the forest. She began to walk around and observe this fascinating place. She thought about what Michael had told her. He was an Angel who had fallen from Heaven and become a blood sucking murderer. It seemed a bit farfetched, but she remembered what she had always heard while growing up. God works in mysterious ways.

The trees seemed to sing to her as the wind blew through their boughs and rustled the leaves. She looked at the endless varieties of fruits handing from their branches. She stopped to smell one or two of the thousands of different flowers that covered the forest floor. The further into the forest she walked, the more aware she became of the breathtaking beauty of this place.

A light shuffling sound caught her attention and she turned to find the source of the noise. Hanging from the golden barked tree was a snake. It was bright green, orange and black. It was hanging from one of the topmost branches of the tree, its head dangling only a couple of feet from the ground. Its body was as big as her shoulders were wide and it had to be at least forty feet long. The 'face' of the creature was the most terrifying aspect though. Its maw was easily large enough to swallow her whole. The two horns that adorned its head, almost like a crown, gave it a very sinister appearance. She froze as the predatory eyes locked directly with hers. After a moment, it seemed to speak to her, although the words were unintelligible, she knew it was trying to coax her move closer.

"This is a dream Sam, get ahold of yourself. You are not staring at Satan. You aren't even in the Garden of Eden. You're drunk and passed out in a motel room." Her voice shook as she spoke the words aloud trying to convince herself she was in no real danger.

The words failed to ebb away the fear that was knotting up in her stomach.

The serpent seemed to smile at her, a wicked, twisted grin. It's long and shiny body tensed right before it struck her, its dagger-like fangs sinking into her neck.

Sam awoke with a start, throwing herself off the bed. She frantically looked around the room, making sure that she was alone and that the giant snake had just been a dream.

One thing kept clawing to the forefront of her mind though. Her mother. It had been years since she had thought about that night. As painful as the memory might be, she knew that she would have to face it soon enough. And even now it brought back the questions that had been eating away at her for years.

As she made herself recall the dream she just awoke from, she started to question her sanity. It took her a little bit to pick herself up off the floor and get her bearings back.

Her head pounded and the pressure behind her eyes was intense. She stood and everything came into focus for her. As she tried to take her first step, her legs wobbled a bit and she belched, leaving behind a nasty taste in her mouth. She went to the bathroom and cleaned up the best she was able before deciding to walk to the coffee shop around the corner and order the strongest brew they offered.

She retrieved her pistol from the nightstand, then went to the lobby, checked out of her room and left the building. She had to squint in the early morning sunlight. The day was unusually warm for this time of year. She had been expecting a brisk walk to the bistro, but was pleasantly surprised.

The little shop was busy, but not overly so. It took only few minutes for her to reach the counter. She ordered a triple shot of espresso and a Caramel macchiato. She waited at the counter until her order came up then chose a seat as far away from the windows as possible. She sat with her head down for quite a while before she picked up the macchiato and took a tentative sip. It wasn't as hot as she had expected and started to drink it fairly quickly. She tested the espresso and found it to be fairly cool. She tossed it back, not caring about coffee house etiquette and stood to leave. The triple shot had helped her feel quite a bit better, the caffeine doing wonders for her headache.

She quickly finished her coffee and left the shop behind, observing the people patronizing the place. She wondered what each of them would do if they were confronted with the things she had just dreamed about. Would they react with suspicion? Would they embrace the ideas? Would they call bullshit and walk away?

She needed some time to clear her mind and she knew just how to do it. She made it back to her SUV and turned over the engine. It roared to life and she began the forty minute drive home.

Once she had reached her house, she jumped out of the vehicle and rushed inside. Mason was doing his customary happy dance as he greeted her at the door, wagging his tail so hard he was shaking his whole rear end. He barked at her and she gently reminded him to use his inside voice. He gave her a soft snort then ran in a circle around her. She kneeled beside him and wrapped her arms around his massive neck.

After letting her furry companion know how loved he was, she went upstairs and took a quick shower. She did not get the now familiar feeling of being watched and knew that she wouldn't. The man, vampire, angel, whatever, had told her that he would visit her tonight and that he would be resting. Even though she had no reason to believe him, she actually did.

After she had finished her shower, she quickly dressed before filling Mason's food and water dish. She gave him another scratch behind the ears before giving him the command to guard the house. She left the house and sauntered to the garage. It was a separate building that her father had built when her mom had gotten sick. He'd used it as a repair shop and had made a pretty penny doing it.

She unlocked the big overhead door and threw it upward. The smell of gasoline and oil wafted out at her and she smiled at the number of memories that came flooding back. She and her dad had spent the last several years of his life working on this car.

She smiled lovingly as she pulled the tarp off of her dad's prized possession, a 1971 Dodge Challenger. She and her dad had spent untold evenings in the garage working to restore and modify this classic muscle car. It was painted Plum Crazy purple with the classic matte black racing strobes down the side. It sat on 295/60r15's on the rear and 185/70r15's on the front. They had purchased Cragar SS rims to carry the beefy tires and give it the classic street rod look.

Under the hood is where most of the work had been done. They had taken the powerful 440 engine out of the car and supercharged it with, replacing the stock balancer with a steel crank hub, Edelbrock heads and a Comp Cams solid lifter cam. It has been bored .030 over and it had dyno'd at 749 HP to the rear axle. This car was a beast and her daddy had taken almost as much pride in it as he had in her.

They had redone the interior together as well. Black leather covered all the seats, a new dash had been installed with a complete set of electronic gauges. The stereo system had been upgraded as well. She was proud to say that she had found this particular car on a farm on the south side of town. It had been sitting in a field rotting away. She and her dad had restored it from a pile of rust into a beast of a machine.

She ran her fingers down the fender, remembering all the time that she and her dad had spent wrenching on this car. It had been the ultimate bonding experience. She knew this car inside and out and could probably rebuild the engine blindfolded.

She gave a wistful sigh as she glanced over at her dad's Harley in the corner. A '97 Bad Boy, a fairly rare bike in its own right. For a few moments, she debated on taking the bike over the car. While it felt good to stand outside now, it would be incredibly cold on the bike. She opted out of the bike and opened the door to the Challenger.

As she turned the key in the ignition, the engine roared to life, the exhaust rumbling so loud that it rattled the open garage door in its tracks.

She eased the car through the opening before shifting into neutral and engaging the parking brake before hopping out of the car to close the garage door.

Throwing the car into first gear, she popped the clutch and the tires spun, leaving a cloud of white smoke behind. She expertly shifted through the gears as she headed north. The rumble of the engine seemed to calm her mind. As she focused on the road ahead and accelerated out of the curves, her mind began to clear.

Finally, she reached her destination, a bridge in the middle of nowhere. It crossed over the White Rock River, though the river itself was little more than a trickle of water cutting through the Earth now.

She pulled off the main road onto a small side road that led down to the banks of the river. She parked the car and cut the engine. As she stepped out of the car, she couldn't help but look around at the beauty of the area. It looked just like it had when she was just a girl. The bridge was almost a half a mile long and two lanes with wide shoulders, all to cross a five foot wide creek. From the wide riverbed and the diminutive flow of water, it was apparent that once upon a time, this had been a formidable river. Now, however, the pathetic flow of water rivaled only that of a dripping faucet. But as a reminder of how time can change things, the once mighty river had cut its scar upon the land only to fade away.

She locked her car and left it as she walked her way alongside the stream, just listening to the trickling water. She hiked for quite a while before deciding to head back. Her mind was awash with images of the man named Michael. She rolled the severity of what he had revealed to her last night over and over in her head. She still had trouble believing that any of this was true.

She still questioned her sanity.

As she neared the area in which she had parked, she was ripped from her thoughts by catcalls and whistles. She looked up and noticed an older model Ford pickup parked beside the Challenger and two men sitting inside the cab. "Hey, baby, that your ride? I gotta say, it ain't near as pretty as you. You gotta be the prettiest piece of ass I've seen in a while now. Why don't you come over here and we can get acquainted?" The driver of the old truck called out to her. He was missing several teeth and it looked like he had not been to a dentist in his life. He had not shaved in at least three days and his clothes were grease stained and grungy. As much as she hated stereotypes, these two were case-in-point meth heads.

She had her pistol tucked safely away in her jacket and was not worried about any trouble they might give her until the driver slid a sawed off shotgun out of the window and leveled it at her.

She mumbled to herself, "And it gets even better."

Chapter 16

MICHAEL SAT outside Velma's house until he saw a light come on. He gave her plenty of time to complete her morning routine before he gently knocked on the front door. A couple of minutes passed before the door opened.

A beaming grin enveloped her face as she recognized her visitor. "Mister! I'm so glad you came back. I was starting to worry about you. Come in, come in!"

Michael stepped inside and smiled as the acrid wood smoke assaulted his nostrils once again. He could also smell coffee brewing. "Could I trouble you for a cup of coffee?"

"Of course you can, make yourself at home." As she busied herself in the kitchen, she called back to him, "You know, you need a key. Can't have you standing outside all hours of the night now can we? Neighbors might get the wrong idea you know." She peeked around the corner and gave him a wink.

"Velma, I cannot. I don't want to be a burden."

Her tone took on an angry edge, "Now, you hush that kind of talk. I won't take no for an answer. Take the damn key and that's that. Now, when you come in, don't worry about waking me, I sleep like the dead. Now, how about that coffee?"

As he entered the kitchen, he saw the key in question laying on the table. He picked it up and held it in front of his eyes. This was one act of kindness that he had never experienced in his years. He gripped it in his palm and squeezed it tightly, as if he were trying to reassure himself that he actually had it and that this exchange had been real. An overly revealing smile came over his face as he looked at the generous old woman.

Velma came to the table carrying two cups of coffee. She had already placed the cream and sugar in the center of the table.

He had found himself in two unique situations in this single sleepy little town. First, he believed that he was falling in love with someone, a feat that he had once thought impossible. Second, he was sitting across from a human being, sharing stories with her about life and love. She knew that he was not like her, yet she accepted him without trepidation. She even gave him the use of her house, something that had never happened in his eternity here. Well, something that had not happened without his special brand of persuasion.

She told him about a cow that had kicked her once while she was trying to get enough milk to feed her children breakfast during the Great Depression. She told him of her late husband, Ted, who had been taken from her by Alzheimer's, of her children and how they had grown up and moved off to the big cities. Her oldest son had moved to New York to work the stock exchange, her daughter, the middle child, had moved to Hawaii to run a tourist resort and the youngest son had moved to Hollywood to become a movie star, though his dreams had yet to become reality.

He listened intently as she spoke, yet his mind was elsewhere. He knew he was being rude, but he could not help it. His thoughts kept turning to Samantha and what he had told her last night. Not once in his seven thousand years had he told anyone else those things. He had to spread the occasional rumor, to be sure. Things like vampires cannot be seen in mirrors, crosses' and holy water hurt them, the severe allergy to garlic and the like, but he had never actually spoken the truth to anyone.

He wondered what had possessed him to tell Samantha, and why he felt compelled to tell her more. A large part of him wanted to believe that it was his destiny to do so. He hoped that maybe once, he was meant to have a companion.

Suddenly, Velma's hand touched his shoulder and pulled him from his thoughts. "Dear, if you're gonna see that girl tonight, you better go wash up and get some rest."

"What? How did you know that I was going to see someone?"

The old woman gave him a genuinely amused look, "It's as plain as the nose on your face. You've got the look about you. Wasn't that hard to figure out, you look like the cat that ate the canary!"

As she left the room, she called out, "You look like one of them twitterpated teenagers!" She started laughing as she sat down in her chair to watch the morning news.

Michael was alone with his thoughts again. He decided that Velma was right and quickly finished his cup of coffee and went to the bathroom to clean up. Once he was undressed, he did exactly what Velma had suggested earlier. He made himself at home. He wrapped a towel around his waist and started a load of laundry. He returned to the bathroom and began to clean himself up.

He took a quick shower, washing the stink off himself. He started to sing Ozzy Osbourne's "Back on Earth" as he washed himself, making sure to keep his voice low enough so that he wouldn't disturb Velma.

After his shower, he rubbed his hand along his chin. Normally he didn't shave but maybe every

6 months. But tonight was a special night. He reached under the sink and grabbed the straight razor and shave cup that he had used before and proceeded to shave himself.

He finished his hygienic duties and wrapped the towel around his waist again. He returned to the washing machine and found that Velma had already transferred his clothes into the dryer. He smiled and agilely made his way back to his room. Laid out on his bed he found several sets of clothing, most of which consisted of overalls and flannel shirts, but there were two pairs of jeans and a couple of black t-shirts with the pocket on the left breast. Of course he opted for the jeans and t-shirts., but folded the remaining clothes neatly and placed them in a drawer in the dresser. As he moved the clothes, he found a pair of cotton boxers lying underneath of everything. He slid them on and climbed into bed.

"All these years and people still surprise me." He chuckled as he slid his arms behind his head and closed his eyes. He had a long night ahead of him and he knew it. If he had been aware enough to do so, he would have marked yet another first. As he fell asleep, for the first time in seven millennia, no dreams came.

Chapter 17

SAM COULD smell the ether coming from their vehicle as she drew closer. She knew that as well as being high on methamphetamines, they were also cooking the lethal chemical in their mobile lab. She could only hope that they were too strung out to realize what was happening.

They stepped from the pickup, the driver careful to keep the shotgun pointed at her. She had stared down the barrels of weapons before and that was scary enough, but staring down the barrel of a shotgun wielded by an addict proved to be more unnerving than she had expected. They instructed her to remove her jacket and she hesitated. Her handgun was concealed beneath the black leather and she knew if they spotted it, things would go south quickly. Her hands shakily reached for her belt buckle instead.

"Why don't you boys come over by the bridge? People will be less likely to stop and try to join in the party if we're out of sight" Even though she tried to sound seductive, her voice shook almost as much as her hands as she fumbled with the stubborn buckle.

The driver, obviously burnt out by years of heavy drug abuse, responded. His voice was distant, almost as if he were no more than the shell of a man pretending to be human. "I said take that fuckin' jacket off. I wanna see them titties."

Sam's face flushed with shame and rage. She turned her back to them, bending over slowly to entice them with a great view of her denim clad buttocks hoping to calm them and assure them that she wasn't going to fight.

The passenger seemed to be turned off by the lack of a fight, but the driver persisted. "Oh, baby. We're gonna have a lot of fun, ain't we?"

Sam stood straight and walked right past them, trying to make her way to the bridge where she might be able to hide behind a support long enough to draw her pistol unseen. However as she passed the driver, he threw his arm around her, jamming the shotgun into her ribs. His voice gave away his excitement and forced the realization of how much trouble she was actually in.

"You are one fiery piece of ass, ain't ya honey?" His breath reeked of stale cigarettes, peppermint schnapps and what she assumed was a week's worth of lunch.

Her stomach rolled.

Her cheeks flushed an even deeper shade of red, this time from sheer indignation. She wanted to ram that shotgun down his throat. As they moved closer to the bridge and further from the beat up old truck and its passenger, she could hear the other man pleading with his friend. "John, it's a fuckin' trap. That bitch is gonna mess your world up, dude. Leave her the fuck alone and let's get outta here!" His voice became almost frantic as he shouted the last few words.

The driver angrily grabbed Sam's neck and shoved her forward, throwing her off balance and sending her sprawling into the dirt.

She cut her eyes and watched them with her peripheral vision, all the while careful to keep her head down. The driver, John, had turned his back to her and was shouting at his passenger. "You listen here, motherfucker, I will tell you when it's a goddamn trap and when this bitch is just beggin' for my cock! So unless you got enough hair on them pitiful little balls of yours, SHUT THE FUCK UP!"

He turned his attention back to Sam and she knew she was in trouble. His whole body was shaking with rage and she knew she was going to be his outlet. He was working his jaw back and forth, grinding his teeth and the veins in his forehead formed a veritable roadmap.

He grabbed her hair at the base of her skull and jerked her to her feet.

That was the opening she needed.

She drove her elbow into John's ribs, causing him to almost drop the shotgun. He took a swing at her and she easily ducked it. She doubled her fist and brought it up in a powerful uppercut, catching him in the jaw and knocking him off balance but failing to knock him out. She seized the advantage as he stumbled backward in a daze and snatched the shotgun from his grasp. Using it as a bludgeon, she hit him across the face with it and he crumpled to the ground. He fell to his knees then backwards leaving him contorted in an extremely awkward position.

She turned her attention to the passenger. He had seemed reluctant to assault her, but she knew he would have as soon as his friend had her restrained. She unconsciously clenched her teeth as she approached him.

He tried to shrink away from her, trying to climb inside the truck. Rage took over and she kicked the door shut on his shins. He howled in pain as she round the open door and grabbed his jacket. With a movement more powerful than she believed she was capable of, flung him to the ground.

"You wanted penetration? Here's your fuckin' penetration!" As she closed the short distance between them, she seemed to grow more confident and more alive at the thought that she was about to mete out some pure, unhindered justice.

She shoved the barrel of the shotgun against his lips. "Open your fuckin' mouth!" Her voice dripped with animosity as she screamed the command at him. As he parted his lips, the barrel scrapped across his teeth and he began to sob. "Give me one good reason not to pull this trigger. One, that's all I need you sick son of a bitch.

The meth addict was sobbing and pleading for his life around the barrels of the gun. His body was trembling uncontrollably and he lost control of his bladder. Sam started laughing when she noticed the wet stain that continued to grow.

"Big bad ass rapist pissed himself. I think letting you live would be a worse punishment than killing you. Take your buddy to the hospital and pray to God I never see you two fuckers again. And if you even *think* about touching another woman, I'll find you. Castrate you, and feed you what I cut off. Do you understand me?"

He nodded, still cradling the weapon between his lips. She removed it and flipped the lever to open the breach. The two shells inside popped out and she deftly reached out and caught them, stashing them in her pocket. As she returned to her car, she unlocked the door and tossed the weapon in the rear floorboard.

As she turned her car around, she made a mental note of the license plate on the old truck.

She would call it in as soon as she got signal on her cell. She saw the passenger trying to drag his unconscious friend to the truck. The rear tires spewed a fishtail of gravel at them as she slammed the accelerator to the floor.

She shifted through the gears quickly as she headed home. She had not decided if she was completely insane, or if what had happened last night had been real. She did know, however, if it was indeed real, she was not going to be caught off guard. She needed a plan. She needed to be prepared.

Chapter 18

MICHAEL AWOKE, feeling refreshed and alive. He was hungry, but not for blood. He craved a good breakfast, bacon, eggs, biscuits and gravy. As he sat up and swung his feet over the edge of the bed, he realized why. Velma had been busy. The scent of bacon and fried eggs filled his nostrils and made his mouth water. He hastily dressed and made his way to the kitchen where he found Velma standing over the stove flipping the bacon in the pan. He coughed to announce his presence.

Velma turned and smiled. "Good morning, er well, evening, sleepyhead. How'd ya sleep?"

Michael could only smile. "I slept well and I must say I did not expect this. I have decided that it is you, who are truly an angel. You had to have read my mind."

The old woman slid the hot pan off the burner and placed the bacon on a paper towel. "An angel you say? Don't know about all that nonsense. I just figured you'd be hungry. A growin' boy's gotta eat, don't he?"

Michael nodded and took a seat at the table. Velma deftly cracked two eggs in the skillet and seasoned them with salt and pepper. Without a word, she turned the eggs and seasoned them again. Moving with an astonishing grace, she opened the oven and took out the biscuits placing the hot pan on the table in front of him. She then took the butter from the fridge and a butter knife from the silverware drawer and placed the items on the table, the knife lying across the lid of the butter container.

She turned the hash browns over so that they wouldn't become too crispy or burnt. She sprinkled a little pepper on them as they continued to cook. As if by an afterthought, she returned to the fridge and retrieved a bottle of hot sauce and placed it on the table by the butter.

Michael sat in awe, watching the woman cook. He had eaten numerous meals, but he had never seen one prepared with such agility, grace and expertise. It was a simple meal, but her movements led him to believe he was about to taste the work of a five star chef.

He found himself anticipating the first bite, something he had never done. Food was for sustenance, he had never had a personal experience with which to make eating human food an enjoyable one.

He had watched numerous vampire movies depicting creatures that were charismatic and flawless, falling in love with the human because she possessed special abilities or was completely different than the rest of humanity. He had also seen the films portraying vampires as beastly and monstrous, no better than rabid animals. He had even forced himself to sit through the latest perversions about vampires that tried to 'mainstream' and ended up in love with a human female and couldn't decide whether or not to make her like him. It was ridiculous.

But this, this was real. This spectacular woman cooking breakfast for him an hour before sundown, was real. This was something incredible, something special and he was convinced that Velma was a gift, sent to him by his Father, his God.

Velma finished the eggs and lifted the skillet from the burner. She seemed to float across the floor, bringing the eggs to him. Tipping the cookware, she slid the over-medium eggs onto his plate and sat the hot skillet on the counter. She then took the hash browns off the burner and gave him a generous portion of them. She sat across from him and took a sip from her glass of sweet tea. "Would you mind saying Grace?"

He smiled nervously. This was something he had not done in at least fifty years. But he nodded and bowed his head, clasping his hands in front of him.

"Loving Father, we thank you for this food and for all your blessings to us. Lord Jesus, come and be our guest at this table. Holy Spirit, as this food feeds our bodies, we pray that you would nourish our souls. Amen." A warm feeling came over him as he finished the prayer. When he looked up, he noticed that Velma had a tear rolling down her cheeks. "Did I say something to upset you?"

"No, sir you did not. I haven't heard that prayer since Ted passed on. It just brought back many a memory. It was beautifully spoken." She wiped away the tear with the back of her hand and reached for a biscuit.

Michael decided that it was best to leave this subject alone and he reached for the bacon. It had been far too long since he had shared a meal with anyone. This was a pleasant change. As they ate, they spoke of the past, shared memories of times long gone and many, many other topics.

* * * * *

Sam arrived home and pulled the Challenger into the garage. She grabbed the California duster from the shelf and gave the car a quick wipe down before covering it with the tarp again. She would usually do a quick detail, but she knew that she had very little time to prepare for her 'date.' Judging by the light outside, dusk would fall in a little over a half an hour.

Mason barked as she slid the key into the deadbolt and unlocked the door. She could see him turning in circles in anticipation. As she opened the door, he almost knocked her over he hit her legs so hard. She laughed at him and scratched him behind the ears and on the sides of his rump. "What's the matter, you attention whore? Did you miss me?"

Mason looked her eye to eye and barked once, very softly, as if in response to her question. He then ran to the back door, his feet scrambling for traction on the hardwood floor as he bolted away from her. He ducked through his doggie door and disappeared into the back yard.

She followed him and watched him through the windows. He was running the perimeter of the privacy fence as hard as his powerful legs would carry him, his lips drawing back to reveal his teeth. This was a look that she had learned was a smile. She watched him make so many circuits around the yard, she lost count. This was a normal thing for him if she was gone for extended periods. He would run until he was exhausted, then he would come inside and lay beside her with his head in her lap. She would scratch him behind the ears as he slept.

She turned away from the windows and ran upstairs to shower. She finished as quickly as she could and picked out a semi-dressy purple shirt and a black skirt. She paired the outfit with a pair of three-inch heels. She returned to the bathroom to apply her makeup and styled her hair.

After she had finished making herself look good, she hurried downstairs and began straightening up the house. It was not in terrible condition, but she didn't want him to see her house even the least bit dirty. She blushed as the thought that he may have already been inside her house flickered through her mind. Busying herself with the task at hand, she pushed the intruding though aside. Inside of thirty minutes, she had showered, applied makeup, fixed her hair, dressed and cleaned up the house.

She went into the kitchen and poured a glass of wine. She didn't want to get drunk, didn't even want a head change, but she did feel a need to take the edge off. She was actually nervous.

She looked through the window above the sink and saw Mason still running around the yard like he had lost his mind. She chuckled and went to the living room to watch TV.

Sitting on the couch, her feet tucked under her rear, she skimmed through the channels. She wasn't interested in anything, just killing time until her guest arrived. She was a little nervous, but with each sip of the wine, that feeling was going away. She was more terrified of why she was nervous.

She was more terrified of her feelings towards him than she was of what he was capable of.

Every few seconds, she would glance towards the front window, checking to see if night had fallen completely. He had not given her a time, but she knew he would not keep her waiting long after dusk. For a cold blooded killer, he seemed to be a perfect gentleman. Her mind began to focus on the dreams she had been having.

Then her earlier thought crept back into the forefront of her mind, had he been in her home before without an invitation? "How is that possible?" she asked aloud. "Don't vampires need an invitation to enter someone's house? I'll have to ask him about that."

She continued to sip on her wine as she patiently awaited her guest's arrival. She found herself checking her clothing several times as she was not used to wearing such feminine attire. She was more of a blue jeans and t-shirt kind of woman. But for some reason she didn't quite comprehend, she wanted to look pretty for her murderous visitor.

This was another thing that baffled her. She was an officer of the law, dedicated to putting murderers behind bars and yet, here she was, primping for a visit with a serial killer.

A nervous chuckle slipped through her lips.

A knock at the door jerked her from her thoughts. She smoothed her skirt as she stood and tried not to seem overly eager as she made her way to the front door, but her steps seemed to quicken of their own accord. She deftly unlatched the locks and opened the door for her visitor. He stood at the threshold smiling that amazing smile.

She raised an eyebrow as she tried to be sneaky with her very first question, "Oh, I'm sorry, you need an invitation don't you?"

Michael stood at the threshold and laughed. "Again, you watch too much TV. That thing will rot your brain, Samantha. No, I do not need an invitation, but manners dictate that I should wait for an invitation."

Sam shook her head, "Everything I thought I knew about vampires is wrong." She glanced at his boots as she invited him in. Just as she thought, they were motorcycle boots. A slight smirk played across her lips as she gave him the invitation. "Won't you please come in, Michael?" she asked with her best overly exaggerated southern belle impersonation.

"How gracious of you, Ms. Brae." He dipped forward in a low bow, continuing her jest. As he stepped through the doorway, his boots made absolutely no sound as he walked across the hardwood floor. Sam watched in awe as the incredibly tall, powerful yet unbelievably stealthy man moved with an unnatural grace through her living room.

He stopped by the couch and held out his hand, "Won't you please join me?"

Sam took a tentative step forward, absentmindedly closing the door. Her short journey across the ten feet that separated her and this supernatural being seemed to drag on forever. She was consumed by fear and excitement as she drew closer and closer to him. Vampires had always fascinated her, but it had been a private fascination. It was a secret that she had shared with no one. She was a good girl, a Christian woman and Vampires had always represented all that was unholy and evil.

My, how things change.

Now, one of the legendary creatures was standing before her, asking her to sit beside him on her couch. A small part of her still wanted to run from the room, while the other, more prominent part of her wanted to giggle like a schoolgirl. She allowed herself to do neither. She finally accepted Michael's hand and sat down with only a few inches separating them.

Michael leaned back and relaxed. He had a casual yet attentive grip on her hand as his fingers seductively slid back and forth over the tender flesh of her wrist. His skin was cool, but not ice cold like the movies would have you believe. He was pale, but not corpselike in appearance and his smell was amazing, like weathered leather and ice.

There were so many things that she thought she knew about vampires that were turning out to be rubbish. She steeled herself, as she had so many questions and she had never been one to ease into anything.

"Okay, Michael, I have thousands of questions about you. Can we just get that out of the way?"

The vampire smiled, his elongated incisors catching the light just enough to provoke a shiver to run down her spine, something akin to the feeling one would get staring down the barrel of a .50 caliber handgun. She knew that she was looking at very deadly and formidable weapons.

"I would be delighted to answer your questions, my beautiful Samantha."

"Please, call me Sam." Her gaze fell to the floor as she spoke. "My mother was the only one to call me Samantha."

Michael apologized and leaned forward to embrace her in a hug. As he slid his arms around her, his lips ever so lightly brushed against her neck, sending explosive tendrils of pleasure throughout her body. She held the embrace for quite some time before pulling away. She was afraid that if she let go any sooner, he would vanish again. "Alright, Mr. Suave, stop trying to sidetrack me." She laughed and gave him a playful push on the shoulder, something she had done when she was younger whenever she was nervous.

"First questions, why do you drink blood and do the fangs retract?"

Michael donned a serious look as he began his part of the interrogation. "I drink blood because if I don't, I lose my powers. Not completely to the point of becoming human, but I do become very, very weak and I feel like I'm starving to death even if I do eat other foods. And no, the fangs do not retract. It would be nice if they did, I could fit in a lot easier that way."

"So, aside from the hunger, you could be pretty much human. Why don't you do it, I mean, if a little suffering could take you from this lonely life you have, why not go for it?"

A longing filled his eyes, "because, Sam, this is what my Father wanted me to do. If your father told you to do something that you knew to be right and just, could you turn your back on his request just to make your life a little more bearable?"

Sam looked at the floor again, "No, I guess I couldn't. Okay, what about the sun. You've told me that you won't burst into flames. Was it you in the woods the other day? I swear I saw you. Does the sun hurt you?"

He gave her that magnificent smile again. "It was me, Sam. I was watching you, trying to decide if you were supposed to be one of my victims. As for the sunlight, I become extremely vulnerable. In sunlight, I'm all but human. I'm still faster and stronger, but my regenerative powers are virtually null. If I am mortally wounded while exposed to sunlight, I will die. The difference between you and I is that after I am either cremated or buried, I will come back three days afterwards."

"Wait," Sam sputtered, "Like Jesus? You're resurrected after three days being dead?"

"Basically, yes. The only difference is that my timer starts after they have a man of the cloth give me my last rights. Believe me, it's not something I like to do. First of all, it hurts like all hell. Second, if someone sees me climbing from my grave, I'm very likely to end up in the hole I just climbed out of with a whole new set of wounds. I guess I only have two reasons why I don't like to die, but they sound like pretty good ones to me."

"Okay, here's a biggie. Have you been in my house during the day? And were you in the bathroom while I was taking a shower?" Sam's tone became very serious as she put voice to the question.

"If I told you I didn't see anything important, would you believe me?" He gave her that perfect smile again.

Sam began to blush. He had just confirmed that he had seen her at her most vulnerable, completely naked and oblivious to his presence. Something she also realized, though she would never admit it is that this revelation turned her on. "You son of a bitch! Why were you playing peeping tom? Huh? I should test the 'I can't die' crap right her and shoot you in the nuts!"

Michael's face became deadly serious. His smile quickly disappeared and was replaced by one of stoicism. "Sam, at the time, I was debating on whether or not to kill you. I'm rather glad I didn't."

It was Sam's turn to don the serious face, "Let's change the subject. I don't think I like where this one is headed. So, what about garlic? What's the story there?"

Michael shook his head and laughed again. "Now that is a funny story. In the early 1300's, I was hunting in Romania. I was in a small village called Oradea stalking a habitual rapist. I'm going to skip the ethics difference between our time and then, but they were significant. Now, while stalking Dumitru, I was discovered due to a lack of diligence on my part. To appease them, as they decided that I should be tortured, I told them that I could not stand garlic. So, they tied the stuff around my neck and hanged me. I suppose it made them feel better. But I am quite fond of garlic. I love garlic bread, to be honest."

"Okay, what about silver? Almost all the legends and stuff say that silver can hurt a vampire. Is that true?"

Michael nodded, "Silver does hurt but it isn't deadly. It has something to do with Judas' betrayal of Jesus Christ because before that, it didn't bother me. Holy water doesn't affect me. It does, however, make me incredibly angry that someone would think that throwing water on a creature of the dark would harm it. You humans come up with some off the wall ideas, do you know that? What else is there? Oh, a wooden stake through the heart, of course that will kill me. Who wouldn't it kill? The point here is that for the most part, I am just like you. The same things that hurt you hurt me. I am just a lot harder to kill, and that I do not suffer from a permanent death like humans do. And lastly, the Cross. Cross' do hurt me, just not the way the movies portray. It is more of an emotional hurt, it reminds me of where I am from and the life I once lived. It reminds me of my time in Heaven, which is barely more than fleeting wisps of imagery and feelings."

Sam could see the longing and pain in his eyes and she hugged him. "I'm so sorry. It seems that you and I both have something to miss."

They held each other for a long time before Sam pushed away. She felt a stirring inside her and she wasn't ready to let go of that much yet. "So, how long have you been here? I mean, on Earth."

Michael sighed, "Seven thousand, three hundred and fourteen years."

Sam's face said it all. She didn't have to say anything before Michael answered her unspoken question. "I know, the timeline you know is off. Let me give you a 'for instance.' Your timeline, your biblical history begins with the creation of Adam. You believe that Adam only lived for 130 years. In fact, Adam died when he was 968 years of age. So many things are left out of the Bible. I mean, would you read a book that describes how they prepared their meals for six hundred pages? A lot of everyday life was omitted to make it less monotonous to read. Can't say I blame them, though."

Sam stopped him because her questions were getting the better of her. "Now hold on. What about the cavemen? We've found fossils to prove they existed."

Michael laughed again. "You humans are always so convinced that you alone are correct. That two opposing views could not possibly coincide. Cavemen did in fact exist. They were not the cave dwelling, club thumping barbarians that you all believe them to be. They were quite sophisticated actually and one day, your archeologists will find evidence to prove that. Evolution is correct to a point as well. Do you think that Adam and Eve looked just like you? The human race has evolved in the last hundred years, and you all still seem to believe that 7,000 years ago, people looked exactly the same as they do now. What I find humorous and concerning all at the same time, is that while your species continues to evolve physically, you are regressing in your mannerisms. Look at the violence taking place in the world today. People have become intolerant of others because they hold different beliefs. Kids are shooting each other because someone called them a name or hit them once. People are being killed for a pair of shoes. I had once believed that humankind would become more and more sophisticated, but instead, you have become more barbaric with better technology."

Sam put her hands up to signal him to stop. "So, everything I've learned about the Bible is wrong? Come on, how much smoke do you expect me to let you blow up my ass? I mean, Adam and Eve were cavemen?"

"I'm not claiming that everything you believe is wrong, just edited to fit a certain ideology. Mankind cannot remember everything, cannot grasp the concept of things that happened in the beginning, so they alter it so that they can understand it better. The history of the world would blow your mind, Sam. But, the Bible contains the highlights that man could understand well enough to write down. It was written as a guideline for living, to teach you how to love, to forgive and how to treat one another. But it seems like most of humankind, even devout Christians, have discarded its teachings and went on to follow their own twisted beliefs. Some spout hate in God's name, people act violently towards others simply because they have different beliefs. I'm sorry, I could go on and on about this, but I want to know more about you."

Sam shook her head, "You know, that actually makes sense." She gave a weak laugh as she noticed Michael preparing to launch into another tirade. She held a finger up to his mouth, "Another time, please. Let my littlebrain soak this much in first. Please?"

Michael gave her that mesmerizing smile and nodded. "As you wish. So, what shall we talk about now? Or would it be too forward if I kissed you?"

Sam's eyes widened and her pulse quickened. She fought to keep herself from lunging forward. "Whoa, slow down there buddy. I mean, you're gorgeous, but I would rather take it a little slower than that. I mean, just yesterday, I was trying to track you down so we could stick you in the electric chair, tonight you're in my living room talking about kissing me. That's a hell of a leap."

"You are right, Sam. I apologize. I just felt that I should try to live up to my reputation."

Sam smirked, "and what reputation might that be?"

"Oh, you know, we vampires are notorious sex fiends." His smile let her know that he was kidding with her, trying to put her even more at ease with him.

And it was working.

"Well, I tell you what, big boy, if you play your cards right, I might let you have that kiss before dawn." Sam gave him a sly smile and felt herself blushing. She had never been this forward with a man before.

She'd never sat across from a vampire either.

Michael couldn't keep the smile from his face as he saw her cheeks tint rose red. "Well, I'll have to stack the deck to insure I get only royal flushes all night then. So, do you have any more questions?"

"Okay…. Well, what powers do you have?"

"Wow, where to start? For the most part, I have all the powers that I'm rumored to have, but only under the cover of darkness. Speed, strength, regeneration, and glamouring for a start. I can appear as anyone or anything I can imagine, which makes it very easy and sometimes excruciatingly fun to strike fear into the hearts of those I pass judgment on, but, only if I've fed within the last 48 hours. If not, my powers weaken and I become more and more mortal as I said before."

"You're an angel, right? Where's your wings?"

Sam was visibly afraid of the answer to this question, even though she was trying very hard to keep it from showing.

"I was an angel. Now, I'm content to be called a vampire. I have become accustomed to that name, and it fits, although I wish it wasn't synonymous with evil." Michaels face grew pensive and his posture rigid as he spoke of his past. It wasn't because he was upset or regretted his choice. He could never regret doing what his Father had asked of him. He was homesick. He missed his brothers and sisters. Being away from them for so long did bother him. But this was the path he had been set upon and he would see it to completion. He looked into Sam's eyes and his mood lightened. Her smile was exactly what he needed.

"I still can't wrap my head around the fact that an angel is responsible for the carnage in town. It makes sense, and I wish I could do what you've been doing, but it doesn't mesh with everything I've ever been taught. What about Dracula and Elizabeth Bathory? Were they really vampires? Or were they angels? Or were they just bullshit stories made up to scare kids?"

Michael smiled. "Oh, Vlad Tepes, or Dracula, was real enough alright. I'm convinced that it was one of my brothers. As for the Countess Bathory, I believe that she may have been one of my sisters. I believe that the count of her victims is inaccurate though. I believe that my brothers and sisters are free to feed from whomever they choose, and I am sure that they have developed a taste for innocent blood. It pains me to think that my brothers and sisters are out there committing these atrocities."

They sat in silence for several minutes, each holding the others hands. Michael finally broke the silence. "Well, that about covers my sordid past, so may I ask about yours? I must admit that I am beyond curious as to what happened in your past to leave the smudge on your soul. But, I will understand if you are not comfortable enough to share that."

Sam smiled meekly, tears already welling up in her eyes. "I am comfortable with you, Michael. And to be completely honest, that scares the living hell out of me. You're a killer. I should be terrified of you, but I'm not. I want to tell you, but before I do, I want to know what you mean exactly by my soul being stained."

Michael stood and motioned for her to follow him. "Come, take my hand and I will show you."

She did as he asked and followed him to the door. As the door inched open, Mason charged, trying to slip out of the widening crack. Michael made eye contact with the large animal and the Rottweiler slid to a halt. He then gave a sharp yip and plodded to the couch. He gave a great leap, clearing the coffee table and landing on the cushions. He plopped down in the very spot Michael had just left.

The vampire gave a knowing smile to the dog and turned his attention back to Sam.

Sam knew that her mouth was hanging open and that she was staring at him. All she could force herself to do was nod dumbly and try not to drool on herself.

He gave her a wink before he stepped outside gently pulling her behind him. She closed the door and winced as the frigid night air hit her. The temperature had dropped sharply since she had returned home. As she noticed that she could see her breath, she knew that it had to be in the thirties outside. But as she looked at Michael, no smoky plume emanated from his mouth. Something else from the vampiric legends turned out to be true.

Michael gave her a knowing glance over his shoulder, "The better to stalk you with, my dear."

He led her to her vehicle and asked her to drive to the Elkhorn Lodge. In Black Ridge, the lodge was famous for two reasons. During the Civil War, one of the bloodiest battles fought took place right outside of the lodge. It had been converted to a hospital where Union and Confederate troops were treated side by side. The Trail of Tears also crossed right beside the building.

She nodded and returned to the house to get the keys. As she returned, she unlocked the SUV and her and Michael climbed inside. She pulled from the driveway, her headlights cutting through the darkness, forcing the darkness to momentarily retreat before once again caressing them from behind. She couldn't help but smile as Michael casually rested his hand on the back of her seat, his fingers brushing through her hair.

"Why are we going to the make out spot?" She had a feeling that he would not try anything, but she was curious as to why he had chosen that spot.

"You will see when we get there. And I do hope that you aren't squeamish." He gave a foreboding chuckle and they finished the drive in silence.

As they reached the Lodge, Michael pointed to a small hill that overlooked the town. "Up there."

She pulled her SUV as close as she could to the hill without having to shift it into 4 wheel drive. Once she had placed the Tahoe in park, she killed the motor and turned off the headlights. She giggled a little, "So, should I climb into the back seat?"

Michael glanced at the rear seat and back to Sam. "As intriguing as that idea is, I think maybe we should take a short walk first. I know it is cold, but if you can trust me, it won't bother you for very long." He unleashed that charming and irresistible smile again.

Chapter 19

WILL WAS working on his seventh glass of scotch. He had been fuming all night about the decision to suspend him and Sam. Sure he was on paid leave, but there was a murderer out there that he and Sam had been busting their asses to catch. Now some other schmuck was going to get the credit for it. And to top that off, something was definitely going on with Sam. He knew in his heart that it had something to do with the murders, more than just her letting the case get under her skin. He was pretty sure that she wasn't involved, but maybe she knew who was.

His feelings for her had surfaced again. Maybe it was the alcohol, but he had to tell her how he felt. He loved her so much and would do anything for her, including taking a bullet for her or covering her beautiful ass if she did indeed have something to do with what had happened at the jail.

He got shakily to his feet and fumbled for his keys. He swayed back and forth as he fought for his balance. After a brief moment, he managed to get control of himself and stood tall. He steadied himself and continued to dig for his keys. His mind was spinning now, as thought after thought of Sam being in trouble filled his inebriated mind. At first, he did consider the possibility that she was actually involved in the murders here in town. He had quickly dismissed that thought and replaced it with another one. Maybe she was only covering for someone. But who? Sam had precious few friends outside of work. As a matter of fact, after the fiasco with her mother, she had all but become a hermit. It was rare indeed to see her out of the house socializing with anyone.

"Yeah, but isn't that what they say about serial killers? They were all reclusive and shit?" he mumbled aloud, his speech extremely slurred. With the speed of a flash flood, his temper boiled over and he swiped his arm across the counter top, knocking all of the papers and brick-a-brack onto the floor. He threw his glass at the wall before he started to cry. The tears cascaded down his cheeks and he furiously wiped them away. He was angry with himself because he had even considered such a ludicrous notion. Sam was a good and kind woman. There was no way she was mixed up in the crazy shit that was going on around town.

She had a heart of pure gold.

He grabbed the bottle of sixteen year old scotch and went to the back porch. He sat in the frigid darkness looking up at the stars.

"God, if you're listening, I need some help here. You know how much I love Samantha, right? So, here's the deal. I want nothing more than to be with her, but I'm afraid for her. I don't know why, I just feel like she's in trouble and she won't talk to me. You know what that poor woman's been through and you know I've always been there for her. So, come on man, cut me some friggin' slack here and let her see how good of a man I am." He stood, stumbled and grabbed the railing before he fell. "I was gonna go see her tonight and tell her everything that's on my mind, but I think you hid the damn keys from me." He loosed a drunken laugh. "Always heard you had a funny sense of humor. Hey, hey, you heard the one about how you made the platypus? What the hell is that thing?" Will lifted the bottle and took a long drink, "What was I talkin' bout? Oh, and that son bitch that's been killin' everyone in town. You wanna do me a huge favor and help me catch 'em? Just help me catch 'em, please God? I'll do whatever you want me to. Oh, and help me show Sam what a good guy I am. Thanks buddy!"

Will held his bottle towards the Heavens before taking another long swig from it. He stumbled back through the house before crashing into his recliner. He did not know that the bottle had slipped from his hand or that he had closed his eyes. Within seconds of falling into the chair, he was snoring loudly.

* * * * *

Sam sighed, bracing herself for the icy blast of air as she opened the door. It wasn't as bad as she thought it would be, but given enough time, the wind would find a way to dig its icy claws into her skin, cutting straight to the bone. She slammed the door and stepped in front of the large vehicle where Michael was already waiting for her. He extended his hand and this time, there was no hesitation as she grasped it. They hiked to the highest peak on the ridge and sat down.

Michael had a bit of a distraught look about him, so Sam started to pry. "What's the matter? I mean, it's colder than a pervert's pecker in a snowman's ass out here, but I'm with you. Isn't that what you wanted?"

Michael couldn't help but laugh at her idiom before giving her a pensive smile. "What I am about to ask of you, I've only done once before and that was over six thousand years ago. It is dangerous, scary and incredibly intimate. You will be closer to me than with any man you have ever met. I am giving you the choice."

Sam mulled over his words carefully. A smartass remark began to surface, but she sensed that this was indeed a very serious situation, so she pushed it back down. She smiled sweetly, scooted closer to him and laid her head on his shoulder. She then slid her hand over his leg and took hold of his hand, giving it a reassuring squeeze. "It has something to do with your blood doesn't it?"

"Again, lay off the TV. But I will admit, the series that came out, the one with Suckie, Sookie, whatever the hell her name was, actually did get several things pretty close to right. Yeah, it does involve my blood. It will allow you to see things as I do. You will hear better and your sense of smell will be tenfold what it is now. You will become stronger and you will feel more alive. You will always know when I am near. Most of the other symptoms will fade over time, but we will always be connected."

"So, we'll essentially be married?" Sam gave a small laugh.

"No, it's more like you become my servant for eternity." He gave her a serious, almost angry look, making her cringe a bit. He held the look just long enough to make her start to shiver before he gave in and started to laugh.

She playfully pushed him and joined in the laugh. After they had enjoyed the moment, she asked him, "What do I have to do?"

Michael smiled and lifted his hand. The fingernail on his pinky began to shift and quickly became elongated and very sharp. He held up his wrist and locked eyes with Sam. "Are you sure that you want to do this? If you believe the movies, books and myths, you will become mine. I will always know where you are, I will know what you are thinking, feeling and sometimes, I will even be able to see what you are seeing."

Sam looked between Michael and his exposed wrist. The butterflies had started to swarm in her stomach. She was thinking about drinking a vampire's blood. She couldn't help but wonder if she had truly gone completely mad. But as she looked at the man in front of her, she knew that this is exactly what she wanted. She just had one question. "This won't turn me, will it?"

"No, Sam. I'm not even sure that can be done. I've never tried because I would not wish a lifetime of solitude on anyone. This is a life that I think very few mortals would be able to adjust to. No, this will allow you to, in a sense, see things through my eyes." A single tear rolled down his cheek as he spoke, catching the moonlight and sparkling like the brightest of diamonds as it made its descent.

Sam reached up and wiped the tear from his cheek, giving him a tender smile as she did. "I'm ready, Michael. Let's do this."

He pressed the fingernail against the pliable flesh of his wrist and almost immediately the blood began to flow. At first, it was barely a trickle, but as he applied pressure above the wound, it began to flow more freely. He offered his arm to her and she pressed her velvety lips to his skin. His blood was sweet, not coppery or metallic. It reminded her of a homemade wine. After a few swallows, she pulled away and looked at Michael. "Is that enough?"

He smiled. "That should be plenty." He delicately wiped the corners of her mouth. As he withdrew his hand, she grabbed his wrist and took his finger in her mouth, sucking the drop of blood from it.

It took her a second to realize what she was doing, her mind telling her to stop even as she began to swirl her tongue around the tip of his finger. She had to force herself to cease the sensual act. There was just something so sexy about this moment. He had shared something so precious with her, in such a romantic setting. The moon watching their every move like a pale voyeur, here in the place she had lost her virginity not so many years ago. And he was just so damned sexy! He was the perfect specimen of masculine beauty, and he was here with her. She had often laughed at the vampire stories, how the women had given themselves so freely to the creatures of the night, falling victim to their charms. But here she was, falling head over heal for this guy after knowing him for only a few hours. It seemed like something out of a fairy tale, but here she was wanting nothing more than to spend the rest of eternity with him, well, that and to rip his clothes off and ravage him right here in the frozen grass. She pulled his finger out of her mouth and gave him an apologetic look. "I'm so sorry. I don't know what came over me."

Michael smiled, "It's the blood. You are feeling what I feel. I should be the one apologizing. Now you know exactly what I'm feeling right now."

Sam blushed a deep shade of red and felt it happening, which made her blush even deeper. "So, um, what exactly is this supposed to do, aside from turning me into an aspiring porn star?"

He tore his attention away from her and looked to the town below. "Look, and focus on them. You will begin to understand."

Sam focused her attention down the hill. She could see numerous white lights moving around. "Are those... people?"

"Yes. What you are seeing are the pure souls in your town. Now, look harder. Focus and make it come to you. Imagine that you are looking through a rifle scope and zoom in. You will start to see things even clearer."

She did as he requested and within moments, she had done exactly what he had said. Everything happened just as he described it. The building and people grew closer to her even though she had not moved. She began to see dark masses moving through the streets. Beings so dark they seemed to suck the night into themselves. "The shadows." She whispered.

"Those are the impure souls. They are people who have committed grave sins against their fellow humans. They are my prey."

Sam sat quietly, attempting to digest the information. She lived in a small town, roughly four thousand people, and from what she had just seen, over a third of them were corrupt. "How is it I didn't know this? I'm a cop for Christ's sake! I should have known that there were this many criminals in my town. How can I protect them if there are this many of them that want to hurt one another?" She had been protecting a town full of good and decent folk, or at least, that is what she had believed ten minutes ago. Now she saw them for the evil, sadistic beings they really were.

"Do not blame yourself, Sam. You are, after all, only human. Humans have a tendency to look the other way when they see something that upsets them. If it isn't relevant to their lives, they ignore it. You see this evil every day, yet you turn a blind eye to it. I see it every day and it breaks my heart that your species is so callous. I have fought so hard to try and help humanity evolve, but they just keep going backwards. They steal, lie, cheat and kill each other for some menial personal gain."

Sam was livid now, her anger threatening to boil over. Her body began to shudder as she balled her hands into fists. "That's just bullshit. There are good people in this world. I know it. But how can so many of them, the ones that I thought were good, be such slime balls?" She tried to focus on their faces, but all she could see were either light or dark silhouettes.

Michael stood and helped her to her feet as she began to cry. He pulled her into his arms and she rested her face against his broad chest. "Do you see now why I have never even tried to turn someone? To live with this knowledge would drive most people insane. That's why, if you wish, I will help you forget what you have seen tonight. But before we do that, did you see any shades of grey?"

Sam sobbed into his chest and uttered a muffled "No" into the fabric of his shirt.

"That is why you are so unique, Sam. You are a little different than most I have met. The fact that you are by far one of the most beautiful women I have ever seen is a bonus. So, while the tears are already falling, would you be willing to share with me what happened?"

She pulled away from his comforting embrace and for the first time since she had drank his blood, she noticed that she was not cold. She didn't even register that it was the slightest bit chilly. She wiped the tears away and stared at the town. "I'm sure it's because of what happened with my mother. Mom had always been a bit unstable, mentally that is. And when dad got back from Vietnam, well, he wasn't quite right either from what my grandma had told me. He was always checking the doors and windows to make sure they were locked. He wouldn't go to bed until he had searched the house three or four times and I guess that drove mom even crazier. I was born in 1981, so I wasn't around for most of this. Growing up was no picnic. They had gotten better, dad had mostly adjusted to life away from the jungle, but mom had steadily gotten worse. She was diagnosed with schizophrenia and bi-polar disorder, not a good combination.

I got married right out of high school and moved out, mainly to get away from her. Don't get me wrong, I loved my mom, but she could get downright mean sometimes. But, as I moved in with Jackson, I found out real quick that things weren't so bad at home.

He became increasingly violent. He beat me relentlessly because the bacon was too crispy, or not crispy enough. He hit me in the mouth with an ashtray because I didn't turn down the sheets one night. Long story short, he came home drunk one night, classic huh? He started hitting be because of some imaginary transgression on my part. It was that night that I realized that I didn't have to let this keep happening. I grabbed my cast iron skillet off the stove and nailed him with it. He dropped like a sack of potatoes. Turns out, I hit him in the temple and killed him right then and there. The scary part is that I felt nothing, no remorse, no regret, nothing. But I couldn't stand to live in the house anymore, so I moved back in with Mom and Dad until I could get it sold.

I was twenty one and mom had gone completely off her rocker. I started police academy shortly after I moved in, thinking that I would be able to help other women like me. You know, before it escalated to where it had with me and Jackson. Anyway, after the academy, I started patrols and the call finally came in, a domestic disturbance at mom and dad's house. I took the call because I knew I could talk her down. I'd been able to in the past, so why not tonight? I got to the house to find mom in the yard swinging around a butcher knife. The front of her nightgown was soaked in blood. Dad was standing on the porch holding a towel around his arm. Mom had cut him up pretty good. Mom was screaming about the tree people wanting to eat her. I tried to talk her down, tried to get her to give me the knife but she wouldn't." Sam began to sob uncontrollably. Her whole body consumed by the violent tremors as she tried to finish the story. "I killed her, Michael. I killed my mom."

Michael was a damn good judge of character and he knew that something horrible had happened to her, but this was unimaginable. He had no idea of the magnitude of the secret she was carrying with her. He tried to hug her, he needed to console her but she held him at bay.

"Not yet, let me finish. Mom came at me with the knife. I knew she was crazy, but she had completely snapped. She stabbed me twice before I halfway got control of the knife. She slammed into me and we both went down. She landed on top of me, but the fight was over. She just looked into my eyes and told me she loved me. I thought she had come to her senses and pushed her off of me. The knife..." Sobs shook her again. "The knife had penetrated her left lung and her heart. When we hit the ground, the knife wedged and she stabbed herself. My mom died in my arms because I didn't know what I was doing. If I had more training, I could have kept that from happening."

She launched herself at Michael, wrapping her arms tightly around his waist. He returned the hug, gently crushing her and whispering into her ear, "Sam, it was not your fault. Nothing you could have done, no amount of training could have prepared you for that. It was just what was meant to be. It is a part of your past that has molded you into the woman I love. Even still, I'm so very sorry."

She ran her fingers through his long, silky hair and felt the anguish flowing out of her faster than the tears she cried. She was shivering now, but it wasn't due to the cold. Michael was right. The icy winter air no longer affected her at all. She pulled away from him and locked eyes. She inched forward, her eyes pleading with him.

As he looked into her beautiful green eyes, he hoped that he was reading the signs correctly and he leaned in to complete the connection between them. When their lips touched, it was if the whole world stopped. Everything around them faded into nothingness. Even the sounds of the night dissipated. All that was left was the beating of two hearts. Pleasurable tingles exploded through their bodies as their lips touched, racing from the tip of their heads to the tips of their toes.

His hands slid to the small of her back and pulled her tight against him as their tongues danced together.

The kiss became more passionate, hungry and needful. Her hands were feverishly running up and down his back, her fingernails becoming insistent at the fabric of his shirt.

She ceased the kiss to lean forward and nibble on his earlobe while whispering, "Is the blood doing this to me? Is that why I need you so badly right now?" Her words were barely discernable through her frenzied breathing.

Michael was also in a frenzied state. He had never felt the touch of a woman like this and found that he was losing control of his urges. He knew that he was destined to walk the Earth alone, yet he had dared to hope that maybe he had found his soulmate. Maybe he would be allowed to love just this once. She had experienced so much heartache in such a short amount of time. She had been forced to endure the worst that humanity had to offer and despite that had grown into a wonderful and compassionate woman. She put herself at risk every night to try and keep the dregs of humanity off the streets. Now, she had accepted him, even though she had originally viewed him as a threat. He did find himself wondering what she would do now. After all, she was the lead investigator on his case.

"Yes, Sam, it is the blood. You are feeling the desire that I have to be with you." Michael's face was flush now. He knew it was wrong to lust after her the way he was, but after so long on earth, it was only natural that he started to feel some of the things that humans did; anger, jealousy, lust, desire and hopefully even love. "I am sorry. We need to stop this before it goes any further. I should drive you back to your house."

Sam's breathing was intense now and her body was on fire. Her legs started to quiver as she thought about driving home and what she was praying would happen when they made it home. Her hands slid up his chest and she could feel the incredibly chiseled muscles under the thin fabric of his shirt.

Michael could see that she was losing herself to the blood fever. He knew it was wrong. If he let her do what she intended, it would be the same thing as date rape. "Sam, we can't do this. You are under the influence of my blood, you're not yourself. I can't do this tonight."

Sam was kissing his neck now, nibbling on his earlobe again as she spoke. "After all the years of stories telling me that vampires had no morals and were completely sex crazed maniacs, I find out they are real, and not only do they have morals, but they're prude too? What the hell? Michael, I need you, I have to have you right now. So, you can either take me home and to my bedroom, or you can watch while I take care of myself."

A wicked smile curved his lips. "Mmm, that sounds very intriguing. I would love to have a front row seat to that show."

Her hands slithered down to his crotch, caressing, touching and tugging insistently. Her eyes silently begging him to take her and he finally caved. "Alright, Sam, I give up. Let's go. I'm driving."

She fished the keys from her pocket before tossing them to Michael and high tailing it to the passenger side. Michael quickly opened the door and fired up the engine. He threw the SUV into reverse and gave it a little too much gas, causing the tires to briefly kick up dust and dried leaves before lurching backward. As he jammed on the brakes, the vehicle slid to a stop. He dropped the shifter into drive and eased down on the accelerator until he pulled back onto the roadway.

He accelerated heavily as he turned onto the road and the vehicle lurched sideways as the rear tires fought for grip. Michael corrected for it, and the vehicle was soon rocketing down the highway.

Sam was writhing in the passenger, almost completely consumed by her own passion. It was almost too much for him to handle. Driving at the rate of speed was proving to be challenging enough and with this woman providing such a relentless distraction, it was a much more difficult task than it should have been.

She had already started to disrobe, slowly unbuttoning her blouse. Her breathy sighs threatened to drive him over the edge of sanity. His foot crushed the accelerator and the motor roared even louder. Michael's keen sense of vision and his superb reflex's made the trip a very short one. However, it was not an easy trip for him. His mind constantly wrestled with his morals and his eyes repeatedly roaming over to enjoy the show that was being provided in the passenger seat.

Samantha was intoxicated with his blood and for him to make love to her in this state would be taking advantage of her and it bothered him. However, she was incredibly beautiful and she was definitely into him. She was into him even before she ingested his blood. He could not ignore the implications of his actions though. He was completely torn. Never before had he wanted anything as badly as he did now. Within the last couple of miles of the trip, he decided that he would see how it played out. If it was not meant to happen, it wouldn't.

They arrived at Sam's home and Michael pulled into her parking spot. While she all but jumped from the vehicle while it was still in motion, he waited until it came to a complete stop and took his time putting it in park and shutting the engine off. He watched her through the windshield as she ran to the front door and tried to shoulder it open. He took a deep breath as he anticipated the worst. He opened the door and as he stepped from the vehicle, he tossed the keys to Sam. She caught them and impatiently fumbled with them trying to get the door open.

As she opened the door, she reached down and absently patted Mason on the head before she began ripping off her clothing. She took the stairs two at a time, leaping up to her bedroom and tossing her clothes down as she went. By the time she reached her bedroom door, she was fully nude. She threw herself onto the bed and could not keep her hands still. She rubbed her arms causing goose bumps to rise. She soon slid her hand down her legs, her hands kneading her taut flesh. She ran them up and down her stomach and over her breasts as she awaited her lover.

Michael entered the room. He had not been so hasty in removing his clothing. He took his jacket off and draped it over his arm. But that was the only article of clothing he removed. He stopped as he saw Sam and the spectacle she was making. Her breathing was already erratic and she was writhing on the bed and staring at him with so much passion and need in her eyes. He pulled off his shirt and slowly walked to the bed. His muscles rippled as he undressed.

Sam watched with wide eyed wonder as he undressed. His jeans fell to the floor and he stepped out of his boots. She reached out and grabbed his wrists and pulled him to the bed. She wrapped her arms around his neck and kissed him with a fiery passion. Her fingernails dug into his back as she tried to pull him even closer to her. She grabbed his buttocks and pulled him tightly against her thighs as their tongues danced together like serpents.

Michael shifted their position so that he was on top of her. He began to kiss her neck, gently grazing her soft skin with his fangs. Her breath caught in her throat when she felt the needle sharp teeth touch her, but was quickly moaning in pleasure on the brink of orgasm. He kissed her shoulders and slowly moved down her chest. His tongue darted against the most sensitive parts of her body as he toyed with her. He couldn't help but smile his long-toothed grin as her body began to convulse beneath him. He slowly kissed a blazing trail down her stomach. His teeth grazed against her thighs as he planted kisses up and down her long legs, lightly preceding each kiss with his tongue. He brushed his lips against her, his breath hot against her skin. While one hand slipped behind her neck and gently pulled at her hair his other hand slid up and down her chest as he placed his head between her thighs and his tongue darted against the sensitive button hidden in the velvet folds.

Sam arched her back as the most intense sensation she had ever felt coursed through her body. Every hair stood on end as his fingers traced over her body. In only a few short seconds, she had reached the most powerful climax she had ever had. Her whole body pulsated with pleasure as she lay on the bed, staring into the eyes of this incredible being. She unsteadily reached for the stereo remote and turned the machine on. The opening strains of 'You're in Love' by Ratt poured from the speakers and Sam gave a breathless giggle. "If you keep this up, this song may end up being prophetic. My God, you are incredible." She gave a contented sigh and ran her finger lovingly through his hair. He slid up her body, his powerful legs pressing against her as he moved, and he kissed her. The kiss was hungry, passionate and almost violent in nature.

Sam felt as if her skin might burst into flames at any second and her body tingled as Michael continued to torment her with pleasure. He rolled her over so that now she was on her stomach. He began kissing her back. His movements were slow and deliberate, designed to heighten the pleasure and make her beg for more.

As his mouth touched her hip, he gently bit her. His teeth pressed hard enough to leave two small puncture marks on her ivory skin. He gently kissed the soft globes of her buttocks, lightly dragging his tongue across them. He slowly ran his fingernails down her back, causing more goosebumps to form. She shivered as he positioned himself on top of her and pressed himself against her buttocks. He gently nibbled her earlobe and traced its shape with his tongue.

Sam was frenzied now. Her blood felt as if it was boiling and she needed him inside her. She forced herself to flip over underneath his weight. She laced her fingers into his long hair and pulled his head backward, exposing his neck. Before she realized what she was doing, she had bared her teeth and clamped down on his throat. Her teeth were of course not sharp enough to break skin, but Michael did jump as he felt this new sensation. Sam worked her hips against him, trying to take him inside her. He obliged and she almost screamed in pleasure as he entered her. Explosions of sheer ecstasy slammed through her body. They moved together in an eager rhythm. She climaxed repeatedly as they moved against each other.

Michael finally found his release. His body tensed as they simultaneously reached climax. He rolled onto his side beside her and laid his arm across her nude and quivering body.

She turned her head to the side to look at him and kissed him again. This time, it was the soft and tender kiss of a woman in love. She ran her hand up and down his arm before gathering up the courage to ask. "Michael, if you're an angel, where are your wings? Did you have to give them up when you fell from Heaven?"

Michael kissed her shoulder. "No, the wings are somewhat... Metaphysical. Kind of like an imaginary friend. Now, in Heaven, you can see them very well, but here on Earth, they work a bit differently. Sometimes, if the moonlight catches them just right, you can catch a glimpse of them if I have fed very well. It's always a fleeting image though. I can always feel them though, they are always there. Maybe one day, you will get to see them yourself." He leaned up and kissed her mouth again.

"Can you fly?"

Michael nodded, "To an extent. I can fly for short distances, so traveling over large bodies of water is out of the question. I'm a vampire after all, not Superman."

Sam laughed as she pictured him in a pair of red boots and blue spandex pants. "Wow. That was not an image I needed in my head."

"What is it you find so amusing?"

Sam laughed even harder. "I was just picturing you in the superman getup." Her words burst out between bouts of laughter.

Michael stood up on the bed and making fists, placed them on his hips and turned his head to the side, striking the perfect superman pose, in the buff. Sam was laughing hysterically now. He gave her a rather comical look and asked her in a perfectly calm voice, "Excuse me, Miss? Have you seen my cape? I'm feeling a bit of a draft."

Sam was holding her sides and gasping for breath between laughs. "Oh... God... Please... Stop!"

Michael was laughing now too. He felt great after all these years of solitude. To finally have someone he could wrap his arms around. Someone he could laugh with. Someone he could love.

He lay back down beside her and pulled her close as the laughter began to subside.

She was trying to breathe deeply in order to calm down. "Oh wow, Michael. I haven't laughed that hard in years. And I have no idea why the hell that was so funny either." She giggled again. "I have a rather forward request." She could feel the heat rising in her cheeks again.

Michael was perplexed. "What is it you would like, my beautiful Sam?"

"I want you to stay here with me. Sleep beside me and hold me today."

He smiled wider than he had ever smiled. He had seen numerous humans in love and he had seen their reactions when something made them extremely happy. But never in a million years had he expected to be the one with the dopey grin on his face. "I would be honored, Sam. But on one condition; you let me cook breakfast."

Sam snuggled closer to him and mumbled "I would love that." She closed her eyes and started to think about what it would be like to live with a vampire. Would it be like the movies portrayed, or maybe more like the series she was addicted to? The only thing that she was sure of is that she would grow older and he would not. She closed her eyes and lost herself in the post-orgasmic bliss as she wrapped her arms tightly around the man that was made for her.

Her soulmate.

Chapter 20

MICHAEL SMILED and quietly watched Sam drift off to sleep. It would be a few hours before he finally succumbed to unconsciousness, so he was left alone with his thoughts. He closed his eyes and the images came. Memories of the past, lives he had taken and the thoughts he had stolen from his victims. Suddenly his happiness seemed only fleeting.

Darkness had fallen swiftly upon the town of Chicago. Michael had watched this man for several nights as he had entered the church and prayed for forgiveness and went about his nightly routines. His name was Charles Spicoli. Charles was in his mid-forties, overweight but overall, he was a pleasant looking man. His soul told Michael a different story though. As Michael looked at him, he saw nothing but the purest black, pure evil. In this man, Michael had found his first dilemma, the man was evil and he had done some atrocious things throughout his life yet he prayed for forgiveness every night. So, was this man supposed to be one of his victims or was he to be left alone? Because of this, he had decided to follow this man to see if there was reason to kill him.

Several nights passed with the exact same routine, always ending at the church right around the corner from his apartment. After he prayed, he ventured to his apartment and went straight to bed. On the fourth day of surveillance, Charles did not go to the church and Michael followed in the shadows.

This time, he hailed a cab and headed east, to the outskirts of the city near the Belmont Harbor. He paid the cab driver and walked to a small house that looked abandoned. Michael followed him into the house and watched as he opened a secret hatch in the staircase. The bottom four steps lifted up to reveal another stairwell that descended deep underground.

Michael knew that he was about to find his answer. He followed Charles down the stairs and into the long corridor lined with metal doors. It reminded him of a solitary confinement wing of a maximum security prison. Through the thick steel doors he could hear whimpering, sounds that made him think of abused animals. The smell of human excrement was almost unbearable, but he pushed on so that he might find the secret that had made this man's soul so foul.

Finally, Charles stopped in front of a door and fished a key ring out of his pocket. With a dexterity that seemed out of place, he shoved the key into the pad lock that secured the door and deftly opened it. As the door swung open, he took up a defensive position as if he expected something to rush him. His hand flashed forward and caught the throat of a young boy, maybe thirteen years old, as the child tried to rush past him.

Michael had seen enough. He willed Charles to see him and started briskly towards him. The large man turned and without a word pulled a knife from a concealed belt sheath and placed the blade against the boy's throat. The sadistic grin that crept across the pedophile's face was enough to make Michael's skin crawl.

Michael stopped and spoke, his voice low and calm as he tried to make the mental connection, "Charles, you want to put the knife down and let the boy go back into his cell."

Charles' face twisted with an inhuman anger and he jerked the blade across the child's throat. Blood poured from the wound. Michael had only a split second to see the body fall to the floor before Charles was on him, driving the double edged dagger into his heart. Michael grimaced as he felt the blade pierce his chest.

It was a bad wound and would have been fatal to a human. He grabbed Charles by the throat and shoved him backwards. The large man stumbled over the body of the child and fell to the floor. Michael stood up, and in true vampire form, slowly pulled the dagger from his chest. He studied the blade closely before giving it a 'Dracula-esq' lick, drawing the blade slowly across his tongue before tossing it aside.

Charles' face had now contorted into a look of pure terror. Michael lumbered towards the murderous pedophile, glaring at him with all the contempt of a man watching a cockroach scurry over his food. Charles was trying desperately to get his feet under him but fear had more or less paralyzed him and he could not find the strength needed to stand and run.

Michael now stood over the sniveling man, "You know what I am and why I am here, don't you Charles?"

Charles shook his head 'no'.

"I am death. I am your judgement. Human kind suffers enough without monsters like you prowling unnoticed through their masses. It is time for your wretched life to end." Quick as lightening, he reached out and snatched Charles by the throat. He lifted him off the ground and slammed him into the wall. As the explosive sound reverberated through the hallway, several high-pitched screams followed. Michael's stomach churned at the thought of how many children this man had abducted. Judging by the sound of it, there were at least ten more.

Michael was now furious. He allowed his rage to guide his actions. He repeatedly slammed this waste of flesh into the wall, splitting the back of his head open. He gave Charles a violent toss and flung him further down the hallway. His body hit the floor and rolled haphazardly, landing in a twisted and awkward position. He tried to push himself to his feet, but he was too dazed from the beating he had just taken.

With a movement too fast for the human eye to follow, Michael was on him again, his fist smashing into his face. He dug his fingers into Charles' ribs, piercing flesh and snapping several of the thick bones. Michael flung him into another wall eliciting more screams from the terrified children. Charles was trying to scream but all that came forth was a muffled gurgle. His breath came in short bursts and blood bubbled from the corner of his mouth indicating that one of the ribs the vampire had just broken had punctured a lung when Charles hit the wall.

A savage grin crept over Michael's face as he slowly closed the distance between himself and the murderous pedophile. His hand shot forward and grabbed the front of Charles' shirt, lifting him so that they were looking eye to eye. "No amount of prayer could wash away these sins. It is an affront to me that you would even consider stepping inside a church." Anger dripped from his words like venom. He opened his mouth, revealing the dagger-like teeth. In a flash he had clamped down on Charles' neck and drank deeply.

The man's blood was incredibly nourishing. It had been several days since he had last fed and finding an individual as evil as this man was truly a gift. In a matter of seconds he had almost drained Charles dry. He stopped drinking and staunched the flow of blood with his hand. "Your time hasn't come yet, monster. You have so much more pain to endure."

Tears were rolling down the fat man's cheek as he shook his head no.

"Oh, yes, much more suffering." Michael slammed his hand in Charles' stomach again and again. The pain must have been unbearable. Michael had completed the mental link between them and was forcing his victim to remain conscious.

With his right hand still grasping the front of Charles' shirt, Michael grabbed his right arm and gave a quick and powerful tug. The sound of bone snapping echoed through the concrete hallway. With another sharp pull, the flesh tore and the arm fell free. He brought his knee up into Charles' groin causing the man to grunt and attempt to double over.

Michael slammed his left hand into the broken man's chest. Although there was very little blood pumping through his veins, he still managed to cough some up as the air was forced from his already pulverized lungs.

The vampire lifted him eye to eye once again and grasped his head with both hands. He stared into the monsters eyes before he gave a quick twist and separated the man's head from his body. He tossed it to the side and set his attention on the padlocked doors.

He spread his will around the room, searching the rooms for children and found seventeen of them locked behind the doors. He took control of their minds as he went from door to door, tearing the locks away and swinging each door open. Each door revealed either a pre-teen boy or girl clad only in underwear. When all was said and done, there were twelve girls and five boys, minus the one that Michael had been unable to save.

He ushered the children outside making sure that none of them could see what was in the corridor, his mind forcing them to see only the pale grey walls. They all waited upstairs while he phoned the Chicago PD. Once he was sure that the children would be taken care of, he quickly disappeared into the night.

None of the children would even remember seeing him or how they had escaped from that hell on Earth.

Chapter 21

WILL AWOKE with a nasty taste in his mouth. His head was pounding and he felt greasy. He looked at the clock and realized he had slept for thirteen hours. It was just after six in the evening.

He stood shakily and headed for the shower. While he waited for the water to warm up, he brushed his teeth and popped two Aspirin into his mouth. He tilted his head sideways and took a drink from the faucet to wash them down. He looked at himself in the mirror and grimaced at what he saw. His eyes were bloodshot and sported dark circles underneath. He had not shaved in two days and the growth of hair on his face made him look ten times more haggard than he believed he should appear. As he picked up the razor, he decided that he just didn't care enough at the moment to go through all that work.

He stepped into the shower and washed away the alcoholic sweat and the remnants of last night's escapades. He felt a little better as he stepped from the shower and got dressed.

Back in the kitchen, he grabbed a bottle of Gatorade from the refrigerator and greedily gulped down the contents. His mind turned back to Sam and he decided that he would give it a little while before he went to see her. He needed to talk to her about all this that had been happening lately. He had also finally decided to tell her how he felt about her. He grabbed the bottle of antacids and took two of them.

"One day, William, you'll get smart enough to leave that shit alone." He grabbed a towel and went back to clean up the mess he had made last night when he had dropped the bottle of scotch.

After cleaning, he sat back down in his chair and tried to relax. He had been on edge since the murders started and even more so since he and Sam had been suspended. He flipped on the TV and surfed through the channels. He had no interest in watching anything, really. He was just doing it to attempt to keep his mind off everything else going on.

He sighed deeply and closed his eyes. He fought to clear his mind, but he kept circling back to thoughts of his lovely partner and what their relationship used to be like. He could still hear her laugh, even though he had not heard it outside his memory in several years. She had become reclusive and private lately, even more so than normal.

He wanted to bring her out of her shell, to make her get back out in public and enjoy life, to forget the events of the past and live for the now. "Now if I only had a damn clue as to how to do that." He sighed again and turned off the TV. He glanced around his house and decided that he had some cleaning to do. He had allowed it to become a pig pen. He started loading dishes into the dishwasher and wiping down the countertops. Once he found his keys, he decided, he would go ahead and head over to Sam's to have that personal conversation with her.

* * * * *

Michael awoke as the moon began to peek through the lace curtains that adorned the windows of Sam's bedroom. She had a very classy setup. The bed was dressed with white satin sheets and a down feather comforter that was white with light blue accents. The headboard and footboard were both made of antiqued brass. He guessed that they had to have belonged to her grandmother as you just didn't see craftsmanship like this anymore.

The room itself was painted in a pale lilac color. All-in-all, it was a beautiful room, albeit a little on the feminine side for his tastes. He turned his attention to the beautiful redhead sleeping next to him. Her breathing was slow and soft. He watched her sleep for quite a while before she opened those exquisite emerald eyes.

"Good morning, beautiful."

She smiled back at him. "Good morning, you sexy beast. Did you ever find your cape?" she chuckled again.

Michael smiled as he noticed how her smile seemed to illuminate the room. "No, my dear, I have decided that the world needs a superhero sans clothing." He shared in her laughter for a moment. "Sam, I must confess, being with you, I feel as giddy as a child on Christmas morning. I am baffled by this feeling."

"I feel the same way, Michael. I really do. I was thinking last night while we were making love about how just a couple of days ago, I wanted your head on a pike. And tonight, you're here in my bed. After watching all of those movies about vampires, you'd think that I'd be immune to your charms. I remember thinking that it was all bullshit, that I could never fall in love with a creature like that. Turns out I was the one full of bullshit." Her face flushed red as she spoke.

Michael lovingly caressed her cheek. "I know what you mean. I've probably seen all the same films you have, and I called bullshit too. I just hope that this is meant to be." He leaned forward and kissed her passionately.

Sam could feel him becoming aroused as they kissed and she slid her hand down his stomach. "I see someone else is awake. Does this mean he wants to play?"

Michael shifted his position so that he had her pinned and pressed himself against the definition of her womanhood. She gasped as he entered her. "Does this answer your question?" he asked in a seductive, breathy tone.

They made love for three hours before they both lie exhausted in each other's arms, spent and in post orgasmic bliss.

Sam was all smiles as she looked at Michael again. "How would you feel about taking a shower with me?"

"That is an enticing idea, but I thought you were going to let me cook you breakfast."

"Breakfast can wait. I want your sexy ass in that shower, pronto. I know it seems stupid, but I have to spend as much time as I can, doing normal shit before things start getting all weird again." She looked at the floor as if she had something to be ashamed of.

Michael tenderly cupped his hand under her chin and lifted her face to look him eye to eye. His eyes shimmered as he spoke, "Don't be ashamed of anything that your heart desires. I would do anything to make you happy, because being with you is all I need to make me happy. As for the shower, I'd love to bathe you."

As they made their way into bathroom, they passed Mason in the hallway. He looked at them with a dopey grin, chuffed and lay his head back down.

Sam turned the water on to heat up and hugged Michael from behind, her hands crawling over his splendid body.

She stepped into the shower first and Michael picked up the body loofa and the soap. Sam gave him a quizzical look. With an ear to ear smile, Michael began to wash her. He took his time, savoring every curve of her body. He washed her entire body before he turned her so that he could wash her hair.

After he had thoroughly cleaned her and explored every inch of her body, she smiled wickedly and began to bathe him, paying special attention to a particular area of his body. Her hands caressed him and explored every taut muscle. To her, this was probably the most sensual thing she had ever experienced.

After they finished their shower, Michael started to get dressed but Sam stopped him. "Let me wash those for you. Come here. Check Daddy's closet. He was a little bigger than you, but everything should fit you okay."

Michael looked through her father's clothes and found a pair of Levi's and a t-shirt with the words 'Mopar or No Car!' sprawled across the back. "Dodge fan?" he asked as he held up the shirt.

Sam, while still wrapped in her towel laughed. "He wouldn't drive anything else, said he'd rather drive off a cliff than drive anything other than Dodge."

She walked downstairs still in her towel and fumbled around in the coat closet. She returned upstairs carrying a leather biker jacket. It had seen numerous rides, and some might say that it had seen better days, but to Sam, it was perfect. "I know it looks pretty rough, but it would mean a lot to me if you would wear this."

Michael was truly shocked. "Sam, I would be honored. It means a lot to me that you would even consider letting me wear this. I will admit, I will have to leave it with you, from time to time. I'd hate to ruin it."

"What do you...? Oh, I get it. Why don't you just stay here? I mean, do you have a place? Or, you know what? Nevermind."

"Sam, I would love to stay with you." He grabbed her and hugged her tightly. They finished getting dressed together and went down to the kitchen. She showed him where everything was and took a seat at the table to watch the man of her dreams cook her breakfast.

Chapter 22

ROSA HAD been awake for a few hours waiting on her daughter and granddaughter to come visit her again. She had enjoyed being able to be a part of their lives again, even if it was from a hospital bed. Throughout her life she had only a few regrets. If it had not been for Frank, she never would have had her beautiful daughter and the family that she now had would not exist. The only regret that she had is that she had never stood up to Frank. She had allowed him to continue to do the nasty things he had and she never had the courage to stop him.

The door opened and Sarah and Hailey stepped through. Most of the tubes and wires had been removed the day before and Rosa was feeling a lot better. Though her throat was still raw and her voice very hoarse, she could at least talk to her family. "How are my beautiful girls, today?"

Sarah and Hailey both smiled. Hailey ran to her grandma's side and grabbed her hand. "I'm doing good Grandma! It's good to hear you talking! I brought my Kindle so I could show you a new game I got. It's called Five Nights at Freddy's. It's really scary."

Rosa made a scared face and pretended to shiver. The movement caused her to wince as pain shot through her body. She forced a smile and told her granddaughter, "I'm looking forward to it. It's not too scary is it? I don't want to pee the bed."

Hailey laughed at that and even Sarah found herself joining in the laughter. She had never expected her mom to come up with something like that. She continued to grin ear to ear as she listened to her daughter describe the intricate workings of the game. Rosa, although black and blue and broken in so many ways, tried her best to keep up with the conversation. She finally had to give her mother a reprieve. "Hailey, honey? Your grandma is on some heavy duty medicine to help with the pain and it makes her really sleepy. We probably need to let her get some rest."

Rosa tried to push herself up in the bed to appear a little stronger for them. "Oh, no dear, I'm fine, really. I am enjoying every second of this. She is such a wonderful young woman."

Hailey continued to prattle on about her game as Rosa and Sarah exchanged a look that told the other, 'everything is going to be all right.'

While they were talking with Hailey, the doctor came in and looked over Rosa's chart. "Mrs. De Lucca, looks like you'll be able to go home in a couple of days. You are going to have to be on bed rest, which means absolutely no getting out of bed. You are going to need someone to help you with your daily tasks." He gave a meaningful glance to Sarah. "Until you are able to move about with little or no pain, that is. Now, I'm going to prescribe something for the pain and some antibiotics. Any questions?"

Rosa shook her head, "No doctor. The nurses had pretty much filled me in on everything else. I'll just be happy to be back in my own bed."

The doctor smiled as he replaced the chart at the food of the bed and left the room. Hailey couldn't contain her excitement anymore. "Grandma? I'll come live with you and take care of you. I'll even cook. I make a mean peanut butter and jelly!" They all three burst out in laughter and they knew everything would be fine.

* * * * *

Michael prepared Buckwheat Crepes with Sautéed apples and gruyere cheese. He had to ad lib a few ingredients, as Sam was not prepared for a five-star chef in her kitchen. However, he was pleased with his creations and happily served them.

Sam was astonished. She had definitely found someone worth keeping around for a while.

He was incredible in bed, very courteous and he could cook. Yep, he was a keeper.

She took her first bite and was in culinary heaven. "Oh my God, Michael! This is amazing!" She tried to savor each bite as the flavors were unlike anything she had ever tasted.

Michael smiled, "I'm pleased you like it." He fixed his own plate and sat down across from her. They engaged in light conversation, even though Sam was pretty well occupied with doting on him and his cooking prowess. After they finished eating, she helped clear the table and Michael started running the water to wash the dishes.

Sam grabbed his hands. "Michael, you made breakfast, and I must admit that at one point in my life, I would have said that it was better than sex. But now that I've met you, I can never say that again." She paused to bite her bottom lip. "Listen, you cooked, I clean. That's the way it works, period."

"As you wish." He turned the water off and gave her a quick kiss. He took a seat at the table again.

"Michael, why did you leave that message in Enochian at the De Lucca Residence?"

"I didn't want you to think that I was just a murderer. I wanted you to know that there was more to this story than what you were seeing. I wanted you to open your eyes to the world around you and see that not everything is as it seems. Well, that and I really enjoyed messing with you." He gave her a wicked grin.

She strolled over to the chair and straddled him. "You are a mess, you know that?" And just why the hell am I so smitten with you?"

As Michael opened his mouth to answer her, Sam's cell phone rang. She picked it up and looked at the caller ID. She was a bit surprised to see the Chief of Police calling her. She held her finger to her lips and answered. "Yeah, Chief. What can I do for you?"

His voice was somewhat apologetic as he spoke, yet held a tinge of suspicion. "Sam, the state boys want to ask you a few questions as soon as you get a chance to make it down here. But we need you in here tonight. They've just about finished their investigation and I don't think you're a suspect anymore. I think they're just trying to tie up loose ends. Listen, they determined that Billings died about forty-five minutes *after* you signed for your weapon, so they know you were nowhere near the cell. To top it off, they found two of those long hairs that keep showing up and those funky teeth marks. Also, there was some kind of symbols on the door. Your guy hit the jail, Sam. We're gonna need you on this one so get your ass down here and get this taken care of. Okay?"

She cut her eyes at her newfound lover, "Symbols on the cell door huh? Did you send them over to the U of A?

"Sure did, and we've already got a translation back. It's some old language, inknockianan, eenocheean. Shit, something like that. Anyways, from what professor what's his name said, it means '*Because you cannot.*' Now, can you tell me what the fuck that means?"

"Enochian, Chief, and no. I have no friggin' clue as to what that might mean." She cut her eyes at Michael again. "This whole case has me baffled. Have you looked at my notes/ there is nothing to go on except for the hair and now these two scenes with the symbols painted in the victim's blood."

The Chief seemed to be reaching the level of frustration she had just a couple of days ago. "Well, you're cleared to return to work after you finish the state interview. So, enjoy the remainder of your day off. I want you back in here tomorrow night. I'm gonna give Will a call and tell him the same. Get rested up and get ready to get back to work. I'm getting tired of getting hounded about how we haven't caught this guy yet."

Sam was smiling as she hung up the phone. "Alright, Michael, how in the hell am I supposed to go back to work and cover your ass when every cop in the state is looking for you?"

Michael gave her a cunning grin, "And just what exactly do you have to lead them to me? A few hairs and some abstract and cryptic messages painted in blood?"

"That's just it, we don't have anything and now I'm supposed to go back and try to figure out how to capture you, the man I love. You've killed people, but you're doing your 'job.' I know I should turn a blind eye, pretend that I don't know anything, but I'm a cop. It's my job to bring you to justice. What the hell am I supposed to do?"

"This is your choice to make, Sam. I cannot tell you what you should do here. All I can do is support you with whichever choice you do make."

Sam kissed him, "You really are amazing. I'll have to work through this one on my own, but I'll cross that bridge when I get there. So, what do you want to do tonight?"

He gave her that wicked grin again, "To be perfectly honest, I just want to lie in bed and cuddle while watching TV."

Sam returned the grin, "Sure, sounds good. Sounds very good."

They were holding hands as they ascended the stairs. As they reached the bedroom, they undressed each other and slipped under the covers. Sam didn't bother with the television. She never even had a chance to pick up the remote. Michael embraced her tightly and kissed her passionately. She could feel the need in his kiss. His hands found her breasts, his fingers deftly teasing her nipple to hardened points. Her breath was already becoming ragged as he stoked her inner fires.

Her hands explored his body again before wrapping around his manhood. She began to stroke him, trying to drive him over the edge before they began to make love. As they locked in a lovers embrace, Michael stopped and lifted his head. "Sam, you've got company."

She stood and quickly pulled on a pair of sweat pants and a hoodie before heading downstairs.

Chapter 23

As Will pulled into Sam's driveway, he decided that maybe this was a mistake. He started to put his vehicle into reverse when he saw her peeking through the window at him.

Too late now, he had been spotted. He shifted into park and turned off the ignition. Taking a deep breath, he stepped out of his truck and tried to build up the courage to do what he had come here to do. Sam opened the door and called to him, asking if he was okay. "Yeah, Sam, I'm alright. I just needed to talk to you for a bit." He walked as calmly as he could to her doorway.

"Will, this isn't really a good time. Can we talk later?" She seemed a little agitated, more than usual.

"I promise this won't take long. I've just got to get a few things off my chest. Please?"

Sam glanced over her shoulder as she opened the door. Will was pretty sure now that she had company, even though he hadn't noticed anyone or seen a car in the drive. "Come on in. But only for a minute, Will. I just want to relax and try to keep my mind off the shit storm that's been going on in town. Did the chief call you? I'm supposed to go talk to the State Troopers tonight."

"Alright, Sam, five minutes." He stepped inside and he was sure he could smell men's cologne, some sort of leather scent. But he wasn't absolutely certain. "Do you have company? Anyone I know?"

Sam's face flushed as she answered, "What does it matter, Will? We went on a couple of dates and things didn't work out. Don't get me wrong, Will. I care for you deeply, but not like you want me to. We just aren't meant to be."

"Sam, I love you though. You are such an amazing woman."

Sam tried to interrupt him, but he held his hand up, effectively cutting her off. "Please let me finish. I took me quite a while to gather up the balls to do this. Just let me finish. I just wanted to let you know that I'm always going to be here for you. I don't care what you get into, what kind of trouble you get into, or anything else. I was just hoping that we could try dating again."

Sam looked at the floor, not because she didn't know what to say, but because she knew exactly what he wanted to hear and she couldn't say it. "Will, I care for you a great deal, you're my partner. Because of that, I'd lay down my life for you. But that's it. I'm sorry, Will, it's just not gonna happen."

She knew her words had hurt and she asked him to sit down.

Will took a seat on her couch and noticed Mason peeking at them from the top of the stairs. "Hey, you big ugly monster! Get your furry butt down here!" He patted the couch beside him and the Rottweiler bounded down the stairs as quickly as he could. Instead of leaping onto the couch beside Will, he slammed headfirst into his chest. "Jesus H. Christ, Mason! What the hell have you been eating? Buicks by the buttload? My God you've gotten big!" He scratched the grinning dog behind the ears and on his haunches. As he petted his furry friend, he noticed something on the couch arm, a single, long blonde hair. He tried to avoid looking at it but his eyes kept creeping back to it. He forced his attention from the incriminating hair and back to Sam. "Listen, I know there's something going on with you but I don't care. I just want to know you're okay."

Sam looked directly into Will's eyes. "I'm fine Will. Things are starting to look up for me and everything is fine. I promise."

Will stood and brushed himself off. He glanced at the hair one last time before opening his arms to Sam. She gave him a hug before walking him to the door. His heart felt as if it weighed a thousand pounds, but he tried not to let it show. He opened the door to his truck and climbed in. As he backed out of his driveway, the tears started to form in the corners of his eyes.

When he was sure he was out of sight of Sam's house, he pulled into the ditch. He placed his head in his hands and began to cry. If there was someone for everyone, he was afraid he had missed the chance to be with his one and only. "But, there's always tomorrow," he told himself.

* * * * *

Sam returned to her bedroom to find Michael sitting on the edge of the bed. "Is everything okay? I heard your partner and it sounded as if he was upset."

"Yeah, he's convinced that he's still in love with me even though he and I have absolutely nothing in common. The only time we actually get along is at work. We tried it a couple years ago, but it just didn't work out." Sam seemed a little distressed so Michael gave her a much needed hug.

Michael didn't have any advice for this situation. He had been all over the world and seen some amazing things throughout history, but he had never had a relationship with anyone. "Well, Sam, this is not exactly my forte. If you ask me if someone is a good person or whether or not you should trust him to watch Mason, I could answer that. But this is a totally different monster. I wish I could help though."

Sam began slipping out of her clothes again. "This is no big deal. I think he already knew what I was going to say, but he had to make at least one last play for me." As she slid off her pants, she sat down next to Michael. He kissed her shoulder and gently stroked her silken skin with his thumb.

She kept her attention on the TV, trying unsuccessfully to play coy. She had never been very good at playing the seductress, but this man brought out the kinky in her. She briefly shifted her eyes to glance at him, a smile tugging at the corner of her mouth. She continued to pretend to ignore him.

He slid his hand down her stomach and across her thighs. She gasped as he slid his finger into her heat. He grinned as the look of ecstasy spread across her face. She twisted towards him and kissed him deeply. Their bodies intertwined as they began to make love yet once again.

Hours passed before they both found release again. Once they cleaned up, they cuddled on the bed again with Mason pinning their feet in place. With the level of comfort they had with each other, it wasn't long before they were both dozing off in each other's arms.

Chapter 24

MAJOR ABRAHAM Haywood was a fifty-seven year old black man. He stood well over six feet tall and had a voice that would make James Earl Jones sound like an alto. His head was clean-shaven as was his face. His uniforms were pressed with military precision. He firmly believed that all you ever have is a first impression and he expected his to mean something.

He had been given the job of overseeing the investigation of the murder of an inmate at the Black Ridge jail. After he had spent only a few minutes in the cell, he wondered if the rest of the murders in the sleepy little town were anything like this, amazingly brutal and without evidence.

With almost forty years of service, nothing he had ever experienced could help him with this. His men had searched that cell as if they thought that an atom might hold the evidence they needed to crack the case.

He was extremely disappointed that the only evidence they found were a couple of hairs and the bloody symbols on the door. This was indeed the strangest case of his career. It had become apparent early on that the detective who had visited the victim earlier the previous day was not responsible for the brutality that lie beyond the steel door, but he wanted to find out what she knew. Maybe if the two of them could work together on this, they might find the one detail that both of them seemed to be missing.

He called the local police chief and informed him of his findings. After making arrangements to meet with Detective Brae as soon as was possible, he hung up the phone.

He decided to break for lunch. He let his investigating officers know and he left for a local restaurant known for its incredible hamburgers.

He stepped outside and took in the winter chill. This was truly his favorite time of year. The cold, crisp air, the openness of the leafless trees and how the cold grip of winter seemed to dull the noise of everyday life.

The Black Ridge PD sat just off one of the busiest roads in Northwest Arkansas, yet, even with hundreds of cars passing by, the sound was barely above a dull roar. He smiled as he walked to his unmarked cruiser.

The little restaurant he had chosen was only a few blocks away from the PD, but the commute there took him almost twenty minutes. Once there, he placed his order and pulled a small notebook and a pen from his pocket and began writing questions for the young Detective Brae. He wanted to be as prepared as possible when he met her later this evening.

When his order arrived, he ate contentedly as he continued to jot down questions.

He had a feeling that this would prove to be a very interesting evening.

* * * * *

It was nearly 4 in the morning as slipped from the bed. She knew she had to call the State Trooper that was heading up the investigation. Mason lifted his head and snorted loudly as she quietly crept from the room. As she passed the bathroom, she grabbed her bathrobe from the door and slipped it on. Once downstairs, she made her call. "Major Haywood? This is Detective Samantha Brae. I was told that you wished to speak with me?"

"Ah, yes, Detective Brae. I've been expecting your call. I was wondering if you could meet me sometime soon, at your convenience of course."

"Of course, Major, I can meet you now if that's okay. Where would be good for you?"

He sounded amused, "Anywhere is good, I'm easy."

Sam had a feeling that for the second time today, she was going to be propositioned, or she would receive a slew of inappropriate comments would be tossed her way. "Well, there's a gas station on the corner of Main and 72. I think that would probably be the easiest for me. I can meet you in thirty minutes."

"It's a date. See you then, Detective."

As she hung up, she gave a sigh of relief. She sat down on the couch and stared out the window as she was beginning to stress about the meeting with this investigator. She knew that it was his job to sniff out lies. She was sleeping with the very murderer she was supposed to be tracking. "Ah, a moral dilemma, one of life's little perks," she whispered to herself. She zoned out on the nights black sky and did not hear Michael descend the stairs.

"I didn't hear you get out of bed. Is everything okay?" His face showed his concern only too well. He stood at the foot of the stairs clad in only a pair of boxer shorts, causing a shiver of excitement to shoot down her spine.

"Yeah, everything's alright. I had to call the State Police and set up an interview over that slimeball you mangled at the jail. They've got a few questions for me. I'm sure it's no big deal." She pulled her knees to her chest. "I have something I want to talk to you about. Have a seat?"

Michael sat down beside her and took her hand in his. He wanted nothing more than to hold her next to him for eternity and the possibility of trying to turn her kept crossing his mind, that is, if she wanted that. "What's on your mind, Sam?"

"Well, I'm just going to spit it out. Just a few days ago, I had a firm grasp on reality. There was a vicious murderer in town, killing good and God fearing folk and it was my job to bring him to justice. Then, in the blink of an eye, everything changed. I found out that the very people I protect are guilty of things worse than murder, things that I can't even imagine someone being capable of. I've decided that I just can't do this shit anymore. I would rather take what money I've managed to save, invest it and just live here. I'll grow a garden, I'll go hunting, hell, I'll do whatever it takes, but I'm sick of the twisted world I live in. so, I'm going to meet with this Major Haywood, then I am going to resign from the Black Ridge police department. Do you think less of me?"

"Sam, nothing you could ever do could make me think less of you, unless it had something to do with barnyard animals, power tools and peanut butter. That might make me think less of you." He gave her a playful grin. "No, Sam, I don't think less of you. As a matter of fact, I wondered how long you would be able to continue to protect those people once you knew the truth of them. I am sorry that I have placed you in this position."

Sam was looking at the floor. She had a lot to chew over and she knew that he would leave to find his 'dinner' when she went to the interview. "Michael, you didn't place me in any position. You just opened my eyes to how shitty mankind actually is. We *are* a bunch of savages, you're right about that. All I need to make this life okay is you. I know, I'm getting all sappy and girlie on you, but it's true. You make me feel like there is some hope for these people, even if their salvation can only be found in death. Please say you'll stay with me. Tell me that you won't leave me." A single tear rolled down her cheek and she knew right at that moment, she was truly in love with him.

"Until time ceases to exist. I give you my word. Forever." He leaned forward and kissed her on the forehead.

She smiled and hugged him tightly around the neck. "You, my lovely little play toy, better go find something to eat. I wouldn't want you to lose that..." she glanced at his crotch, "appetite you have." She bit her bottom lip as she felt the urges stirring inside her again. "Go. Get that cute ass upstairs and get dressed before I go looking for the peanut butter and power tools." She laughed again as she stood and pulled him to his feet.

Michael was almost in a full belly laugh as he ascended the stairs. He loved her twisted sense of humor.

Sam followed him up the stairs and also began getting dressed. She grabbed a pair of thermals, her thick blue jeans, a thick wool sweater and a long sleeve 'Ride to Live' shirt. She had already decided that she would take the Harley tonight. It was cold, but that was no longer an issue. She had a feeling that the cool night air and the open road would be needed to calm her before and after facing the Major's questions.

Michael also got dressed, choosing the clothes he had worn here, blue jeans and black t-shirt over the clothes Sam had given him. He was going to feed tonight and did not want to ruin anything. He pulled on his boots and got ready to leave. Sam was still dressing as he stepped behind her. She bent over to pull on her thermals and he took advantage of the situation, grabbing her hips and pulling her tightly against him. "So, I'll see you soon?"

"You bet your ass you will. I'll be home in no time. This shouldn't take me more than an hour, two tops, depending on how many questions this guy has. I should be here when you get back though." Sam smiled as she stood up and leaned against his muscular chest. She turned her head to the side, placed her hand on Michael's right cheek and pulled him in for a kiss.

"Okay, you're making it really hard for me to leave. I'll be back as soon as I run my errand and find a place to clean up. I'll see you soon." He wrapped her in a tight embrace, kissed her again and headed for the door.

"Hey, don't worry about finding a place to clean up. There's a shower in the garage. The keys are hanging in the cabinet by the fridge. Take those with you, and try not to leave a trail... Never mind, you never even leave footprints." She gave him a weak smile.

"Thank you, Sam. I'll see you soon." He turned and headed down the stairs. He almost did not want to feed again. He started thinking that if he didn't, maybe he could grow old with Samantha, live a normal life with her. Those thoughts proved to be fleeting though. He had a duty to his Father and he had performed it for over seven thousand years already. He shook his head and took the keys she mentioned, though it almost physically pained him to leave her.

* * * * *

Sam finished dressing and gave Mason a quick rub down. The large dog was acting perfectly content for the first time in his life. He gave her one of his menacing smiles before licking her arm. "Mason, I've got some business to take care of, but I'll be home for good soon, okay? On guard." The dogs ears perked up and he leapt from the bed and began a circuit around the room.

She locked up as she left the house and headed to the garage. Once inside the large building, she pulled her leather jacket out of the small closet in the workshop area and slipped it on. She took her gloves out of the pockets and started the bike. While she finished donning her winter apparel she started the Harley-Davidson to let it warm up.

By the time she had finished with all the zippers and threw open the garage door, the bike was purring smoothly. She straddled the large machine, pushed in the choke and shifted the bike into first and eased outside. It took her another couple of minutes to climb off the bike again and pull the door closed. "I've really got to invest in a garage door opener."

Back on the bike, she kicked it back into first and rolled on the throttle. She smiled as she thought about the reason why the cold air that was blowing against her skin no longer bothered her. It was a beautiful night for a ride. She dropped the throttle and blasted through the darkness. She rounded a corner and saw several deer jumping over the brush at the edge of the roadway.

As she rolled into town, there were very few cars on the road. She noticed several waiting to pull out and she expected any one of them to whip out in front of her, but none of them did. She pulled up to a four way intersection and waited for another car to pass in front of her before making her turn. As she straightened out of the corner, she noticed an older blue and white Ford pickup waiting to pull out of a residential neighborhood. She didn't give it a second thought as she swung into the gas station and pulled her bike onto the sidewalk outside the front of the store. She killed the motor and dropped the kickstand.

As she swung her leg over the bike, she was already removing her gloves. As she walked past the windows, she saw that the Major was already waiting for her. She sighed and gathered her courage to face the man.

She pushed open the glass door and took a seat across from the investigator. He introduced himself and launched right into the questions. "Detective Brae, you were the last one to visit Mr. Billings on the night of his death. Did you notice anything out of the ordinary while you were in the cell with him?

"No sir. He was drunk and running off at the mouth. He managed to piss me off pretty bad with the crap he said, but other than stinking the place up, nothing out of the ordinary."

He started to ask her something then hesitated. "What exactly did he say to you?"

"Well, I'm paraphrasing here, but he pretty much told me that the reason he killed them was because..." Sam had to talk several breaths to calm herself enough to continue, "Because they were too needy and the little girl acted too good for them."

Major Haywood was truly shocked. "Are you serious? Wow, I knew the world was full of sick people, but that's just insane!"

Sam could hear the rage in his voice and knew that he sympathized with her feelings toward the dead man. "When I left there, I drove back to work to start my shift. I never touched him, but I will admit to thinking about it."

"Well, Detective, I'm glad you caught the guy, I just wish that our justice system would have had a chance with him. I'm sure he would have had a great time in prison. Alright, I have a feeling that he got what he deserved though. Do you know anything about the symbols on the door?"

"Not really. I know that there was another scene with some of the same brand of weird shit. The De Lucca house. That one translated to 'the guilty are punished so the innocent can live' or something like that. Other than that, I have no clue."

"Well, to be honest, Detective, we had it translated and this one meant, 'because you cannot.' Now, if you ask me, that's directed at someone. And since you were the last one there, I think this guy is leaving you messages. I think you might know him."

Sam was caught off guard. She had definitely not expected this. "I've thought the same thing, well, except for knowing the killer part. I think the psycho is taunting me. I think he's made it personal but I have no idea why."

"I see, so you have no knowledge of who might be committing these murders?"

Sam almost laughed. "That's what I'm saying, Major. I don't have a damn clue. All I know is that I want this interview to be over so I can go do what needs to be done. Some things have changed in my life and I know that dealing with trash like Billings doesn't fit into my new master plan."

"So, after all this, after all the work you've put into trying to catch this psychopath, you're just gonna walk?" The Major was clearly shocked by her revelation.

Sam sighed, "That's it. I've given up countless hours trying to protect the innocent only to find out that they're not so friggin' innocent. I'm just tired of everything I do being part of a bigger lie. The world is unjust and I refuse to be a part of this bullshit any longer."

Major Haywood smiled and touched Sam's hand. "Listen, I know it's a bullshit world we live in, but it's all we have. If we don't try to clean it up, who the hell will? You know as well as I do, if we all just give up, our world is gonna end. If this is really what you want to do, I understand completely. Hell, I've contemplated it myself. I just hope you'll reconsider. Apparently you're pretty damn good at your job or your chief wouldn't have fought tooth and nail to keep you on the force. So, I've got a favor to ask of you, in light of everything that's happened here, I want you to consider coming to work for me. We need good detectives that have a good head on their shoulders."

He reached into his shirt pocket and withdrew a business card. He scribbled on the back of it before passing it to Sam. "If you decide you want to give the State Police a try, give me a call. I put my home phone on the back as well."

She gratefully accepted it before standing and offering her hand. "Thank you, Major. I may be giving you a call. You have yourself a good evening." She turned and left the confines of the gas station and took a deep breath as she stepped into the crisp night air. Breathing easier knowing that this part was over with, she decided she would return home and enjoy some more time with Michael. Quitting her job would wait until tomorrow night.

She straddled her bike and fired it up. She zipped up her jacket and pulled her gloves on. As she roared out of the parking lot, she didn't notice the blue and white pickup pull out behind her.

Chapter 25

MICHAEL CREPT through the town, his mind not on the hunt, but on the beautiful Samantha. He wondered how her interview was going. He half-heartedly looked for his next victim, though he found him rather quickly. He had set his eyes on a young man this evening. He looked into his heart and saw the dark deeds that he had committed and knew this was to be his meal. His prey's name was Javier Menendez and he had shot and killed three college students as part of a gang initiation. Later on, he had beaten a man to death because he was bored.

As he stalked his prey, they moved through side streets and he knew instinctively that this young man was up to no good. Finally, the reached their destination and his intended victim began casing a house. Michael could see that the occupants were home and awake. He knew right away that this was going to be bad.

In the blink of an eye, Michael had grabbed the young man and slammed him to the ground. Even though the force of the attack was enough to break his ribs, there was no sound. Michael leaned close and whispered into Javier's ear. "You know why I'm here, don't you?"

The young Hispanic looked terrified as he stared into the icy blue eyes. It took him a second to screw up his courage and tried to be intimidating. "Esa, you better let me up, or you gonna be in some serious shit. You don't know who you playin' with."

Michael laughed, baring his long and razor sharp teeth, causing the wannabe gangster to piss himself. He lifted his eyes to the house that Javier has planned on breaking into. "What was your plan once you got inside? Were you going to kill them all? No, you know what? I don't care. Your past speaks volumes about you. Tonight, you will die, so you had better find your peace."

He drove his fist into the Latino's face, shattering his nose. He repeated the blows until most of the bones in Javier's face were broken. He grabbed him by the throat and tossed him across the street as though he were a child's toy.

As Javier hit the ground rolling, he began to cry. His whole life he had been the tough guy and now he was powerless to fight back. He fought his way to his feet and tried to run, but Michael was already there.

Something connected with Javier's kneecap, snapping it backwards and sending him tumbling to the ground. He howled with pain as he hit the ground. He was shocked as his attacker was already on top of him, pounding his ribs, taking him right to the brink of unconsciousness.

Michael saw his lips roll into the back of his head and he stopped the beating, long enough for him to regain consciousness. He gripped his throat and lifted him off the ground Javier was now making raspy gurgling noises as he tried to speak. "You have yet to make your peace, Javier. Or have you forsaken your God?"

Javier shook his head violently and meekly touched his chest. He clasped the cross he wore under his shirt and slowly brought up to his swollen lips. He kissed it and began a prayer.

As Michael leaned forward to sink his fangs into the Latino's neck, a feeling of wrong washed over him.

Sam was in trouble. He quickly tore Javier's head from his shoulders and dropped where he stood. He focused on Sam, trying to get a feel for where she was. As soon as he knew, he closed his eyes and pictured the crossroads that were about a mile from her house.

She was headed home.

Chapter 26

JOHNNY BURNS sat behind the wheel of his '72 Ford pickup, waiting to make a left hand turn onto the highway when a woman on a motorcycle caught his attention. He had just stopped to drop off some of his home cooked goods to one of his best customers when life had given him something to be thankful for. His lifelong friend, Dan Phillips was sitting beside him and gave him the 'holy shit' look.

"Dan, you saw that shit, right? That's the same bitch that broke my jaw and took my shotgun, ain't   it?" Johnny was between enraged and excited. He was sure that it was, but he had to ask his friend to be sure.

"You're fuckin'-A right it was. I say we shoot the cunt as soon as she steps outta that store." Dan wasn't as excited by the prospect of taking a life as his best friend was, but after she had humiliated him by making him suck the end of that shotgun, he was more than willing to help kill her.

Johnny sat quietly for a moment, clicking his teeth back and forth while running his fingers over his scalp. "No, we're gonna follow this bitch. Catch her when she's not expecting it and shoot her right in that smug fuckin' face of hers." He struggled to keep his voice calm even though he was as high as a kite and extremely pissed off.

They sat in the parking lot with the engine idling for about twenty minutes before she came out of the store. Dan had been fidgeting with the stereo and picking at his arms while they waited. Johnny however, was too angry to mess with anything. He kept his attention on the red-headed woman. He wanted revenge, but he knew if he got busted right now, he would spend the rest of his life behind bars and that was not his idea of a good time.

As the bike roared onto the highway, they pulled out and stayed a fair distance behind her. They followed her through several turns and eventually started down a country lane. It was one with which Dan and Johnny were both very familiar with. They had set up meth labs on this road on numerous occasions. They knew that their chance was rapidly approaching.

The road came to a four-way stop about a mile from where they were so they sped up, closing the distance between them and the bitch that had humiliated them both.

Dan handed Johnny a shotgun. He didn't mind going along with the plan, he just didn't think he could be the one to pull the trigger. He clenched his teeth and waited for the deafening blast.

Johnny came up behind the Harley as it was slowing to a stop at the intersection. He jammed on his brakes and slid to the right of the bike. He jammed the shotgun out of the window and stared directly into the red-headed bitch's eyes. As he leveled the weapon with her pretty face, he had to ask her, "You fucked with the wrong guys, this time, didn't ya, whore?"

A note from the author

Thank you for purchasing my novel and I look forward to presenting you with the second novel in the Noco De A Oresa series, When Angels Fall. Look for it on Amazon very soon! Or join my Facebook page to get (hopefully) daily updates.

First, I want to thank everyone who had encouraged me in the creation of this story. It's been a long hard road and I know I could be a bit difficult when I got discouraged. Thank you all for standing beside me. You all mean the world to me. If there weren't so damn many of you and if I wasn't tired of staring at the computer screen, I'd list you all. Sorry, love ya!

Secondly, I would like to invite you to drop by my Facebook page and leave me a comment as to what you thought of the story. I would love to hear from you! Just try to be civil. If you don't like my work, go find another book to read. I invite all comments, positive and negative, just keep them civil and please, NO SPOILERS!

www.facebook.com/intheblackofnight

Thank you and God bless,

D.M. Milne-Jones

Noco De A Oresa series

1 – In the Black of Night

Detective Samantha Brae discovers that vampires are indeed real, but everything she knows about them is wrong. She begins on a deadly journey as she discovers just what lurks in the black of night.

2 – When Angels Fall

Coming Soon!